THE
DEVIL'S
ONLY FRIEND

Mitchell Bartoy

THE DEVIL'S ONLY FRIEND

ST. MARTIN'S MINOTAUR
New York

THE DEVIL'S ONLY FRIEND. Copyright © 2006 by Mitchell Bartoy. All rights reserved. Printed in the United States of America. No part of this book may be used or reproduced in any manner whatsoever without written permission except in the case of brief quotations embodied in critical articles or reviews. For information, address St. Martin's Press, 175 Fifth Avenue, New York, N.Y. 10010.

www.minotaurbooks.com

LIBRARY OF CONGRESS CATALOGING-IN-PUBLICATION DATA

Bartoy, Mitchell.
    The devil's only friend / Mitchell Bartoy.—1st ed.
        p. cm.
    ISBN-13: 978-0-312-34089-6
    ISBN-10: 0-312-34089-3
    1. Rich people—Fiction. 2. Automobile industry and trade—United States—Fiction. 3. Police—Michigan—Detroit—Fiction. 4. Detroit (Mich.)—Fiction. I. Title.

PS3602.A843D478 2006
813'.6—dc22

                                                                    2006044506

First Edition: October 2006

10 9 8 7 6 5 4 3 2 1

For my wife

ACKNOWLEDGMENTS

I would like to acknowledge the gracious support I've received from Phil, Patricia, and Megan Abbott. The folks at the United States Postal Service have helped in so many ways that it would be impossible to list them here. In particular, I'd like to thank Terry Traylor and Cindy Tobias for their understanding and encouragement. To my family, to the APWU, to Bonnie and Joe and Margo and Robin and all that gang—many thanks are due.

THE
DEVIL'S
ONLY FRIEND

PROLOGUE

Detroit, Michigan, 1944

While the city went up in flames, while the Negroes wrecked their own shops and the cops and the National Guard shot and beat down the mobs—well, I got the hell out of there. I cooled my heels for a couple of weeks and took in some sun. I drank beer and rested in a place where nobody knew me, and to pass the time I walked along the shore of Lake Huron, out at the very tip of Michigan's thumb. For a day or two I tried to figure out the angles, what the nasty business would mean for the future. But it was too much for me, and so I just stared out at the waves breaking against the rocks and the pebbled sand and the big freighters crawling along at the horizon. When I got back to Detroit, I found that I was still a free man, in spite of all I had and hadn't done. As an officer of the law, I had sworn an oath to protect, to serve, to uphold the laws that had been hammered out by the earliest men of the city. But it had been many years since I had been so green and so full of myself that I could give away my faith so easily. I had fallen away.

I walked into the police headquarters on Beaubien, and it didn't get me arrested. Nobody said a word to me as I walked up the stairs to Captain Mitchell's office.

Looking back, I guess I could have found something more to hash out with him. There were things left to be straightened out. Mitchell had been close to my father, as close as anyone had ever been. I knew there were things he might have told me that would sink into the vat of dead memory if I could not find a way to sit and talk to him. He might have told me that Fred Caudill was a good man—not just to say the words but to tell exactly how my father had found a way to be a good man. Mitchell might have been able to show me the choices my father had made, what he had taken, what he had left. I was just simpleminded enough to come upon an interest in history in my middle thirties. But the big riot had left things bitter between us, and I hadn't really come to the captain's office to talk. It might have seemed like the only honorable thing left to do; but my lack of imagination meant that it was just the simplest. I flipped my detective's badge in its charred leather case toward him and turned away from that part of my life.

It looked like I was all set up. I was feeling like I could do anything I wanted. There was still a little money left from the botched deal with auto baron Jasper Lloyd, and I thought I might have a chance to settle in with a good woman. For a short time, at least, it looked like they weren't going to call me in for any of the blood I had spilled—I knew enough to make it ugly for them if they did.

I kept thinking back to that moment when I walked out of headquarters. It was early enough in the day that the July heat wasn't deadly. I was breathing easy, and I could have chosen to follow any path. No obvious thing would trip me up. For the first time in a dozen years or more, there was no reason for me to care where I was or what the clock had to say. The air was fresh as the air ever gets deep inside an industrial city, and I tried to ignore the faint trace of worry that dogged me—had I been kidding myself? I had managed to shrug off a boatload of trouble, but maybe I couldn't slip out of my own scarred skin after all.

I didn't go to see Eileen right away. It was a Sunday, and I knew she'd be home. I walked and walked, meandering with my one eye up and down the streets of Detroit, from time to time spying a corner where I'd cracked a

wino's head or an alley I'd chased through with my brother Tommy—
Tommy, who'd gone halfway across the world to get himself killed. On foot,
as I'd been for so many years as a beat cop, you can smell out a city, or at
least the small part of it you can get to before your dogs give out. Tucked in
the nooks and crannies between the big buildings of downtown, in apartments and flats along the back alleys, people were cooking. Most of the
men were either gone overseas to fight or else working their seventh day on
the lines, but the families that were left were sitting down to an early Sunday supper. It only made me think how few friends I'd made in my thirty-
six years.

Finally I took the bus up Campau and got off at Davison. I came along
the alley that ran behind the auto dealer and the garage with gravel
crunching under my hard shoes. The rose bushes that Eileen kept along
the alley drooped with old blooms. I thought she might be out in the back,
working at the yard, but there was no trace of her. Inside the garage they
were pounding out fenders, patching up cars that would have to stay in service until the war could be won and the factories could turn again to making new models. I walked over the little patch of grass in front of Eileen's
place and stepped up onto the big porch.

I knew what kind of man I was just then. It hit me. As my finger pressed
down onto the button of the doorbell, it came to me *for the first time* that
Eileen probably thought I was dead. When the riot broke, she knew I was
right in the thick of it; and I hadn't been decent enough to send word to
anyone that I was all right. While I was gone, while I was taking fresh air in
Caseville, walking on the beach, I'd thought of her—but I hadn't ever considered what she might be feeling for me.

I could see it plain enough when she opened the door. For a moment as
the wave of emotion seized her, it seemed that she could not quite tell
which of her three lost men was standing before her. Was it her husband,
my brother Tommy, who had been killed in the war? Her only child, Alex,
a boy of fourteen, who had been driven away by my bungling? I was the
third man, the last choice, reasonably, but I had changed. She had seen me
wearing the glass eye before, of course, but now it was as if she couldn't
quite place me. Because of all the sorrow she'd been dragged through, she
held herself back from feeling for a killing second.

Then she stepped through the screen door and fell onto me. The way she was shaking, I thought she would tear us both to pieces. I wrapped myself around her and held tight, but I felt the shadows of doubt and guilt I had not managed to bury. I wondered if there was anything that could still hold us together.

CHAPTER

1

April 6, 1944

In general I don't care to hear any word of advice, and I do my best not to give any out.

But there's just the one thing.

If you've managed to work yourself into a good job, steady work, the kind of a spot where you can keep a little respect for yourself, you should think for a time before you chuck your detective's badge at your captain's chest and walk out on the whole thing. That's how I found myself in a little rented flat in a three-story building on the east side, whiling away the hours and whittling away at my dwindling stash of money.

After the riot and all the mess of the previous year, I thought I knew what I'd be doing. I thought I might take a little job to keep me occupied. I had a vague idea that I could carry on a regular affair with Eileen. But it wasn't so. Through the summer and the fall of 1943, I prowled around the city and continued to eat myself up inside. With Eileen I'm not sure how it happened; it was like a record that had skipped off track. It wasn't right from the beginning, and then thoughts of Alex and Tommy and my father got to be heavy enough to darken everything. Gradually she soured toward me.

I moved from my rented house, which was too big for me, into a tiny flat. Then I spent so many hours stewing out on my little landing on the fire escape that I knew everything about the neighborhood—everything that could be noted along the interior of the block, along the alley that all the buildings backed into. I watched as daughters crept out for secret meetings with boyfriends; I noticed that husbands were more likely to smack their women as payday drew near and money grew tight; I came to know where the rats hid from the light during the day. You see a clearer picture of how people live when you look into their back windows.

Even with all the old ladies peeking through their curtains and all the old gents scouring the riverfront for Nazis night and day, Detroit was still a place where you could be left alone. I wasn't sure if any of my neighbors knew anything about me or what I had done. They knew my name, most of them. But you can't ever tell what people will say about you, you can't control how people will talk. I was just glad to be able to sit unmolested on the little landing on the outside fire stairs, halfway between my floor and the floor above.

I brought up a quarter sheet of plywood to keep the legs of my little kitchen chair from going through the grate. Though the rail was loose and rickety, it was wide enough for me to rest a can of beer or a cup of coffee on it. During the day, and just after school let out especially, the neighborhood kids chased up and down the fire escape and the alley, but then they were called to supper, and things were quiet enough for me to sit and think. Usually I crept out as dusk took hold.

Then one evening in April, after I had weathered the worst of the Michigan winter and early spring, sitting out sometimes even as the snow whipped through the alley or settled softly over me like a blanket, I swung out my window thinking that I'd be warm enough to sit till the moon crawled away. But as I started up, I felt the buzz that jolts you when you realize you're not alone; there was a man I didn't know sitting above me in my chair, the orange tip of a cigarette bobbing between his lips. The pale light from the street lamps down below threw a shadow over his face, but there was a weak flickering glitter in his eyes. I couldn't very well back down the stairs in such a case, and so I clomped up the remaining steps and said hello.

"This your chair?" he said, rising. "I guess it is."

"That's all right," I told him.

He got up stiffly and stepped clear. "I can't do right by stealing another man's chair."

There wasn't much to do but sit down. The slender stranger stood with his back against the stair rail for a time, pulling smoke from his brown cigarette and pluming it outward. The steady wind that came through the alley drafted the smoke quickly upward, spiraling away. I was wearing a work vest to hold off the cold—a vest that had been my father's—but this fellow just stood there in his shirtsleeves. Fred Caudill would have glad-handed him; he'd put out his hand as a natural thing to any man, friend or stranger, who came within ten feet of him. My brother Tommy would have put out the mitt, too. I sat and let my eye go out into the distance.

"My name's Ray Federle," the smoking man said. "We moved into the building last week."

"Pete Caudill," I said.

"Got the wife and two girls," he said. "Needed a cheap place."

"Yah," I said. "It's cheap all right."

My eye started to see a little better in the dark, and I could see that Federle was still a young man. He lit up smoke after smoke, and each time he passed the fire from the old one to the new, he chucked the dead butt over the rail. It was impossible not to watch them as they fell and splashed sparks on the alley below.

"Good Friday tomorrow," he said. "You follow that stuff?"

"No." I had fallen out of caring what day it was. With no regular job to press me, I had no cause to mark the days.

"For the Catholics it's a big deal on Easter," said Federle. "They get to eat again."

Federle's talk made me think of my mother in her house all alone—of family meals and laughter, gone now. Easter—I knew I'd be eating alone again.

"I got a job rolling fenders at Chrysler," he said. "How about you? You on the bum?"

"I get by," I said. "I work when I need to."

"Did you lose that eye—"

"I never went to the war," I said. "But I got a couple fingers missing, too. You want a look-see?" I waved my bad hand for him.

"If I'm too fresh with you, I don't mean anything by it. I got a case of nerves."

Federle was not quite as tall as me, and he gave up thirty pounds in the matchup. It made a question flicker through my mind: Were we high enough where a man would be killed if he fell from the landing, or would he only break his legs?

"You're lucky you didn't have to go," he said, rubbing his thumb over the black stubble on his chin. He tapped a light cone of ash from his cigarette, and it tumbled like snow over the hairs of his forearm. "It ain't no picnic."

"It's bad?"

"Let me tell you," he muttered. He held out his cigarette in the dark, as if his arm gestured to a faraway place that he could somehow see before him. "Sometime I'll tell you about it. It'll make your hair stand up like a porcupine. The wife don't want to know."

After that we were silent for a long time, as much as an hour. I could mark the time by the sounds of supper dishes being washed, children getting bathed, lights blinking out, the nails of mongrels clicking down the alley, rattling trash cans. Now and again a stumbling couple crept down the alley, taking the darker path toward the Alderton flophouse for an hour's entertainment. I thought I could hear a mystery play from someone's radio echoing down between the buildings. *Another day gone*, I thought. *How many more?* As much as the moon could make it stand out from the black sky, the smoke from Federle's cigarettes trailed away from us like silt kicked up in a slow-moving stream.

"Late at night," said Ray Federle, "when it's quiet like this, and people are lying down to bed—kissing their babies and tucking them in and whispering to them that everything's going to be all right—you'd think it would be a peaceful time. How the darkness comes down to soothe all the bad business and set you down to rest..."

He broke off to pull one last long drag from his cigarette. The ash came close enough to burn his fingers, and he twitched the butt away. I could see that his eyes were wide and staring and empty and his jowls were slack.

"That's when the spiders come out," he said.

My first thought was that it was still too cold, too early in the year, for spiders to be out spinning all night; but then I saw him bring two long fingers slowly up to tap his forehead, which was shining oddly with sweat. He stared out blankly into the night for a few moments more.

"Off to work," he said finally. "Boneyard shift."

He climbed stiffly up the steps toward his own window, hoisted it open, and went through with some difficulty. I made my way down to my own place and turned out the lights. Coming in from the night and then putting my face close to the lamp dazzled my eye. In the dark I stood for a time, trying to make out the solid parts of my paltry room. Filmy sheets of white bloomed and faded before me, and I turned to see them all around me. Gradually I became adjusted to the darkness again, and the ghosts left me alone. I sat at my little dinette table and wondered if sleep would come for me.

CHAPTER

2

Friday, April 7

A city like Detroit moves right along without you. If you don't have much to say or offer, people will just walk right around you like you were a lamppost or an old box somebody left on the sidewalk. For me it was a comfort. I had to guess that it was the same for any number of other men in the city—but how many of the million or so stories could I really know or care about? Some fella's wife cuts out with the kids, he takes to the bottle, he lets his place go to seed—that's regular life. In the papers every week you could still read about the debutantes in the Pointes coming out at balls. While the dog-faces went to rot in the mud overseas, a regular crop of socialites came out every year, and their pictures always made them seem pretty and untainted by guilt. You could always read about some big shooter at Chrysler's or at Lloyd Motors donating some chunk of money to a pet charity, to send a crate of cigarettes or a thousand decks of cards to the boys overseas. But most of the people in the city were just grinding themselves away at their work. They'd die soon or late, and that would be the end of them. They knew it damn well—and for the most part they'd step out of their own skins to keep from admitting it to themselves, to keep from saying it out loud.

I should have been set up by then. With the kind of time I'd had for thinking, I'd been over it a hundred times. If I had found a thing to put my hand to when I was young, if I could have settled on some line of work that suited me and kept my mind on getting ahead, maybe I'd have been somewhere. Money wasn't on my mind. However it had happened, I had skipped the track. I could have made more of all the days that had passed by me; I could have filled my life with living more than I had. It seemed that there was nothing that could stop my mind from dwelling on it, from gnawing at the memory. It made me want to cut things down to the bone.

It seemed like things might work out with Eileen—my dead brother's wife. I kept thinking it might still go along like it does in the movies, but with the cracked-up lives we'd both had, any pretty story we could spin would just go wheeling away. There was the nagging feeling that I had made a mess of things on purpose. I had intentionally fouled up every close feeling I stumbled into because I felt that my ugly face wasn't fit to show anyone up close. What was worse, I hadn't made anything out of all the extra chances I had been given. All along the road—I had mapped it out in my dreary moping a thousand times—everyone I had ever known had been nicer to me than I deserved, had thrown a break or a good word my way at every step. All of that had been wasted on me. I had always been a disappointment to my father, and it would kill him to see me now: a brooding, useless man.

Things started to get even messier when Walker turned up at my door. After the race riot of the previous year, folks became more keenly interested in who showed up in their neighborhood. Black Bottom, Paradise Valley, the colored west side: There were places in Detroit where Negroes could live, where they might buy houses or property without running into a mob. My own place wasn't far from the line, but when a colored man as dark as Walker came along in the neighborhood, tongues began to wag. Especially when he showed up so early in the morning that people were still in their nightshirts, still mopping up the egg yolk from their breakfast plates.

I was wiping out my one frying pan, letting the bacon fat drip into a tin can, when I heard boots clumping up the hall. Somehow I knew the boots were coming for me; I expected every day that one ghost or another from my past would come calling. And so I was not surprised to open the door to see Walker's passive mug. Half a year had gone by, but he seemed to have aged more than that. I guessed that he had worked through the night, and that he would go home to a wife and a bed after he could get away from the business that had pulled him to my door.

"Detective," said Walker.

"No more," I said. "You know that."

"That's the name I have for you," he said. "I can't think of you any other way now."

A more ordinary man would not have answered the door in his shorts and a torn undershirt, but I didn't give it a thought. Walker didn't seem to mind, or at least he wasn't giving that much away with his face. He wore several shirts buttoned over an old turtleneck in place of a jacket, and kept the whole mess tucked into his work trousers, which had been patched at the knees and along the hem. Walker held a dusty knit cap with one hand at his side.

"I guess I ought to let you in," I said.

"Thank you."

I shifted out of the doorway, and Walker stepped in. With the tin can still in my hand, I waved him over to my chair at the little table. I had cleared away my plate and coffee mug, but greasy scraps from my breakfast still marked the surface.

"What's it all about, Walker?"

"You don't want to ask me about my health, or ask after my family?"

"The both of us know my manners don't work that way," I told him. I hung up my frying pan on a wooden peg that came out of the wall near the sink and put the greasy can at the back of the counter.

"Well, I didn't come here to roist you, Detective. But you can see I've—"

"You shouldn't call me detective," I said. "I've left all that behind me."

"I'll need to call you something."

"Only if your business here takes overlong to wrap itself up."

Walker said nothing. He shifted in the chair and angled his fingertips together on the table. He would not have come, I knew, for some trifling thing. He was polite enough to keep from looking around my place. Still, it burned me to think of how filthy everything was, how hollowed-out and empty it seemed—no pictures on the walls, no food to offer a visitor, no books, my bed unmade, the floor unswept. I should have been glad to see him, as I knew him to be a good man, a sturdy man, even a friend. I should have gladly offered him my hand.

"Why don't you just call me Caudill?" I said. "I call you Walker, don't I?"

"I'd better call you Mr. Caudill," he said.

I couldn't tell whether he was joshing me.

"I don't want to forget myself in this neighborhood."

"Well," I said, "I don't give a good goddamn how you call me. You don't have to call me anything."

Walker pulled a curling photograph from his shirt pocket and smoothed it over a clean place on the tabletop. He turned it toward me. Because my only other chair was on the fire escape, I had to stand over him.

"My baby sister," he said softly. "Felicia."

I picked up the photo. Somebody long ago had put a thumb on the picture, and now the girl's face seemed fuzzy at the cheek with the imprint. She was not remarkable in any way for a Negro woman except for the little nurse's cap she wore and for the way she pulled her lips down over her protruding teeth.

I shrugged. "So?"

"She was killed about two weeks ago down toward Cleveland."

"Listen, Walker, I—" I looked again at the picture. The woman's eyes seemed to look out more sharply now that I knew she was dead. "I can't do anything for you."

"They found her at the marsh at the edge of the old Lloyd axle plant. I don't know what they build over there now. That whole place now is locked up tight for the war, just like all the plants. They have army guards patrolling along the fences."

"Well, Walker, what did you think I could do about any of that?" My knees began to tremble at the sight of Walker's poor face. I wished that I had never put my other chair out on the fire escape.

"I don't know. You've spoken to Mr. Lloyd—"

"Old Man Lloyd would rather he'd never met me," I said. "I haven't seen him or had any word from him since the first night of the riot, you know that. And I understand he's just about ready for the glue factory." I had saved the Old Man's life that night, which must have been quite an inconvenience for such a wealthy man.

"Detective, I don't have anything to offer you. I have run around with the Cleveland police and it seems like they are over and done with anything to do with this case. Unless something jumps up and bites them on the rump, so to say, they won't ever find out who did this. Now, you know how I lost my job on the force—"

"All right, Walker. You know I did what I could with Captain Mitchell. What else could I have done? What sway did I have?"

"Detective, I—"

"Jesus Christ, Walker! Can't you stop calling me that?"

He put his head down like I had slapped him. The nap at the top of his head was going thin and flecked with curls of gray. He pulled a shop rag from his back pocket and used it to swab the grease from my table. He tipped back his head and looked up at me patiently.

"I don't try to lay any blame about everything that happened last summer," he said. "I don't see how we could have dug ourselves out of that hole we were in. But Felicia left two little ones, and their daddy isn't reliable—so it looks like we may have to take them in. We're stretched a bit thin, but that doesn't bother me. I just . . . You can see how a thing like that can be important to a man. I mean, your family can be important."

Walker did know how to cut into me. There wasn't any way for him to know that I still hadn't been able to locate my nephew Alex, that I had botched things up with my sister-in-law Eileen, that I had arrived at the end of my rope. Walker and I had not spoken since the previous summer, on that morning before I tossed my badge at Captain Mitchell. But Walker could see how I was living—that I had whittled myself down almost to nothing. The apartment was bare except for the few pieces of furniture I hadn't sold . . . and I had been talking to him all the while in my bare feet, unshaven, in just my shorts and a ratty shirt. I counted myself lucky that I had at least taken the trouble to put the patch over my eyehole that morning.

"I'm not looking for a miracle, Detective," said Walker. "Maybe you could just ask around a bit."

I stood breathing heavily for a few moments, heat rising over my chest. I looked closely at Walker. His hands were swollen and scuffed up from work, and I could see from the dullness of his eyes and the general withering of his face that he had not been sleeping much or resting easy.

"What are you doing these days, Walker?"

"I pick up work tossing freight," he said. "I do some driving. How about you?"

The question surprised me. I blinked and shrugged. "Not a damn thing."

"That's nice work if you can get it," he said. "But it doesn't do well by you, from the look of things."

I looked around the flat. It took only a glance or two to make an inventory of my things.

"I'd just like to know," Walker said. "I'd like to know what happened down there. I won't even say that it's to get revenge on anybody." He turned his eyes to me. "It's my sister. She come out of the same mother and father as me. I'd like to be able to think about the whole story of her life and be able to put an end to it."

Does he know about all the people I've lost? I thought. My memory had been so abused that I could not remember what I had told Walker about myself. I guess I knew that he was trying to help me in some way because he knew how important a family should be to a man. He knew that I had fallen away.

"I'll try to help you, Walker," I said. "I doubt it'll come to much."

"I can't pay you."

"Pay me!"

"For your time. I don't ask for charity. If there is some service I can do for you … my Emily puts together a fine meal …"

"Listen, Walker, don't think about it. I'm only saying I'll ask around. That don't cost anything."

"I appreciate this, Detective. But let me say—not to be frontways with you—you might want to clean yourself up a little before you head out in the world."

"Yah," I said, drawing my hand over three days of jawbone stubble.

It grew quiet enough for a time to hear a telephone ringing somewhere in the building. My feet scraped over the dusty wood floor as I shifted from side to side.

"Well," Walker finally said, standing up. "I'll leave the photograph. If you can, I'd like to have it back."

"Sure."

Walker turned away and walked carefully to the door like an older man with an ache throughout the body. I felt a sudden shame that I hadn't even thought to offer him anything to drink, not even a glass of water.

"I'm sorry about your sister," I said. "I know how that goes." I was thinking about my brother Tommy, really—not two years gone. But then the memory of my own baby sister came back to me. Twenty years had gone by since the influenza had taken her, more than twenty years—and now I had fallen to such a state that even that sharp memory had begun to fade.

"You don't need to be sorry," said Walker. "It wasn't any fault of yours." He let himself out and pulled the door shut. His footsteps seemed to drag away forever.

I wanted to crawl back into my bed, but the bright light of morning washed away the idea. Walker's sister seemed to stare out at me accusingly from the photo, and so I had to turn it over on the table. This, too, made me feel a pang of guilt, like the woman was alive and could take it as an insult; but I was used to it. I worked hard to squander the rest of the day, thinking and stewing in my little room. I reasoned that I could hold the photo for a day or two and just tell Walker that I had failed to turn up anything. Nobody had ever believed that I could be credible as a police detective anyway, and Walker had seen it for himself. Everything I had tried to work on had been botched in one way or another. My partner had been killed, Walker had lost his position on the force, and I had failed to do anything to prevent the riot and the flames that had scorched Detroit.

I could forget about helping Walker. He would not blame me. His sister was gone, and there was nothing to do for her. During the remainder of the day—Good Friday—I didn't go out. I kept myself occupied by listening to the radio, dialing away whenever news of the war broke into the music. It became another whole day I had wasted in my life. By dusk I had convinced myself to shirk it off, and by the time darkness really took over I thought I had forgotten about the bucktoothed woman. But I had to keep inside my apartment because I did not want to think about meeting Ray Federle again on my little landing, and by Saturday morning the thought of

Walker and his sister had worked me over hard enough to push me up out of bed with some intention. It burned in my gut whether or not I wanted to think about it. It was his sister, after all, and there were children, too.

This was how it had started the other time. I had let my feelings get strong after Bobby and I found young Jane Hardiman killed in the nigger's apartment. Why should I have cared so much about that rich man's girl? There was nothing to be done for her, and it had not ended happily for anyone. I wanted to shrink back from the feeling that Walker, such a good man through and through, had brought up in me. But it was no use.

As I scraped a dull shaving blade across my cheeks, in the mirror I watched the delicate hole where my eye had been. The eyelids opened and closed like a baby's mouth as I stretched and shifted my cheeks in shaving. *What's it trying to say to me?* I thought. I was in such condition that I felt a twinge of guilt when I covered the eyehole with the patch, like I was strangling a living thing. *What am I doing?* I thought. *What am I doing?*

CHAPTER

3

Saturday, April 8

There wasn't any elevator. There was a stairwell to the east and one to the west. I always went west because it was the darker of the two and because no one else ever used it. But I hadn't made three steps downward when I saw the woman and the two children in the stairwell, stopped on the landing below and looking out the window to the street. A slender woman, pale—she turned to stare at me with huge dark eyes.

"You," she said. "You're that Caudill?" She kept a baby crooked in her arm. The infant, too, stared at me with overlarge eyes.

"I'm Caudill," I said.

She lunged at me and slapped me a good one right across my face. Even the popping noise it made was shocking. I was stuck there on the tiny landing. I couldn't even bring my hand up to ward off the blow.

"Bringing that nigger up here! With my baby girls in the building!"

The older girl turned away from the window at the commotion but showed little expression. Her eyes were as round and as dark as her mother's, and her skin was pale. The baby just stared at me, stared not at my eye as babies do but at the black patch that covered the hole. The older girl stood picking at her fingers until the woman jerked her away down the stairs.

I guess my cheek must have been red. I was only a few steps away from Mack Avenue when I finally placed the woman: Federle's wife. It made me wish that I'd locked the door to my room before I left, though there was nothing worth taking or wrecking inside.

I had stopped at a bank earlier in the week to pull enough cash from my safety box to last me the week, and the folded money chafed at the top of my thigh. When I stopped at a drugstore and took a stool at the counter, I could feel the metal clip rubbing. From the inside pocket of my old jacket I pulled the picture Walker had given me. I thought that I should never have allowed him any hope about what I could do. When I thought of the future in any regard, I saw a blank, a nothing. I could not seem to get my imagination working.

Someone had written on the back of the photograph in a woman's hand: "Felicia Downey 1936." There was an address as well, written in the same hand but with blue ink rather than black. I took this to mean that the address was more recent than the photo. What of it? What could I do? I had sold my old Packard, and to get down to Ohio I'd have to ride a bus or take a train. I didn't know Cleveland or have any people down that way.

I stepped into the telephone booth and closed myself inside. It was small enough to put me in mind of a coffin, a coffin too small for my shoulders to fit in comfortably. I went through all the coins in my pocket calling around until I got the number for Hank Chew, one of the crime-beat reporters from *The Detroit News*. A number of the bloodhounds from the *News* and the *Free Press* kept their offices right inside the police headquarters down on Beaubien. They worked through the weekend because it was usually the time when all the raciest crime, the most sordid episodes came to light. There was a general clamor for a bit of scandal in the Sunday papers. I talked the switchboard girl into buzzing Chew's line for me, and it rang enough times for me to be sure he wasn't at his desk. As I pulled the piece away from my ear, though, I heard the click of an answer.

"Chew," he said.

"Hiya," I said. "It's Pete Caudill."

"Caudill! We been wonderin'."

"You been wondering what?

"Wondering if you blew out of town. Wondering if you were dead."

"Well, I wouldn't spring to call you long-distance," I said, feeling already that I had made a mistake in calling him. "I'm still around, but I'm not around as much as I used to be."

"Pretty quiet though, eh?" said Chew, gathering steam. "Not like the old days. Quite a rabble-rouser you were, quite a gent with the fisticuffs. Made me a bundle in those days. Haven't been to a smoker like that for years." He broke off for just a moment, and I thought I could hear him taking a drag from the pipe he kept in his watch pocket. "Now that I think of it, there's a thing or two I'd like to ask you, Caudill. You still in tight with Old Man Lloyd?"

"Jesus Christ, who told you that?"

"Well, well."

"I haven't had a word with that old bastard. What's the story? Can't a fella just call to be friendly?"

That pulled a laugh from him. "Nobody ever calls me to be friendly. Nobody ever calls but if they want something out of me."

"Okay," I said. "I never did like you, Chew, it's true. We were never friendly. Talk around the station was that you're a pig-poker."

"Meet me over to Drake's," he said. "Buy me a beer and I'll let you go on insulting me."

"Give me some time to get over there," I said.

"Sure. I got nothing but time and a deadline."

I put down the phone and stood in the booth thinking—trying to set something up, some lie that would satisfy Chew so I could get what I wanted from him without spilling anything I didn't want spilled about my botched caper with Jasper Lloyd and the Black Legion the previous summer. The papers had made a jamboree for themselves for weeks out of the mess, and I knew that Chew and his fellow hacks were sharp enough to have put me in the know about it. I had managed to keep clear of it all, and I liked it that way.

Even though I had gotten awful tight with a nickel, I walked along Mack only until I could flag a cab. We went down the avenue pretty quick until we were caught up in the thick part of downtown, just under the Penobscot Building. What Chew meant by Drake's was the English Tavern in the Hammond Building. Drake wasn't the name of the fella who ran the place—and as far as I could tell, he wasn't English. The place got to be named Drake's somehow by all the men who put their elbows to the bar over the years, not by any sign or point of actual fact.

It was still a bit too early for the place to be full of businessmen taking their lunches. The war had been good for one thing, at least—there was so much work all around town that shifts were running all across the weekends, bringing more business to places like Drake's. In fact, I don't think the joint was even properly open for the day. But I opened the door and stepped gratefully out of the wind and found Chew on a stool at the bar.

He was dressed in his usual getup: a clean white shirt twice the size he needed for his small frame, held tight to his body by a buttoned-up tweedy vest. He leaned back to the bar with both elbows propping him up. One dangling hand held his hat and the other gripped the top of an empty mug like a spider.

"Caudill," he said. "Walkin' in like the Devil himself."

"Sure, Chew," I said. "It's well known the Devil wears beat-up duds."

"Well, now, Caudill, according to certain unimpeachable sources, the Devil might slither into a place dressed as any old thing—a serpent, say, or a politician."

"Devil or no, I didn't have any trouble getting you to meet me down here." I eased myself onto a stool next to him.

"I'm open-minded," he said, grinning. "A libertine. Is it too early in the morning for a drink, Caudill?" He swung himself around to face me and knocked his mug loudly on the bar. "I'll spring for a round."

"I won't keep you long enough for you to get that back," I said. I pulled Walker's picture from my jacket and handed it to Chew. He put his hat back on his head loosely and took the photo gingerly with the inky tips of his fingers. Holding it and tilting it in the weak light, he peered carefully at the front and then the back. Nothing in his expression changed. *It would be a mistake,* I thought, *to get into a poker game with this man.* After a few more moments, he slipped the photo into one of the many pockets in his vest.

"In a day or two," he said, "I'll ring you up."

"I'll have to call you," I said. "There's no telephone in my place."

"Why don't you stop by the office?" This he said with a funny smile. He knew well that I had not set foot in police headquarters for the better part of a year—since I had walked out on Captain Mitchell and the brotherhood of the force.

"Maybe," I said. "Maybe I'll pop in for old time's sake."

"You should see if they'll let you back on the force," he said. "You've lost the twinkle in your eye, Caudill."

"I'm through with all that."

"Quitters never win, you know that. From my way of looking at it, it's always better to be on the inside than the outside of things."

"I'm getting by all right," I said.

"I'm sure you are," he said. He seemed to radiate good health—the sign of a man who thrives in his work. "The boys and I have been working on a number of things. You remember that hullabaloo we had here in the summer? About the time you quit the force?"

"I don't read the papers."

"You don't have an interest in it?"

"Like I say, I get by all right."

"Would you have any interest in the indictment that's coming down for Jasper Lloyd?"

I hesitated for just a flash—a flash Chew took in without any reaction of his own.

I said, "I heard Lloyd was counting down the days."

"Maybe. Maybe not. Could be that's just the story his lawyers cook up to keep him from getting dragged before the grand jury. Could be, in this case, that sooner or later the Old Man will need to spill his guts about a few things."

"What do I care?"

"It's no use pretending, Caudill. I know you need to care."

"You don't know anything," I said.

"It's only a matter of time before the whole story unravels," he said. "If you could help me out with some of the details, it could be worth something to me. From the look of it, you could use a friend on the inside."

He was bluffing—I guessed. I knew that it was a matter of personality for the news hawks to be constantly on the prowl for stories. They could poke and prod until something popped out. And as for Chew being on the "inside," as he termed it—the newsmen were universally hated by the officers and most of the brass. They were like pilot fish swimming for scraps, suckerfish, bottom-feeding parasites.

"Listen, Chew, I came down to ask you a favor. Even this I don't care about so much. That colored woman in the photo isn't any relation to me. I'm only looking into it for a friend."

"A friend name of Walker?"

"You know Walker?"

"Not yet."

I was fairly sure that Chew was only fishing, but my brain wasn't able to think quickly enough to get to all the angles. I tried on a smile. "Walker can't tell you anything."

"Sure he can," Chew said. "Everybody's got something to say. Maybe it doesn't amount to much by itself, but if you start to hear a few names or places more than once, you start to put together a picture in your mind—"

"Jesus Christ, Chew, can't you just look into this one thing for me?"

He finally let loose. A beaming smile wrapped around his whole face and he slapped his little paw on my shoulder.

"Don't be so serious, Caudill. I'm not asking you to sell your soul!"

It didn't strike me as funny, and I noted with worry that a few knots of businessmen were beginning to wander in for their lunch hour.

"I can't help it if I like my work!" Chew said. "You wonder why Ernie Pyle tramps around in the mud with those rat-bastard Krauts lobbing grenades at him? Who wants to be cooped up in an office all the time?"

"Just let's see what you can dig up on this colored woman," I said. "And then I'll see if I can think of anything to tell you about this hullabaloo you're so worried about."

"In good faith I'll ply my trade for you, Caudill. In good faith. Don't forget now." He tapped two black fingers to the brim of his hat in a sort of salute.

"I'll be seeing you," I said, standing up. Though I did not look back at him, I was sure that Chew had already begun to troll over the arriving customers, grubbing for another story, any odd bit of dirt that he might file away on a slip of paper.

The wind slapped me again as I left the sheltered door of the tavern. As always, I didn't know what I would do next. But it seemed that I would have to do *something*—and I hoped it wouldn't turn out so messy as the last time.

CHAPTER

I had to make sure my mother wasn't dead. It was about that time of the month when I looked in on her, and I was already out and about. She was pretty well set up in her little house outside the big city in East Detroit. Though she kept a telephone, and I might well have called her, I forced myself to visit in order to see if anything had fallen off the house.

I took the Gratiot line as far as 8 Mile and hoofed it the rest of the way. It was only a few blocks, and for most of that the wind was at my back. The neighborhood was quiet. The stiff wind, without any tall buildings to channel it sharply, spread over everything and put a chill in the air. Spring rain had collected in the ditches that lined the street; something farther down had stopped up. There had been talk about installing regular storm drains and putting sidewalks in, and I knew that soon the fair city of East Detroit would put the bite on me for a share of the cost.

Even though I owned the house, I stood at the door and knocked like a salesman. When the door finally opened, I was prepared for unpleasantness, yet I was still surprised when a strange woman appeared before me. She was as wrecked in appearance as my mother but possessed greater vigor.

"Yes?" she said, keeping her foot planted inside the door.

My instinct was to plow right through, snapping the ankle of the woman blocking passage to the house that I in point of fact owned free and clear. But I only muttered, "I come to see my mother."

"Oh," she said. "You're that Pete." She looked me over anyway just to be sure, as if a gypsy might come into the neighborhood with a patch over his eye and a mangled hand—and know enough to claim to be me.

"Well, is my mother in?"

"Oh, sure, sure," the hag said. "She'll be so pleased to see you."

She stepped back a bit but still crowded the door, so that I had to squirm not to brush up against her as I passed. It might have been emphysema, but I thought I heard disapproval in the way she took in her breath behind me. Then she followed so close at my back that I could feel her tiny slippered feet scuffing at my heels. I had known the woman only a few seconds, and already I disliked her; I could see why she might get on well with my mother.

"Hey, Ma," I said, stepping through to the kitchen.

"Oh, Peter, how nice to see you." Her eyes glanced at me for a moment and then drifted off.

For the benefit of the woman, I bent down to kiss my mother on the cheek. From the dishes stacked in the sink and from the crumbs left in my mother's whiskers, I judged that they had just finished lunch.

"My dear friend Paulette," she said.

I let go a nod to the woman.

"She stops in to sit with me. She lives with her son right across the back fence."

"That's good," I said.

"And his wife. Two beautiful grandchildren. The new baby." She held up a photo of a homely baby with her shaking hand.

Paulette was still standing behind me with her arms folded. Her spine was twisted somehow, though she seemed healthy enough. I let myself down in to the chair opposite my mother across the little dinette table. There were only two chairs in the kitchen.

"I only came to see if there was anything that needed doing here."

"You could drive me to the market."

"You know I got rid of my car," I said.

"Never mind then."

"My son has a car."

My mother said, "They have a little nigger boy who delivers from the market. I get what I need that way. It costs a little more ."

"If they can get jobs," said Paulette, "they'll want to move in. You see?"

"The house is all right?" I asked.

"He lives in the Sojourner Truth. How does he get here? He takes the bus."

"I told you," said Paulette.

"I can go to the market for you, Ma. It's only down the block."

"It's all right. I have a little rolling basket."

"She has a rolling basket."

That seemed to settle the matter. My mother took in a trembling breath and let out a heavy sigh. She arranged a few photographs of her neighbor's grandchildren on the table. I thought she would remain lost in her mind for a time, and I was about to get up to check through the house.

"I had a visit from my daughter-in-law yesterday," she said.

"Eileen was here?" I said.

"She comes to see me. She takes the bus."

"She looks okay?"

"Tommy's girl."

"It's good she should visit," said Paulette. She seemed to enjoy standing above us as a sort of referee.

"If you had a car," said my mother, "you could bring her over."

"Well, I don't have a car."

"Alex couldn't come with her. He was busy with the school, with his schoolwork."

I could feel Paulette's eyes sharpen on me. It was clear that she knew something about it. Maybe she had been there for Eileen's visit.

"Alex isn't in school," I said. "He's run off. You remember?"

"Tommy's boy, I remember."

"She remembers. Of course she remembers," said Paulette. She put a hand to my mother's hunched shoulder.

My mother was still fumbling with the photographs. As it had been for some years, I couldn't make out what she was thinking, if somewhere behind her craggy face she was torn up by it all. Her eyes were lost in sagging, wrinkled flesh, and when they appeared at all, they were as beady and as unlit as a mouse's eyes.

"Eileen says that the boy . . ."

"What?" I said.

"She has a beau. Tommy's gone two years," she said.

"She should have a beau," Paulette said. "Pretty as she—"

"Nobody asked you about it," I said. "Shut your piehole."

Paulette's shapeless mouth hung open for a moment. Then she clapped it shut so that her lips made a thin, drooping line.

"When your father and I were young, we were beaus. Maybe you don't remember."

Paulette began to draw herself together.

"Your father ran off, too. Did I tell you? He was my beau in those olden days."

Paulette leaned close to my mother. She tried to round up the loose photographs from my mother's fumbling fingers.

"Don't get upset, dear," she said. "The Lord works in mysterious ways."

She never looked at me again. After putting a kiss on the top of my mother's head, Paulette turned away and hobbled through the little front room, pulled her long coat from the tree by the door, and left. She was wearing lavender cloth slippers with a kind of hard rubber sole. I could see a bit of the white flesh of her legs below her coat because her stockings had fallen around her ankles.

"You shouldn't let that old bag bother you so much," I said.

"She doesn't bother me. She's my friend."

"You keep an eye on her when she's here?"

"She wouldn't take anything. She doesn't need anything. Her son takes care of her."

We fell into a silence. I let my eye wander around the kitchen. Except for a general griminess, the place looked tidy enough. Just the few dishes were out, and I couldn't offhand see any pressing thing that needed to be done.

"Did you want something, Peter?"

"I guess— I only came to see how you were doing."

"I mean do you want something to eat?"

"No."

"You should let your mother fix you something to eat."

"I should, but I can't take anything right now."

I tried hard to see any sign in her expression of the directness of her speech, but she could not meet my eye. I hoped that she would not make any mention of the Easter holiday that would fall the next day.

"Eileen got a better job," she said. "A raise."

"It's good that she's working," I said.

"She should be home with the boy."

I made no answer, and as the silence took root, I could see that she was getting lost. She seemed to be staring deeply at the palms of her hands, limp on the table. Except for her breathing and the bit of palsied shaking it made in her shoulders, there was nothing happening in the little kitchen. The measured ticking of the tall clock in the front room came faintly to my ears, vague enough to ignore for a while. It struck me how unbearable it must be to have lived your whole life and to have nothing to show. Then the electric icebox ticked on and the motor began to hum, and I pulled myself to alertness again.

I stood up and looked down at her. Then I pulled out the folded wad of dough from my pocket and peeled off enough bills to make a hundred. These I placed on the table, near enough to brush against her fingers. I hoped Paulette would not return before my mother had the chance to squirrel away the money.

Of course it was all on me. The boy was gone, and I had at least in part driven him away. Eileen had a beau—someone from outside the family— why shouldn't she? It was clear that I wasn't any good to her. And my mother? There wasn't anything to prevent me from showing her a little tender feeling, a little understanding. She was alone, and I was her only living child. But I could not bring myself to do it. I could not let myself be the man I knew I ought to be.

Lately I had felt my heart seem to labor in my chest. It seemed to flutter in a slow spasm now and again, even when I was sitting in my chair on the escape, doing nothing. I thought it might stop beating altogether, and I wondered how I'd feel if I knew with certainty that my life was slipping away. I wondered what I'd want to do then, how I'd wish I had lived. There was another thought that formed itself dimly, and I tried to push it back to the dark part of my mind: My life *was* slipping away at that very moment; it had been slipping away all along.

Though the sun was high up in the sky that day, it couldn't do much against the wild wind. As I left my mother's house, I turned my collar up and jammed my hat down against the cold.

Walking back toward Gratiot Avenue, I considered again if I could pin down the day I had gone astray. It might have been a day in early fall of 1943 when I went really wrong. After the mess with the riot and Captain Mitchell and Jasper Lloyd, after Lloyd's executive Roger Hardiman had been killed and there had been some settling of the score for his daughter Jane's murder, I should have been resting easy. Eileen and I had been going out now and again, stepping gingerly because we had been made skittish by loss. The shadow of Alex, her only son—somewhere on his own in the world—was always there, but we were used to sharing our places with shadows. I think the knowledge or the hope that Alex was still alive gnawed at us, but again, we had been accustomed by then to a world where our expectations were kept tight.

I had made a visit to my mother's place in East Detroit on a day in late September of 1943 when the trees had not yet begun to drop their leaves. All the heat of summer had been stored in the earth, or it seemed that hell pushed heat up from inside the melted ground below. I always ran hot, anyway, and the prospect of visiting my mother did nothing to cool my mood. I had not given up the old Packard yet, and I drove easily north to her place, noting with melancholy how so many cheaply built shops were springing up along Gratiot, how many boxy houses were ripping up what had been green and open only a year before. If I stayed away from her for a month or more, there might have grown the husk of a service station or a hat shop on a strip of road I knew as empty. It was impossible to hold on to anything, to keep the things you knew from changing. Even though I should not have had any emotion about East Detroit—my mother had only lived there a short while—it was just the same as any other place I might have counted on. Whenever some razor-edged memory of my young days in Detroit surfaced from my brain, I was always caught by the understanding that the landmarks

I had used to set those memories in place had all been changed or de-stroyed.

I stopped at a couple of places to pick things up for my mother, food for her and seed for the birds she loved to feed in the yard. As I carried it all in a big box up to her porch, I could see her looking out the front window, placidly gazing from behind the gauzy curtain at the new houses across the way. Everything in the area had a sense of rawness, of rudely built newness. The houses were plainer and made largely out of cheaper materials. For my mother it must have been much worse to think about what had with-ered away since her childhood. She had lived too long already: beyond the deaths of four of the five children she had carried into the world, beyond the murder of her husband. She had seen me change from a rambunctious boy to a shallow youth to a sour man in his middle age, maimed and distant. Maybe there had been a time when she felt pretty.

"Hello, Peter," she said. "You brought something."

"Yes, I did."

"I don't need anything."

"You have to eat, don't you?"

"I don't eat much."

Some days she was calmer and seemed more at peace. She had her fin-ger tucked into a book on her lap.

"I could cook for you, Peter, if you told me when you were coming."

"That's all right. I eat out."

"It's not the same."

I carried the box into the house and put the items where they belonged. There was trash to be taken away, and spoiled food in the icebox, and so I put all of it into the box I had brought. Over the throw rugs that covered the wood floor, I could see the paths my mother had worn during her days alone, back and forth in her limited track: the kitchen, the bathroom, the front room. The chairs she used carried the print of her backside. Her shoes were formed to fit her badly shaped feet and bloated ankles. There was a long coat she wore most days she went outdoors, even when it was steaming with heat. This held the shape of her stooped back even as it hung on the coat stand by the door.

"Eileen is fine," I called to her.

She made no answer, and I figured that she had lost herself in staring out the window again.

I walked out the side door and went into the garage. Since my mother did not drive, the garage served as a depository for all the items from the old house and from my rented house, which I had recently given up. Worthless truck was piled up against all four walls and tucked up into a loft made from old floorboards I had nailed into a platform. I meant to retrieve an old rake and some shears for Eileen from the garage. My father's old workbench sat along one wall, and I would have to hoist it aside to get at the rake.

The bench was not overlarge but it was heavy because it had been made from a number of boards glued together like a butcher's block. I supposed my father had made it himself as a younger man. The legs were as thick as my arm and looked as if they might have been turned in a rush on a lathe; they were hewn with uneven grooves all along their length. The top had been hacked and burnt and drilled so that its surface was splintered and uneven. Where the great vise had been attached, the grime was not as thick and the wood was not as splintered, and so I gripped the bench there when I tried to move it.

I found I could move the bench only an inch or two from the studs of the garage wall, and as I did it, pain tore through my back and shoulder, where I had been slightly injured by a bullet from Roger Hardiman's derringer just three months earlier. It ran through my mind that I was getting old and out of shape; I pictured my father shifting the bulky thing with ease. Between the swearing and the grunting and the heaving, I made little progress. *I'll go on a regimen,* I thought, *I'll take up boxing again, work the gym.* Each time I held my breath to shift the bench another inch across the concrete floor, I felt the veins in my head throb. I knew that even a young man could die in an instant if his blood spilled out into his brain. *That's the way to go, rotting out here for a month before my mother thinks of looking for me.* Finally one front leg snapped off the bench at the top and the whole thing fell slowly over. I fell, too, and just managed to avoid getting pinned under the big block. Worry had come to work so quickly in my mind that I couldn't help but imagine how my leg bones would snap under the massive weight of the bench. I gritted my teeth and tried to shut down the sinking nausea in my gut.

I picked up the snapped leg and felt a wave of emotion. It wasn't that I had any use for the bench. But I knew it was something that had been of much use to my father, and I could see what the work of his own hands had done to the worn wood. Some of my father's working tools were there in the garage, forgotten and useless for a man like me. My own extra things were there, too, my shoulder rig and my gun-cleaning kit, my record collection, some books I had read.

All of Fred Caudill's children were dead but one. What remained of his blood in the world amounted only to one misshapen son and one lost grandson. It seemed by my own lack of strength or faith that I was fading away, too, and I felt sad for my father. By all accounts he had been a good man. He had worked and worked his whole life and tried to hold things together. I was saved at that moment by my lack of ability to believe that my father could be looking down at me from some great hereafter. I was spared that shame.

I picked up the broken leg and examined it more closely. There was a big threaded plug in the end, probably an inch and a half in diameter, that had snapped jaggedly from its anchor in the underside of the benchtop. The wood was old and had dried, and so I was able to work the plug loose from the leg. From the surprisingly light heft of the cylinder of wood I guessed that the hole had been bored out and threaded all the way through to the other end.

I put my littlest finger into the leg, lifted it and peered inside, wondering if I could rig something with more modern hardware to reattach it. A thick roll of bright green bills slipped out of the end of the leg, then another and another. There were eight rolls of bills altogether in the leg. I unscrewed another leg to find it full of another eight rolls of bills, larger in denomination, and a third leg that held only two rolls.

This marked the time when my father had stopped stashing money away because he had been taken to Fighting Island and murdered. I had no doubt that the money had come through Frank Carter, Jasper Lloyd's flinty chief of security for so many years, and ultimately from Jasper Lloyd himself. My father had done work for the Lloyd Motor Company during the labor troubles of the 1930s, this much I knew to be true, and it only stood to reason that he should have been paid for it. I turned and pressed the tight rolls of money in my fingers. They had all been secured carefully with butcher paper and strapping tape, and they felt almost as solid as ash wood. If it was this work for Carter and Lloyd that had brought about my father's murder, then I could see for myself what the life of a good man was worth in the world. *What about me?* I thought. *What am I worth?*

I was soaked through with sweat in the cluttered garage. I rounded up all the rolls of bills on the floor and sat down to consider them. From a guarded place came a heaving blast of hot sorrow; I cried for myself and my father, and for everything I had done to disappoint all the people I had known.

CHAPTER

5

There are places where you can't see across to the other side, and in itself that would make Lake St. Clair a big lake. But situated as she is along the chain of Great Lakes—like a heart-shaped hernia below Lake Huron—she suffers by comparison. The lake goes only to a depth of twenty feet in the channels. It keeps the waves low and makes for good sailing, good fishing. In winter, the shoreline freezes and the wind blows away the snow, and you could skate from the Detroit River north to the St. Clair River if you were crazy enough to try it.

There are pockets in Detroit where the money runs deep. Down in Indian Village and close to Belle Isle, east of downtown, you can see how it is. The houses sit squarely on their big plots of land with an ease that can't be faked on the cheap. Grand Boulevard spreads right down to the bridge to Belle Isle, and in that neighborhood you could get a cop to help you by stubbing your toe. The debutantes and private-school boys prance along in their tennis clothes without any worry about the war or about finding gasoline or butter or new stockings.

East of Indian Village, beyond the eastward edge of the city, you can ride along Jefferson Avenue, following the Detroit River and Lake St. Clair right up to a place where the houses stand even farther apart on even broader stretches of property. The Grosse Pointes had blossomed before I was born into a haven for the lumbermen, factory owners, and fur traders who had made their fortunes in Detroit or who had brought it to the big city from outposts in the wild north, the upper peninsula of Michigan. By a queer blessing of geography, my mother's house in the city of East Detroit was hard by the Grosse Pointe area, not far from the water, and it was easy to make my way over to Whitcomb Lloyd's place along the lakeshore. There were a number of dazzling mansions nearby, but the Lloyd house had been designed to trump them all, in location and in size. Jasper Lloyd had employed some of his architects and builders to raise the place as a wedding present for his only son, Whitcomb, during the great flowering of the automobile giant's fortune. I had come to a vague understanding that the elder Lloyd now spent his days puttering about the estate, though it was far from any large plant in his empire.

I had a cab drop me off alongside the road. I was just stupid enough to let the taxi putter off before I had any idea if I'd really be able to get in to see the Old Man. It was only a short walk from the road to the gatehouse, and so I strolled at my leisure. There was a guard there dressed in a nice suit, and I guess he was used to derelicts approaching the place. He should have put me away, pressed a button to summon the Grosse Pointe safety men, but he heard me out.

If it had been me inside the gatehouse, and I had seen a man like myself approaching, I would have been put off by the sight. I was clean-shaven, it was true, but the eye patch and the outdated suit were a kind of signal. And the fact that I had just walked up from nowhere with an expectation of seeing the richest man ever to live in Detroit should have put the guard on edge. We had all seen during the tough times how men could veer off the path of reason. I had been forced to knock down a few men who had been put out of their apartments or lost their homes; they had the wild look I imagined I had now. But I explained to the guard who I was and what I wanted, and he calmly picked up his telephone and called the big house.

He was more like a mechanic or a gardener than a guard. After he put down the telephone, he walked me through the garage. Six or eight vehicles were lined up on the inside, including the big V-12 Franklin limousine that carried Jasper Lloyd whenever he traveled about the city. The big car sat atop a turntable built into the floor that could point it toward any of the three exit doors. Some of the cars were almost as old as I was, but they were all in perfect repair, spotless and shiny under the open trusses and high windows of the garage. A 1923 Lloyd Cargo Van, with Lloyd Motor Co. painted in red letters in the old style along the sides and back, was a proud reminder of the Old Man's working days. It seemed that the building had become more of a museum than a working garage, and I wondered if there were half a dozen more buildings just like it on the estate.

They made me wait, but after a time they sent a car out to pull me in toward the house along a sharply designed drive lined with poplars. I had seen photographs of the place, but still it seemed unreal. Around the last bend, the main building seemed to loom up suddenly. It was all designed to be overwhelming, and so I turned my head away until I felt the car come to a stop.

Jasper Lloyd's ancient cadaverous head lolled on his pillow. He was propped up on his bed in a state exactly between lying down and sitting up, and it was clearly impossible for him to find any comfort, even with all his millions to coddle him. He rolled his pale mustard-yellow eyes and trained them on me.

"I knew you would make your way over to me eventually, Caudill," he said. "You see we're in this together."

"Only you're living in a mansion."

He considered it. His eyes played about the room they had set up for him. Underneath a single satin sheet, his rail of a body seemed to writhe minutely for balance.

"I would trade places with you," he said, "if such a thing could be arranged. I've played over the idea in my mind a thousand times."

"You could find a better carcass than mine."

"You're in the prime of your life, Caudill. You might consider a brightening of attitude. You might work another fifty years in your time. They could be pleasant years or—"

"Is it safe to talk here?"

"They bring flowers every day," he said. "Sad to say, I am unable to check thoroughly for hidden microphones. I'm at the mercy of my son and his wife now, at the mercy of their servants." He wriggled up a bit on his cushions. "I ring a little bell when I need something. So far a nurse has answered every time."

"Be plain with me," I said.

"I get so many visitors, Caudill. It's tedious but necessary. The many relationships I've formed over the years must be tended to. I can't well drop away at the end of my time with unfinished business. But I must say, Caudill, of all my visitors—"

"Can you get up out of that bed?"

"It's frowned upon." He considered the idea for a few moments—his tired eyes looked out at the trees, went all over the four corners of the little box they kept him in. Then he slithered his hand up along the side of the bed till he found the button for the electric buzzer.

In a flash a slender fellow of middle age appeared at the door. He was dressed in a nicely cut suit with all the trimmings: cuff links, tie pin, pearl buttons. Yet the suit gave him an air of subservience, as if he had been forced to monkey up to please the old man.

"Yes," he said.

"Bring a chair for me, James," said Lloyd.

"A chair, sir?"

"A rolling chair. Mr. Caudill and I are going for a tour of the house."

The man stepped out and returned with another trim fellow and an old bentwood wheelchair. They briskly went through the business of transferring Lloyd to the chair. As they did it, I looked away. There wasn't any reason to look at an old man festering in his bedclothes.

"Where shall we go, sir?"

"Back to your cribbage, James. I'm sure Mr. Caudill is capable of pushing me along."

Both the dandy fellows gave me the eye, but they knew the routine well enough to hold their objections. I thought they might lag along behind us out of sight, but I could hear their footsteps falling away from us as Lloyd and I wheeled out of the room and down the long hall. I pushed him past the photographs of people I didn't care to know that lined the walls, past the paintings and the sculptures that sat on tiny pedestals. It was what a rich man's house should look like.

"My son is in South America," Lloyd piped. "His hand in the business takes him far afield. You might think he's seeing to the management of our plantations there, but I know what's in his heart. I imagine he's climbing a mountain or some such nonsense. Now of all times. And his wife is in California with her tea-party movie friends."

It was necessary to take an elevator to the ground floor. In the cramped space, I got a little too much of the stale smell of the old man. We rolled along the length of the house until we came to the great open room that enclosed the swimming pool.

"I used to swim for my health as a younger man," Lloyd said. "But I have not taken to water for recreation since you threw me into that filthy river almost a year ago. The doctors tell me that some of the water set into my lungs, and that it's caused a good deal of trouble for me since."

The water in the pool was glassy smooth. I wheeled Lloyd to a little table at the far end and sat down near to him.

"You'd rather I left you on the yacht with those men? A quicker death than just wasting away?"

He pursed his old lips and darted his tongue to wet them. His mustaches were silky and white, like a baby's hair, and they had shaved off his customary goatee.

"It's true I should be grateful," Lloyd said. He trained his eyes on me. The warmth and moisture in the air seemed to perk him up a bit.

"I've heard there's trouble for you," I said.

"There is always trouble, Caudill. Always a jury for this and a jury for that. It's a fabric of lawsuits that holds the business world together. This indictment," he said with phlegm rattling in his lungs, "this indictment doesn't cost me any sleep. They'll never get a thing out of me, if that's what worries you. My time has come and gone. Harder men than these have stood against us."

"If it's the G-men, they won't come to play footsie with you."

"The federal men take their orders from behind the curtains, just like any other hired men. They make a wage—they are allowed to make a wage if they fall in line."

"You say so."

Lloyd could muster just a spark of the fire he once had. There was only the flicker of dim hope to keep him animated. His eyes were moist and rheumy and he had lost so much vitality that his lower eyelids drooped down so you could see their pink insides. His sagging jowls worked around as he sat in thought.

"I fear now for my son," he said. "And secondarily for the company that bears our name."

It seemed unlikely that any spy could overhear our conversation; I could barely make out the old man's reedy drone myself. I can't say why he unpacked his heart to me—I had seen very old men lose their dignity before. Whitcomb Lloyd—"Nit Whit," as he was known privately to men like Hank Chew—was Jasper Lloyd's only son. He was the president of Lloyd Motors, a position secured not with his head for business but with the force of the company stock still held by the Lloyd family. As Jasper Lloyd explained to me, Whit had not shown an interest in the workings of industry. The younger Lloyd had enjoyed the family's sudden wealth, and had shown only that wealth could be enjoyed best when frittered away. Young Whit was a sportsman, a hunter and a climber, a skier, and in general an inveterate traveler, even during wartime, more apt to be found playing tennis in Palm Springs than in the boardroom of the company he was obligated to lead. He fancied himself, Lloyd explained, after the model of the intrepid British explorers of the previous century.

"He had lived all his days here in the Middle West," said Lloyd. "Until I sent him abroad to be schooled as a gentleman. The grandchild of farmers."

"I can't say what you ought to do about it," I said.

"But you're here to help me, aren't you, Mr. Caudill?" He muttered this so softly that I wasn't sure I heard right.

"You're thinking of Frank Carter," I said. "Or my father, maybe." Because I regretted having called Hank Chew, I thought I had come only to ask Lloyd for help in looking into the death of Walker's sister. I had been vague with the guard at the gate. Now I wondered how it could be possible for the Old Man to have some other plan for me.

"You couldn't hope to be half the man Frank Carter was," said Lloyd, stiffening his backbone and swaying in his chair. "Imagine it! Mr. Carter once commanded a force of over three thousand security men for me. He was instrumental in the formation of one of the greatest industrial

concerns in the history of the human race. The cancer that came upon
him—so suddenly—in the midst of such a grand enterprise. A man such as
yourself, Mr. Caudill, you couldn't possibly see the whole of it. You
couldn't honestly aspire to replace such a man."

"I don't see *why* I'd aspire to be your toady, old man," I said. "Why did
you let me in here at all?"

"I left a standing order to have the men let you through to see me if
you ever came," he said. "I knew you'd return when the money ran out."

If I had smacked him then, his brittle bones could not have held against
it, and I would have killed a giant, the last of the old titans. I stood up and
began to walk away from him. *Does he know about my father's money?* I wondered. *Is it possible that he can get into my safety box at the bank?* I didn't walk fast,
but I had gone a good ten yards or more before he gulped in enough air to
call after me.

"It's that witch Estelle Hardiman! She aims to ruin me!"

It was the only name he might have mentioned to stop me. It brought
up a flash of anger in me, and I walked back so quickly that the old man in-
voluntarily raised an arm to shield himself.

"She blames me for what happened to her husband. Of course she can't
prove anything!"

"I'm glad she's after you and not me," I said.

"But she's hell-bent—forgive me—on looking into things! I'm convinced that she's been pressing this investigation, this grand jury now. She's
connected to everything here in the city, and she'll hound me to my grave."

"Keep your voice down," I said.

Lloyd had worked himself up enough to make sweat come out over his
withered lip, seeping down to soak the neatly trimmed, silky whiskers.

"I'm finished. I'm finished. In itself this is fair enough. For my part in the
whole sordid affair, for the aid we gave in the early days to those vile men—
however little I knew of it—I must accept culpability."

"So you'll spill your guts to the jury. Just tell them everything, then."

His face puckered and his eyes could not keep from searching about the
big pool room.

"It's not for me," he insisted again. "My son ... my grandchildren ... the
city, how it's grown ..."

"So you'll just save the guilt for another day."

He became more measured. "I'll settle my account before the Lord like any other man," he said.

"As long as you can weasel out of the noose for the time being."

"Surely, Mr. Caudill, you are aware that your own involvement is far more direct than mine will ever be shown to be."

"So that's it."

"I'm not threatening you. I've asked for your help. You have an exasperating way of goading me into discomfort! I'm too old for this nonsense! I'm certainly willing to cast you to the wolves in order to protect my own interests. The war, these Germans, the Japanese are insane! They'll fight to their very last man! The work mustn't be disrupted!"

"Settle down, will you? If you kick off now, they'll pin it on me."

"Make light of death now, Mr. Caudill. Soon enough you'll confront your own mortality."

"Not so soon as you, I think."

Lloyd's chin drooped and his eyes traced a long crack in the floor tile before drifting out of focus. I watched him, but not too keenly. Maybe his old brain was dredging through some old memory, a time when horses snorted and pulled their carts through the dirt roads of Detroit, when he had been a young and hungry man.

"A young woman was killed and dumped inside the compound of one of our plants in Cleveland," he said finally, pursing his mouth.

"That's a case for the Cleveland dicks, isn't it?"

"It would be, yes, certainly. They've been gracious enough to allow an investigation discreet enough to deflect attention from the company. But now there's been another murder—a woman in Indiana."

"What am I supposed to do about any of that?"

"You see that it's all a part of a plan—a single murder, why, in a time of war, especially, a random act of violence might not prove so difficult to manage. But you see that they've crossed state lines, now. They've made it a federal case! That Hoover has been dogging me for years, and now, with war production so crucial—"

"Why would anyone think the two murders were related? Other than where they were found?"

He looked blankly at me. "The facts of the case."

"You'll have to be more plain with me."

"You haven't said whether you're interested in helping. For all I know," he said, "you're out to get me, too. Certainly you've not expressed a great deal of concern for my predicament."

I sat down and thought it over. Only a week earlier I had been all set up to go nowhere in my own time. It suited me. It wasn't a life to be proud of, but then I had never had that anyway. I couldn't blame Walker for dragging me in. He was only looking after his sister, naturally enough. I could have turned him away, as I had turned everyone else away. But now it looked like Lloyd had been ready to send his man James or some other drub out to drag me in anyway. I was bound to find myself muddied up in it, one way or another. I'd already made the promise to Walker, and my social calendar was empty of engagements.

Lloyd could see how I was going over it in my mind. "I expect you'll be asking for some cash now," he piped.

"Sure," I said, shrugging. "Throw me some dough, why don't you?"

CHAPTER

6

In the end I didn't take any money from him—just as well, considering. From the Old Man's secretary I got some papers and photos and a letter of passage with an embossed gold seal, which was supposed to get me into any of Lloyd's plants to have a look around. I had never put any faith in paper, but I took the packet anyway.

Evening came along before I could make my way back to my hole-in-the-wall. Since Ray Federle had more or less ruined my haven on the fire landing, I stayed in and spread out the papers from Lloyd on my little table. I guessed that Walker's sister had been found well inside the perimeter of the Lloyd plant in Ohio; it wasn't clear if the Lloyd security men in Cleveland had moved the body off the property to the swampy area outside the fence or if that was only a story for the papers. A few photos showed the area of the property where she had been found—what looked like a slag heap or a machinery dump toward the rear of the complex. There were no photos of the body, though, nothing showed blood, and I was glad for it. There wasn't much in the packet of papers I couldn't have scrounged for myself, and there wasn't anything that could make Lloyd look bad. It was just papers. Without an idea how it all went together, no one could use the packet to make any case against Lloyd. He didn't care anything about the women; he just wanted me to stop any more mess from happening.

Of course I was useless as far as this went, even more useless than I had been during my brief time as a police detective. After leaving my mother's house on Holy Saturday, I had simply shown up at Lloyd's gate. Lloyd could not have known I would ever show up there. How had I even known that he was staying with his son there on the east side? I must have read it somewhere in the paper. Why would I even believe what was printed in the daily rags? Yet every indication was that Lloyd had been waiting for me; he had been thinking of me all along. It was possible, I knew, that Lloyd might have been stringing along any number of palookas over the years, and he had only to wait for the unluckiest to show up at his door when something messy needed to be fixed again. But there was an odd feel to it; why should Walker's sister be involved? I had never given a specific word to anyone but Hank Chew.

I was startled by Ray Federle's sharp rap at my window. I could see his wide-eyed face peering in from the outer stairs, his palms pressed to the glass, a cigarette held to the side between his lips. As I lifted the window to let him in, I realized that it would be possible for anyone to enter my little room this way.

"Hiya," he said.

"You could use the door."

"Yeah," he said. "I'm funny sometimes." He was in his shirtsleeves, and he was rubbing his arms from the cold. "I wanted to apologize for my wife. I heard she really gave it to you."

"I've been smacked up by plenty of women."

"She worries about the girls," he said. "I was gone for so long, and now—"

"Next time I'll know," I said. "She won't get a drop on me. Kids or no kids, she gets the hard ticket out."

He smiled an empty smile, sucked a drag from his butt, and laughed the smoke out dryly. "It's only fair," he said. "It's only right. She won't give you no more trouble. She's sorry." He glanced around my place, and I could see that he had an interest in the papers on my little table.

"I'm about to hit the hay," I told him, though the night was still young. "If that's all you had to say."

"Okay! I only wanted to tell you how sorry I am."

"It's nothing."

"She's a good woman," said Federle. "She deserves to have a good life."

"Well, I don't stand in the way, so long as she keeps her hands to herself."

"Sure, sure." Federle tried to grin again, and this time it came out with a bit of feeling. "I'll tell her you're not mad. Is that all right?"

"Tell her what you want to."

"Okay, Pete." He made his way back to the window and hoisted a leg up on the sill. "I don't have a key to get back in my door," he said.

I could see that it was hard for him to move through the window and out onto the stairs. He was still young enough to have a spring in his step, but when he moved, something held him back. It seemed likely that he had taken some injury in the fighting. He would not have been sent home unless he couldn't go on. *Maybe he's got a wooden leg,* I thought. *Or two wooden legs.* But for the time I didn't care to ask him about it. If he had to tell me, I knew he wouldn't be able to keep it corked up.

After he was gone, I closed the window and turned the latch to lock it. I'm sure I did. While Ray Federle was still clanging up the metal stairs, I pulled down the shade and tried to think of a place to stash Lloyd's papers. I began to get thirsty for a drink.

I went better than two hundred pounds, even if some of it had turned to lard by then. I told myself that they must have come into my room at two or three in the morning—it's the only part of the night when my sleep gets so deep. To soothe my conscience, I told myself that they must have clobbered me in my bed right away, or maybe it was ether or chloroform. Either way, sure, I had the welts to show they didn't want me squawking while I went. If I ever looked closely at the little room I kept, at the way my building was set up, it might not have seemed possible that they could have carried me out without rousting the whole place given the size of me and the general cheapness of the lumber that went into the walls and floor. What a story! In my shorts they took me out and carried me to a car or a truck and drove me some distance across town. *They must have,* I thought, *they must have—or else I sleepwalked into it, and that doesn't seem likely.*

How could they have done it without anyone hearing? First thing I remember after lying down to bed is my feet in the water. It felt like swimming up out of a deep sleep, struggling to wake yourself up inside that darker world because your dream or your nightmare in some way matches up with the real world. If someone's knocking hard at your door in real life, you might dream about chopping down a tree with a hatchet. Because my feet were wet, I remember thinking that I was set to pee the bed, and so I forced myself to come to my senses.

My head got clear pretty quick.

Not much light came into the room, but I saw right off I wasn't anymore in Kansas. My heart threw an enormous heave of panic because I could not move. I was in a big room with an old wood-beamed ceiling. Some hard guys were there—one stood to either side of the long tank of water beneath me. *An electroplating tank?* They had me strapped faceup to a board, a sizable piece of lumber. My belly was lashed hard to the board with a cord tight up under my rib cage and another just at the top of my hips, my chest was lashed under my armpits, and my hands were roped together on the underside of the board. I couldn't move or even feel my elbows, either, but my legs were loose. I gave a start and my eye danced around the room.

They dunked me under the water for a few seconds and then brought me up.

"Jesus Christ," I said. "What is it?"

"You're a guilty man, Caudill."

I didn't say anything because I figured I'd need my breath.

"A dirty man."

I could not tell which of the two thugs spoke because each had a kerchief over his mouth and nose. They were close enough to touch—if my hands had been free.

Down I went again, not far, but far enough to keep my face under water. I could turn my head, crane toward the surface, but I could not move enough to let my mouth break into the air. How many seconds it lasted I couldn't say. Before my lungs burst, though, they brought me up again.

They waited for me to stop retching.

"Mr. Lloyd's troubles don't concern you."

"Sure," I said.

"Or do they?"

Again I chose to keep my breath.

"You're not talking, Caudill."

It seemed that they were switching off in their speech like a vaudeville act. *How many?* I thought. *One or two?* Even their voices seemed the same, if my ears hadn't been fouled with water. They had the timing of a comedy team. Both men had blue eyes, and I could see that they had muscles enough because they were naked from the waist up. But the real beef was at the other end of the long board. A pair of oxen, jumbo-sized boys, leaned their elbows on the board like a lever to keep me above water. I couldn't seem to make out their faces either. *Two big guys and two bigger guys.*

"You'll talk plenty before we're through."

"You'll sing like a bluebird."

"More like a blue jay."

It didn't seem funny to me.

"We'd like you to tell us about Jasper Lloyd."

I could see there wasn't any point in trying to be hard. But still—

"We're not bad men."

"Not too bad."

"We're all Americans here."

"In the service of our country."

If they were giving a signal to the lever men, I didn't see it. My eye was blinking furiously from the filthy water. When I went under, I kept still long enough to see the smaller pair wavering over me, looking down into the water. Then the thrashing started. You can't keep from thrashing. Sooner than the cords would ever break or come loose, my shoulders would pop out of their sockets. I knew it, but it didn't stop me from thrashing. My heart started whacking and my head cracked back on the board and my teeth were grinding. My only eye was burning like a welding torch in the socket, and I was sure that I'd be blinded entirely. But that was only a flash of worry.

Coppers? T-men? Some of Lloyd's own goons?

I guess I was racking all over the board before I finally sucked in water. If there was a certain moment when I gave up living and decided to suck water into my lungs, I can't say. I only remember how I retched up water and vomit after they finally lifted me out again. All that bile and filthy water washed out of my mouth and nose and fell warmly over my neck. My ears roared. I might as well have been dead—I was dead enough. The heaving and coughing I had to do was tearing and popping my muscles and my lungs because I was lashed down so tight to the board.

The masked men had stepped back to avoid the spatter, but now they moved back toward me. They didn't seem to be in any particular rush to get someplace else.

"Why don't you be friendly, Caudill?"

"Why don't you like us?"

"We like you."

I was coughing and spitting and cranking my head around to see what I could see. Even though I knew it just meant that they'd dunk me again, I sucked in as much air as I could, trying to live a little longer. If you don't have time to think about it and you have make a choice about living on for a little while or dying right away—you'll pick to live a little longer.

"Whyn't you just talk to us a little?"

"Don't be standoffish."

"It's a waste of my breath to talk," I said, gurgling slimy liquid through my voice box to make the sound. *Isn't that funny?* I thought.

"We'll be nice now."

"We promise."

Something like electricity it must be. Your brain flashes even if there's no light. You blink on, you blink off. You maybe can or maybe can't remember what happens to you. Your brain keeps sending the juice down the spinal cord even after your sense is gone; it makes your legs flail and your muscles pull even though it's tearing your skin off your flesh, pulling flesh from bone. Your brain wants to go on living even after it's not worthwhile.

What did I tell them? Maybe I told them everything I had learned from Lloyd, a bunch of nothing. Maybe I told them about Jane Hardiman, about my brother Tommy, about the nigger boy I had killed accidentally so many years ago. Maybe I wept for my father, for my eye, for my lost fingers. If I told them how I thumbtacked Lloyd's papers up under my kitchen countertop, over my silver drawer, if I blabbed or cried or begged for my life, it was out of my hands. The only thing I can bear to remember out of it all is how sick with disgust I was that my own life could be so small as to end like that.

CHAPTER

7

Sunday, April 9

She was standing over me with a silvery trowel in her hand. I thought that she might have kicked me to wake me up or to see if I was dead. Green grass with twinkling frost or dew obscured part of what I saw. She stood so close to me that I could see partway up her skirt when I began to be able to move my eye. She wore heavy stockings. When I began to stir, she turned away toward a bed of budding flowers and neat shrubs.

"Such a life of misery for you, Mr. Caudill," she said. "More and more pitiful with the passage of every day."

I thought I knew Estelle Hardiman's practiced voice, despite the tinny ringing that was constant in my ears. Though it required some effort to position myself to get a better look at her, I managed to twist my head and shoulders. I was sprawled out on the thick grass of a big estate. The house stood at what seemed a great distance. *It's so green, so green,* I thought. I had been dumped toward the back of the Hardiman property, near the service road. It was in that house that I first met Roger and Estelle Hardiman, first came to really feel the sting of what I could not ever have.

She had dropped to her knees a short distance away and now puttered along the edge of the grass with her trowel. Her fanny was toward me. Though she was a thin woman, the flesh at the back of her legs sagged sadly down toward her knees. I watched her working for a few moments, unable to move. She stabbed her trowel into the dirt, twisted nimbly to her feet, and turned to gaze down at me. The warm light of the sun, low over the lake, lit up her face and her glittering eyes.

"You've made me a widow, Mr. Caudill. I don't blame you, exactly, but you'll pay nonetheless."

She left a decent pause for my response, but I could not speak. The breeze over the open grass chilled the wetness in my bare eyehole.

She stepped closer to me and stood glowing with the promise of vengeance. "Do you remember the first time we met? That was the night I learned that my daughter Jane had been murdered. As I recall, you offered not the merest gesture of condolence."

I thought, *I'm sorry, I'm so sorry,* but I said not a word. I could not bear to look at her, and so I rolled my bitter eye to watch the slow progress of a horribly old servant as he made his way toward us from the house.

"It's a pity you couldn't have had more feeling for Jane. She was really... She was becoming a remarkable young woman. You should have known her. She of all people could never have deserved what happened to her."

I knew her. I did know her.

"A surly man you are, Mr. Caudill, surly, backward, and rude. This lack of civility is the plague and bane of modern life, and again you are *emblematic* of this *tragic... discourtesy.* To present yourself in such a way—near to naked on a lady's lawn, and so early in the morning... *on the morning of Easter Sunday.* But you'll see that I am a woman of great resilience."

The servant came near and unfurled a coarse woolen blanket. He stooped shakily and spread it over me and walked back toward the house. It made me think at once how cold I must have been.

"How fortunate for you that I am a woman of Christian charity. You might have frozen to death if you had stumbled onto any other lawn."

My thinking was pretty clear by that time, and I wanted to say something sour, a bitter thank-you. But my tongue was so swollen that it filled my mouth. The blanket seemed to press on me so much that I could take only shallow breaths, and my throat began to clench and throb with panic of suffocation. It seemed that I was becoming unfrozen, and now the pain of every part of my body began to twist. I was able only to produce a blatting sound like air escaping from a dead man.

"I think you'll live, Mr. Caudill," she said. "I think you'll survive to feel things more deeply from this point forward. First comes the pain of childbirth, and then the attachment of love—which is really a kind of pain, to be so attached to another human being that you must yourself feel the sting of every disappointment and all the loneliness she feels each day. Then of course there is the pain of separation. A number of strong feelings—such is the lot of poor mortals. But first and last you should remember the pain, Mr. Caudill. I promise to do my part to help you remember."

That was all she said to me. She turned away and walked up the slope toward the house, shaking. It wasn't long before they came to load me in the meat wagon. They gave me something to put me out, poked me in the arm. For that brief time before I winked out, I let my mind rove. If I remember right, I thought warmly of Eileen, though she was lost to me. I thought of my old man, and I wondered where I might get my hands on a gun.

CHAPTER

8

Tuesday, April 11

My front teeth were cracked and ragged. I couldn't keep from running my tongue over the newly sharp edges. It didn't hurt except when cool water sloshed into my mouth or when my breath pulled too much cool air over the broken parts. There were other places where the back teeth had chipped or where whole corners had cracked off. My fat tongue worked over the familiar smooth surfaces and the new rough ones. It was as if I'd gone away for a long time and returned to find my familiar landscape changed, as if I'd slept for twenty years. But my teeth were the least of my worries.

Three different doctors had given me so many stitches that they couldn't give me a real number as to how many it took to sew up all the torn skin over my arms and belly. One Jewish doctor with a bald head tried to josh with me that they wanted to bring in some new doctors to practice their sewing, but he saw pretty quick that I wouldn't go along. He kept smiling at me with his horse teeth, too close to my face. They had to change the bandages often because I would not stop bleeding. It felt like I had been boned and shredded, like a sack of wet bread, leaking and swollen and soft.

I guess I made it hard on them. They were used to seeing wrecked-up bodies and sick people, but I suppose it wasn't so common to see someone like me, just roughed up for the hell of it. They wouldn't give me a mirror. But I could see how my whole body was black and purple, even yellow, from being torn up so much on the inside. The swelling was awful, and where the skin had been plain torn off, scabs came up and then cracked and more blood seeped up in black rivers to fill the cracks. It wasn't only blood, either. From the raw skin of my wrists came a stuff like vegetable oil, clear and thick. The oil came, too, from the tips of my fingers and from the corners of my fingernails, where the skin was cracked and stretched from the swelling.

I was doped up all the time but it didn't make my mood good. It only made me mad that I was a little goofy. It was the first time I had to be in a hospital bed since my fingers and my eye had been blown away. I had to shit into a pan until they would let me get up.

Pretty soon that bastard Hank Chew came to see me. He rapped with his rings on the glass of the door and breezed right in.

"Oh, Caudill! You're an affront to my senses!"

"Go on out of here, then. Filthy buzzard."

"Gone on a bender, have you? A bit too much of the stuff?"

"That's the story," I muttered. "Fell off a streetcar."

"Well, it stretches the limits of credulity."

"That's your problem."

"Listen, Caudill, aren't we friendly? Didn't I agree to help you out?"

"That's nothing to me anymore," I said. "Forget about it. I'm not in any shape now to worry about somebody else's problems."

The pain by that time had become so general over my whole body that the irritation of Chew's presence was like the chirping of a cricket. He strutted about the room and then perched on the edge of my bed so he could speak closely to me.

"A man needs friends, Caudill. You need to keep up the ties that bind. You could have used a friend two nights ago, am I right?"

"Open up the curtain a little, Chew," I said.

He shut his yapper and looked sharply at me. Then he got up and tried to work the curtains. There wasn't anything to see outside but the tops of some trees, but I felt closed in.

"That's a professional workover," he said, leaning back on the sill. "An admirable job. You expect anybody to believe that you were tossed around by some guys at a bar?"

I shrugged and turned my bleary eye toward him.

"Out-of-town guys, were they?" Chew was delighted in his way to be close to something vigorous and physical, so full of blood. His eyes roamed over the damage with admiration. "Come on, Caudill," he said. "If it's a good story, I'll get at it one way or another. You'll come out better if you put your two cents in with me now."

"Move away from that window."

I might have slept if it was quiet. It was an effort just to keep up with what Chew was saying.

"I can work around you, Caudill. I'm not the biggest guy or the fastest guy or even the smartest guy, but I never give up. You can see that."

"If you keep sticking your nose in, you'll be the next one they come after."

"I'm not afraid," he said quickly. "I keep one eye open all the time. I can take care of myself."

"Still," I said, "still, you've never been worked over like this, have you?"

"No, I haven't. I guess I haven't been in a really good scrap since I was a boy. Is it bad for you?"

"If I have to pay, I'll pay," I said.

"What's that?"

"What did you dig up on the Negro girl?"

"She wasn't up to any good in general. Messed up in the dope and—you might say—lax in her morals."

"I could have figured that much out myself."

He squinted down at my eye. "Doesn't that bother you? Laxity of moral fiber?"

"I don't get you, Chew."

"Well," he said, pushing down his brows, "it was easy enough to pull from the police files. She'd been nailed on a couple of easy fingers, got off with fines both times, both down in Ohio." He scribbled something onto his scratch pad and squirreled the paper away in his vest.

"What's she got to do with Lloyd?"

"Nothing, far as I could figure. Plenty of men come in and out of that plant down there every day, looking for something to take their mind off their troubles. But... maybe you know something more about it?"

"You know I saw Lloyd the other day, then, ah?"

"Well, it's common knowledge."

"The Old Man says— Why don't you tell me everything you know before I start to blabbing?"

"Sure." Chew's face glowed with a smile. He came close again. "I couldn't scare up any kind of hard evidence," he said. "But a fella I know told me that the woman had been sawed up in pieces and left in a pile out in the open. Not just the usual wrangle-and-strangle dump job."

I tried to picture it with my foggy brain. I hadn't seen it with my own eyes, and it was hard for me to really feel anything about it. I said, "You've seen something like this before?"

"Somewhere or another there's always some of that going on, sure. Or do you mean more lately?"

"Well, I read in the paper that they found another girl outside the plant in Gary."

"You told me you didn't read the papers."

"I've been laid up."

"They found her outside the plant or inside?" Chew asked.

"I wouldn't know," I said.

"About the girls I've got only a morbid curiosity. Until it happens here in Detroit, anyway. It's the Lloyd angle that gets me."

"I can say the Old Man is plenty interested."

"Why did he let you in to see him? What's he want from you?"

"Well, he doesn't want me talking to you."

Chew threw up his arms and worked his little pencil through his fingers like a magician.

"Don't you remember how you called me the other day begging for help?" He seemed to have some genuine emotion about it. "Didn't I drop what I was doing to come down and see you?"

"Out of the goodness of your heart."

"That's how friends work, Caudill. I do a favor for you, you throw a little something my way. When you're a grown-up man, you mix your business in with your friendships. You don't think you'll find a friend who'll just heap you up with love and affection like your mother, do you?"

"I hope not."

"I see how it is," Chew went on. "I'm on a newspaperman's salary, and Jasper Lloyd has cash to throw around—"

Who can say how long Ray Federle had been standing in the doorway? He made no sound, but Chew and I both got the chill of it at the same time. We turned to see him there holding his hat in his hands. The entrance to the room was in shadow, and his round eyes glowed out at us.

"This fella bothering you, Pete?"

Federle stepped in with a gentle smile forced onto his face.

Though it hadn't crossed my mind before that moment, the sight of him made me think that he had been a part of it. It didn't figure, and I didn't really believe it, but I couldn't keep a flash of fear from lighting me up. I saw that Federle carried a bundle under his arm as he came toward the bed.

"I brought some clothes for you."

"They won't let me go."

"Sooner or later," he said. "They won't keep you forever." He looked Chew over. "I'm Ray Federle," he said, shifting the bundle to his other arm so he could put out his hand.

"Chew. Hank Chew."

"Friend of Pete, are you?"

"Not so friendly as I might have thought," said Chew. "I'm just heading out."

"Chew is a newspaperman," I said.

Federle looked more sharply at him and shifted his feet on the floor.

Chew ripped out the pages with writing on them from his little book, folded them carefully, and tucked them into his vest. Then he moved to the door and grabbed his coat with some deliberation.

"Comes a time, Caudill," he said, "give me a ring."

Federle watched him go and then positioned himself facing the door.

"Newsman, ah? Think you'll make the papers now?"

"Not yet," I said. "I don't think so." I could see that Federle was looking for some signal from me to put him at ease, but I couldn't produce one. I eyed the bundle. "I won't ever fit into any clothes of yours," I said.

"It's your things. The coppers were inside your place tromping over everything, and I asked if I could grab a few things for you." He moved silently around the bed to sit in the chair.

"They just let you in?" I asked him.

"I told them I was a veteran and all." He smiled and rubbed his palm over his thigh. "I come out on a disability."

The chair by my bed was set up in front of the window, and it was hard to look beyond Federle's slender figure to see the trees. I guess I drifted off for a time—or just closed my eye—because it startled me to hear him speak again.

"Some kind of case you're working on with Chew?"

"Case?"

"I heard you talking."

"Chew is like a buzzard. He's always looking for a story."

"I could help you out, Pete. Let me help you out. I can handle myself. You're in no shape."

"Don't you already have a job?"

"They got me pushing a broom," he said.

No matter how much they doped me up, whether I was awake or asleep or distracted by talk, I couldn't escape the pain. I couldn't stop thinking. I couldn't just jump up and tear my body away and go soaring off. I was trapped inside myself, and there was no escape. It brought up a panic that set my heart to racing, which brought more throbbing pain to every part of me that had blood.

"Listen, Federle," I said, talking low so he'd lean close, "any chance you could get your hands on a gun for me?"

He sat back in the chair. "Sure, I could, probably. But—ah—what exactly were you thinking of?"

"Something I could hold in my hand. Something that wouldn't show under a jacket."

He mulled it over. "Sure. Maybe I can see. But what's the case?"

"I'll be out in a couple of days," I said. "I'll come and see you."

I could see how it hurt when he pushed himself out of the chair. Just a small grimace he tried to clamp down on.

"Get some sleep," he said. "That's what you need." He looked down at me tenderly, like he wanted to say something more. But then he resigned himself and walked stiffly out of the room.

To watch him go I had to shift my head, which jangled my neck so much that I saw colors. I couldn't see how I had ever been friendly enough for Federle to make him want to latch on to me like he had. Maybe he had been through something over the ocean. Maybe I reminded him of somebody else. Except for me—a sour, tangled man—the room was empty, and I was left with the idea that I should not have involved Ray Federle in the mess I was about to make. He had a woman and kids to think of. I wasn't clear in my thinking.

I could see a number of robins and some starlings sitting at the top of the paper birch outside my window. Smoke or mist from somewhere drifted upward and faded into the sky. In the bowels of the hospital something knocked and whined and echoed through the walls. There was melted together the smell of bleach and piss and vomit and a relentless humming that finally lulled me to sleep.

CHAPTER

9

Wednesday, April 12

When I woke up she was pressing her kerchief to the side of her nose to keep from having to blow it. Tears streamed down both sides of her face, and she dabbed here and there to keep the water from going down her neck. To my fuzzy eye she seemed to quiver, holding back sobs.

My effort to speak brought a catch in my throat and a hacking cough. If Eileen had not been just inches away I would have spat the blob of mucus and filth from my mouth. Instead, I just choked it down and clenched my gut to keep from retching.

She rose and put a hand on my bed rail.

"Pete, for God's sake," she said.

"God's sake nothing," I croaked.

She leaned her plump hips against the rail and let her hand come down lightly on my shoulder. She touched my hair and ear and my cheek, and I winced because the touch was something like pain.

"Who could have done such a thing?"

"Some hard fellas."

"But why?"

"Hell."

"They only just called me," she said. "Why did you wait so long to tell them to call me? I could have come yesterday."

"I didn't think about it," I said. But I was thinking, *I never told anybody to call you.*

"It looks bad, Pete."

I rolled onto my back and tried to sit up a bit. The pain had subsided but I was getting more and more stiff and swollen. I could barely see because my cheek and brow had puffed up to cover my eye.

"Have you got a mirror?"

She turned and fumbled with her clutch. Her swooping little hat stayed tight to her head as she bent over; it matched her short coat and her skirt.

"Here—but you shouldn't..."

She opened her compact and handed it to me. I couldn't stretch my arm out far enough to see my whole self, and my hand shook so much that my reflection reeled. They had brought me a new patch for my eyehole, shiny and cheap-looking. Blood vessels had broken all over my face, and the swelling and redness made me look fat and old and dyspeptic. I brought the little mirror so close that I could smell Eileen's powder, a delicate odor that sharply reminded me of the time I had been close to her. The brown part of my eye looked the same but what had been white was now shockingly red all around, not just bloodshot but strongly and solidly red, like a demon's eye. The bright light of morning hid nothing. I closed the makeup kit and gave it back to her.

"It'll get better, Pete. Things will get better." She had at least stopped the tears, but worry screwed her face away from how pretty it was.

"It's ugly to look at," I said.

"The swelling will go down."

"Did you tell my mother?"

"I'll go over there today," Eileen said. "I can bring her by."

"Don't say anything to her. Don't say anything to anyone."

"All right."

She was still shaking a little. With the kerchief still wrapped around her finger, she clutched at my hand.

"I'm glad you came," I said. "But you should stay away."

"Have you fallen into something again?"

"That's what it looks like."

"I have to help you, Pete, if I can. You can see that's true, can't you?"

She had put on a few pounds, and she seemed uncomfortable with the weight. With her free hand she tugged down her jacket and smoothed the skirt.

"You can stay at the house while you heal up. I'm working now but I can cook—"

"I heard you got a fella."

"Well, Pete."

"It's all right. He's a good guy?"

"We've been out to the show a few times."

"It's good for you," I said.

"Does it make you jealous?"

Maybe it was the first time I had tried to smile in a while. "Sure," I said.

"It's a shame how things work out."

"Listen now. It's for the best if you just keep away from me. For a girl like you I'm nothing but hard times. I don't mean to be that way. Go on with your fella and—"

"Don't be overdramatic, Pete."

"I'm trying to say I care what happens to you."

"I know you do."

She sat back down in the chair and crossed her ankles. Her hands picked at the kerchief in her lap. Gradually the lines of worry eased from her face, and she looked at me seriously for a long time.

"What do the doctors say?"

"My shoulders are torn up. Probably I won't play baseball anymore. My back is funny. My feet are tingly. You wouldn't want to see how they stitched me up."

"Do you want to tell me about it?"

"I'll tell you someday. When we're old, it'll seem funny."

She glanced around the room for a clock.

"I'd better go," she said. "I told them I'd be back before lunch."

"Go on," I said, now with a bone of regret in my throat. "Again I have to tell you how sorry I am. I'm a sorry bastard."

She got up quickly and leaned as well as she could over the rail to get close to me, close enough so that her familiar sweet smell brought a rush of emotion. I pressed my lips together and soon enough tears welled up in my eye. I blinked them away.

"How did you find out I was here?"

She stood up and tugged her jacket down again. "Somebody called. They left a note for me at work," she said.

"Who called?"

"Pete, I couldn't say."

I pressed my eye shut and took in as big a breath as I could. It was like a tendril of malice that could reach out to brush her cheek. Had I told anybody to call her? Were the four goons putting another touch on me? My hands were too swollen to squeeze into fists.

"Don't come back here," I said.

"I won't."

"I'll come to see you after a while."

"Just let yourself get better, Pete. Please, please."

She came down again to put a kiss to my hot forehead, and then she had to push off me a little with one hand on my chest to get back upright. It feels just like tearing wet paper when your stitches rip.

"I'm so sorry, Pete. I have to go."

She grabbed her bag and skipped out. I listened to her heels clicking down the hall and began to think about how to drop the rail on my bed.

CHAPTER

10

Eileen was the only one I cared about, the only one who could get me worked up. I cared about her son Alex, but it wasn't the same. The boy had gone off on his own, and it gnawed at me to think that the blame fell to me, but I had no worry that Alex could hurt me like Eileen could. She was like a gate right into my gut. I suppose the sentimental guys would say heart.

It's the sort of thing that comes to you in a dream, and so I was not sure that I had actually ever been on Estelle Hardiman's lawn. Nobody was talking about any of it at the hospital, least of all me. Certainly in my dreams I've had to answer to the ghosts of my guilty past many times. I wake up and doze off so many times on a regular night that it's like cream swirling into black coffee; I can't always keep straight what's real and what's just bubbling up from memory and imagination. Of course, I wasn't in the best shape. A little pain can brighten your senses, but such a mess of it brings the fog in.

Estelle Hardiman cared not a bit for me. Maybe the boys who had worked me over were T-men or G-men, or maybe they were just out-of-town thugs she'd imported from Palm Springs or Brooklyn. From the way they tossed me over, I knew I was only a nuisance to them, and not worth a proper disposal. They were looking for something on Lloyd, the only fish big enough for the old broad to put her hook into. But if Estelle Hardiman was on the inside of the whole thing, then the whole game was rigged beyond my ability to tip. I couldn't turn to the police or trust any judge to see it my way if I wound up in the slammer. Since I wasn't a copper anymore, I couldn't go where I wanted like I owned the place. If I walked into any trouble carrying a gun, I might wind up in the can, and if I wound up in the can, I knew there was a good chance I'd bump into some punk I'd rousted at one time or another.

I couldn't put down the rail, so I slithered toward the foot of the bed on my belly and lowered my feet down off the corner. I pressed my face down into the blanket to quiet the moaning. All up and down my whole backbone it seemed like an ice pick was jamming first up one side and then the other. When my feet hit the floor I yelped just like a dog, like any animal would. Though my back was shot to hell, my legs were all right, and so I was able to stand after a few minutes of wrangling clear of the bed. It didn't hurt, but I could tell from the warm fluid oozing over my skin that I had torn up the stitches on my arms and chest.

Then I realized that I did not know what they had done with the bundle Federle had brought. There was a kind of bin or locker they used to store linens, and I staggered across the room to it. A young volunteer with a beet-red birthmark on her face like a map of Italy stepped into the room and gasped.

"Oh, dear!"

"Nurse said I could take a crap on my own," I said.

"Well, let me help you."

She came over and tried to take hold of my elbow.

"Go on," I told her. "It's part of my treatment."

"Just to the lavatory."

"All right, but just be careful, can't you?"

I put out my mangled hand and squeezed hard on her little mitt when she took it. She had to hide her surprise at the odd contour of my hand but to her credit did not pull away.

"Listen, girlie, what time do you get off?"

"Why, I don't know."

"They work you like the devil around here, do they?"

"I—I only just started today."

We reached the door to the little toilet.

"If you'll stick around until I do my business, maybe I'll lay a little sweet talk on ya." I put on a broad smile so she could see my cracked teeth, and I made my red eye wander all over her. But for the birthmark she wasn't bad off.

"I—I—I'm—"

"What's the matter, you got a fella already?"

"I—I—I—yes. Yes, I do."

"That's all right, then. But if he don't keep the candle lit, you'll think of me?" I pulled her clammy hand toward me and leaned my big head down so close that she had to bend backward to keep away. Then I let loose, stepped back into the head, closed the door, and hoped she'd run off without telling anyone. Truth was, I needed a trip to the toilet anyway. But I stood with an ear to the door for a moment, and then stepped out to retrieve the bundle of clothes. I went back into the toilet and locked myself in.

There wasn't much room to move, but there was plenty of stuff to hold on to. I pulled off the hospital gown and took a good look at what they had made of me. Blood had mushed around under all my white skin, and there wasn't an inch of me that wasn't some odd color, from the top of my ruddy forehead to the blackened nails of my toes. Bandages had been taped over the deeper stitches, but they were now darkened in spots with seeping red. The stitches I could see wandered like rivers where I had torn myself against the binding cords.

But it was my face that was most amusing. The light in the bathroom seemed set up to make you look ugly on your best day, but still it made me grin to see it. My whole head was swollen and round. Unlike the rest of me, the face was a uniform bright red, as if I had been caught forever holding my breath. My dark, greasy hair was combed back, but the swelling made it stick out over my ears. My eyeball, too, was bright red all around the brown iris, though the swelling of my cheeks allowed only a slit to show through. The cheap patch they had given me was glossy like satin and added a formal flair. The best part was the smile. Through all the gnashing I had chipped the corners off two of the front teeth, and now the grin looked crazy and overwhite, like a mutt with the rabies.

Since I was getting only half lungfuls when I breathed, the exertion of making it to the lavatory left me panting. I opened Federle's bundle and found a set of clothes neatly packed around a pair of shoes. The shirt and shorts and trousers were so daintily packed that it struck me immediately that his loco wife must have done it. But I remembered that Ray Federle had been in the service, and even in my degraded state it touched me that he would take the care to fold my frayed and dingy shorts like a nursemaid. I found my wallet tucked inside one shoe and a pair of socks in the other. My money and my operator's license were still inside the wallet.

I kept thinking that they would come and start pounding on the door to the head. Getting out of the gown had been easy, but getting into the shirt was hell. My hands had not been injured so much, but my fingers were swollen to twice their normal size. I don't know how long it took me to button up and to tie my shoes, but it seemed like time enough for some nurse or doctor to set an alarm that I was out of my bed. Finally I shrugged into the jacket and managed to button it in front. Really, I didn't look bad, but from the neck up it was a catastrophe. Federle had not thought to bring a hat—with my bean the size it was, none of my hats would have fit anyway. I figured I'd just have to be seen only walking away from that point on.

Everybody uses the elevator in a hospital, even when it would be quicker to use the stairs. And another thing—no working stiff will roist you if you're walking through any part of a hospital where you don't belong as long as it looks like you're on your way out of the building. I lumbered my way to sunshine with only a slight jangle of pain at each step.

It took some time and a bit of wrangling at the bank to get them to admit they knew me. I smiled a lot because I liked the effect it seemed to have on people. They couldn't get me into my safety box because I didn't have the key with me, but I did empty out my regular account. It was enough money to float for a few days.

I was all set to take a flop down by the river near the cement factory. I knew some guys there who knew how to go all around under the city in tunnels. But then I thought I might as well go back to my place. Sure I was afraid. But sensibly there wasn't anything more they could take from me. They had run right through me. Then again, you can't always depend on people being sensible. It would have been sensible for me to load up all my truck and go down to live in a swamp in Florida. There was just the alligators to worry about down there, I had heard, and they were generally more trustworthy than the average guy.

The super at my building gave me an extra key for my room but only after I had to hear about his bad foot and how his children were no good and about all the trouble I had caused. I could see that he only wanted a friend to listen to his troubles but I just took the key and walked away from him. He was still talking as I made it out of earshot.

Across the street and up at the far end of the block there had been a little guy watching for me to come. He was leaning on a post there by the newspaper boy's box, and he rolled into the phone booth to make a call just as I stepped into my building. And so as I clumped slowly up the back stairs, I figured somebody would come to see me eventually. It didn't make any difference who it would be. Maybe it had been Chew's boy, or Lloyd's, or Estelle Hardiman's, or the volunteer's boyfriend. Maybe there had been a number of guys I hadn't seen all up and down the street. They might all come to see me at the same time, and we could make a regular party out of it.

Already I had some regret about leaving the hospital. Though it was dead boring there, and though I could not get used to the stench of sickness, at least they brought me food and drink. They were taking care of me. Without the medicine, I knew, and without a nurse to properly change the bandages, the pain and the possibility of infection would be worse. It wasn't likely that I could sleep as well in my own bed as I had in the hospital, either. There wasn't any real plan brewing in my mind, any urgent course of action. In fact, I didn't have any recollection of making a decision to leave. I thought maybe the swelling had damaged my brain. I thought, *What a difference it would make if I turned into a retard.*

As I turned the key to slide back the dead bolt on my door, I was thinking that it might be nice to listen to the radio. I wondered what progress Ray Federle had made toward finding me a gun. It was only then that something knifed into me: Eileen had told me that someone had left a note for her at work. *Federle?* Even with my brain as addled as it was, I knew it was not possible that I could have told him anything about Eileen. Why should I have believed it was him? *Probably the coppers called her. Sure, they knew me well enough.*

I was too far gone to think much about it. But however much I tried to push back all the murky thoughts drifting through my brain, I had to admit to myself that I had fallen into something bigger and messier than I was prepared to slog through again. *Who bolted the door like this? Who else has the key?* I stepped inside and pushed on the door till it clicked tight behind me.

My place had been tossed, but gently. Drawers had been pulled and turned out, but all my meager junk had been placed in neat piles. They had opened up the back of my radio and left the six screws that held it together in a row at the back of the counter. It looked like a joke a kid might play. Not much had been broken or torn apart. The bed looked like it had been tipped over and put right again. I did not need to make an inventory to know that nothing of value had been taken or broken—there was nothing of real value to me in the place. I kept a few photographs in the box at the bank for sentimental reasons.

I shuffled over to the silver drawer, took it all the way out, and set it on top of the counter. Though I couldn't get down properly to see up under the counter, I stuffed my hand inside and found that Lloyd's papers had not been removed. I had tacked the envelope right close to the front, and as far as my fat fingers could grub, the papers seemed just as I had left them. In trying to force my groggy head to consider what else of value might have been taken, I fell into a sort of stupor, leaning on the counter crookedly, numbly. That was it. I had come to it. As a man I wasn't even worth a proper knockover.

There was the one thing—and I had put off thinking of it because I knew how much trouble it would be to replace it. I had augered and filed a little hole in the brass lamp that sat by my chair. In this little hole I kept the key to the bank box that seemed to hold everything worthwhile I had managed to glean in my sorry life. The majority of it, I knew well, had been earned by my father. Since the lamp operated mainly with a switch on the wall plate, it was hard for anyone to notice that the key wouldn't turn like a switch or that there was a real knob on the back of the base to let the juice through. I walked over, kicked my ottoman upright, and eased myself down into the chair. Because I had changed, the chair didn't fit me like it had before; but I was able to relax because I could see that my key had not been discovered.

Even though it was the middle of the day, I fell into something like sleep. My mind wandered over everything: my unlocked door, Federle's woman, my mother's garage, Jasper Lloyd's foul breath. I don't think I ever stopped rambling along like that—half awake—before a low knock on the door brought me to attention.

I had stiffened up so much that I could not move from the chair.

"What?" I said.

Muffled speech seemed to echo through the wood.

"It's open," I said. "Just come right in."

There was no answer, but now I could hear or feel the knocker's weight shifting in the hall.

"Come in, you ass! Come in!"

I was seized by a fit of coughing that propelled me to my feet, crabbed over with my hands on my knees. The knob turned, the latch clicked, and the door opened a sliver. I kept hacking and gasping until I dredged up a rubbery clot of something from my lungs. I spat it out into my hand and noted that it was flecked with blood.

"Mr. Caudill?"

I wheeled to see Lloyd's slim secretary, James, standing timidly inside my door.

"Well?" I said.

"Are you all right, sir?"

I stomped toward him so he could get a good look. He kept his horror pretty well hidden, but I was afraid he might slither back through the door, so I turned away and limped to the kitchen area.

"Your jacket, sir," he said. "It's ruined."

"That's fine. I got it at St. Vincent de Paul's."

"But you've bled through the back. You've run off from the hospital."

"It's a bad habit," I said, turning again toward him. "I do what I want."

He considered his words for a moment. "Mr. Lloyd wonders if you're in any condition—"

"I'm all aces," I said, trying out my grin on him. "I'm peaches and cream."

"If you're in any condition to assist him further."

"You can see what kind of shape I'm in."

The secretary had a neat businesslike timidity, and there wasn't any reason to treat him badly. It seemed possible to imagine that he was a decent fellow in his private life.

"We can arrange for personal medical care," he said. "A nurse—"

"Can you get me some penicillin?"

"I should think so," he said. "I can send a nurse to look at the bandages. The stitches will have to be removed."

"Ah," I said, and then I swallowed and tried to clamp down on a blinding surge of pain that raked my sinuses. "Why didn't you tell me that the girl was chopped up?"

"What girl?"

"Look now, don't dummy up on me. Why didn't you tell me about the girl at the Cleveland plant? Now this other girl—"

"I'm not in a position to tell you anything, sir. I'm careful to perform within the limits of my function. I only keep things in order for Mr. Lloyd."

I knew it wasn't any use bracing him—and I knew I wasn't in any condition to play rough with anybody, even a secretary. For all I knew, James was a golden gloves champ. He'd go about flyweight, but I was already coming apart at the seams. I waddled away from him again, pacing to relieve the pain in my lower back.

"Mr. Lloyd is anxious to make some progress."

"Well, Jesus, why don't *you* look into it?"

"I'm not sure I enjoy Mr. Lloyd's complete trust."

As best I could tell he wasn't trying to be funny. He kept his words guarded, but I could see by his face that he was speaking more personally now than professionally.

"I don't know," I said. "I don't know."

"You've faced danger before. I don't believe I'd fare as well as you, given the circumstances."

"Listen, I just got the habit of walking into trouble. I'm not anybody to rely on. I could go south any time."

"Mr. Lloyd doesn't believe you will."

The secretary waited me out. As a practical matter it's hard to stand stock-still for such a length of time without doing something with your hands; but he did. I was flummoxed by the whole load, and panting all the while from the pacing and the pain. A chill ran through me when it hit me that I wasn't sweating at all—did it mean something?

"I've brought you a badge of sorts."

It wasn't a regular badge like a police shield but more like an identification tag. At any of the auto plants it wasn't unusual to see the men and women with tin tags on their coveralls, but this one was larger and heavier, and it looked like it might be worth a little something if the silver was pure. He held it up for me by its little clip. The rounded Lloyd trademark was enameled in red, and the rest of the raised text had been topped with blue, like a blueprint. It looked official, sure enough. My full name was spelled out, and Jasper Lloyd's facsimile signature scrawled out at the bottom corner. I took the badge from him.

"The badge will allow you unfettered access to any plant controlled directly by Lloyd Motors."

"What about the paper you gave me?" I said. "Wasn't that supposed to get me into the plants?" It occurred to me that James might have arranged the whole beating to see how loyal I was, but I was ranting in my own mind.

"I'm instructed to tell you," he said, "that notice has been given to allow your passage. The badge was my idea. I've found that—you're to report any difficulty—"

"So now I'm Lloyd's flunky? Is that the kind of job that draws a paycheck?"

"Certainly I can arrange for some payment," he said. "A cash arrangement would be preferable."

"I know a fella who needs a job. A colored fella."

"I'm really not in a position—"

"Forget it," I told him. "How much cash are you carrying with you?"

"None at all."

I felt too dry to keep talking, but I didn't want to have to offer him anything to drink. There was only spigot water and alcohol. We were still standing just inside the door to my place.

"You can get some money, ah? Deliver it where I tell you?"

"Within reason," he said.

"Hold on—you have a pencil?"

He slipped one practiced hand into his jacket and came up with an outsized fountain pen. From another pocket he pulled a little blank card of stiff paper. It reminded me so much of Chew that I gave a shudder. I gave him Walker's name but I couldn't think of the street number.

"You've a figure in mind?"

"Ten thousand?"

"Five?"

"Why not?"

I was beginning to like the fellow, and he continued to win me over.

"Mr. Lloyd thought you might lack adequate transportation." He dangled an ignition key on a ring from his pinky finger.

"Well—"

"I've parked the car down below," he said.

There wasn't a thing to do but go to the window to have a look. Down in the alley sat an old roadster, illegally parked.

"Lloyd sent over a Chrysler? He couldn't send something newer?"

"There's a bit of travel in the steering," said the secretary. "But you'll find it suitable." There was the trace of a smile in his voice. "The engine has been modified."

"Anyway, it beats the streetcar." *It's like a dream,* I thought. *What have I fallen into?*

I caught him looking at his wristwatch as I turned back toward him. He stood patiently while I crossed the few feet toward him, and he dropped the key into my shaking palm. His face was placid in the main, except that now and again his eyebrows would get close together and his head would tip to one side.

"You'll want to make a visit to the younger Mr. Lloyd. He maintains an office at the big plant. He's forced at present to curtail his travels due to some pressing business with the board of directors."

"Sure."

"Good luck to you, sir. Good-bye."

So far I hadn't done anything. I kept the key pressed into my palm and wondered how far I could get if I left right away and kept driving until I hit ocean. How long would it take me to get to a place where the sky was big and the clouds swept away farther than you could see? Along the back roads the hayseeds might part with some of the gasoline they'd kept in rusty tanks since before the war, and I could put the windows down on the Chrysler and let the air whip away the ringing and the buzzing that now plagued my ears. I could just walk out to the middle of a great field of wheat and lay down until I melted into the earth.

CHAPTER

11

I started drinking right after the secretary left, though it was only mid-afternoon. I was surprised to find a pint of whiskey in my cupboard with the seal still on it, and I put it to good use. The doctors will tell you how bad liquor is for the old carcass, but that's only true in the long run. The booze cleared out my sinuses right away and eased my breathing. Before long I felt right, and some of the pain in my muscles loosened and drained away. If my liver rotted out in a few years, it was a proper trade-off for an evening of comfort. I thought I knew enough not to drink myself into a wicked hangover.

Since I didn't have anything else like a weapon, I spent a good hour or two trying to put a proper edge on my meat cleaver with a tiny whetstone. It was not a blade to do a butcher proud, and I knew that my swollen grip was not firm, but it was better than nothing, and it was soothing enough to keep me from thinking too much. As the day faded I gave up trying to sharpen my only other blade, an ancient paring knife with a broken tip and a wooden handle that rattled against the tang and the rivets.

I became tired from the booze and from all the work it took to heal. What I needed was sleep, a solid block to let my body take care of itself. It was early still, but I capped the dribble of whiskey left in the bottle and got up to pull the shades. Something made me pause at the window. I was light-headed, and I looked for a good place to fall over. The spell passed, but I stood for a moment more, all abuzz from the booze. I heard someone in the hall coming to my door, and I knew it was Federle.

He rapped in a syncopation, like a secret code.

"Pete? Pete?"

It seemed to take me a long time to get to the door.

"Pete? Pete?" More knocking.

When I pulled the door open, it made a puff of cool air on my red face. I don't think I knew how tall Ray Federle really was until that moment. He was very slender, and he had a kind of restless energy that seemed to burn him up from the inside. It reminded me of the partner on the police force I had known so briefly—Bobby Swope, until he was gutted.

"Hey, Pete. Listen, I didn't know you were going to bug out of the hospital so fast."

I stood aside so he could enter.

"It's better I come through the door, eh?"

I shrugged and walked over to the counter.

"I'm on tonight," he said. "They're giving me some hours. Don't pay much, though."

My legs trembled as I stood with my good hand propping me at the counter. I did not want to face Federle, because I was afraid he had done what I asked him to do.

"Got a light on, eh? It's all right. The liquor will dry you up—takes the swelling down. We used to drink grain alcohol when we could get it."

He had moved closer to me, and I could feel heat from him. I felt dully that I needed to piss.

"What do you know about me, Federle?"

He stopped in his tracks and considered it. "Not so much, I guess," he said.

"Did I ever tell you anything about myself?"

"Ah," he said, "you don't need to if you don't want to."

He stood calmly before me. I was screwing it over in my mind, what Eileen had told me. Now I wasn't sure if I had only imagined it or heard it in a dream. "Have you been talking to anybody about me?"

"Pete, why would I? I told my wife I had been to see you, sure." He furrowed his forehead. "Who do I know around here?"

"A friend of mine told me you left a note for her at her job," I said. "Does that make any sense to you? How could she have called you by your name?" *Am I thinking straight?*

A dark and steady cast came over Federle's face. "Somebody's putting one over on you, maybe," he muttered. "It looks like somebody has it in for you."

"Well," I said, "never mind about it. Maybe...I'm a goner anyway. Maybe I heard it wrong."

He looked me over with some concern. "If your bandages are bled through, you need to get them off," he said. "You got anything clean to put on?"

"Maybe some gauze."

"You can tear up a shirt if you need to. It don't need to be fancy." He walked off to rummage through the medicine box in my bathroom. He had an armload of truck when he returned.

"You're like Florence Nightingale," he said. "You've had some medical training?"

"That's all stuff that sits in there. Never been opened." It was finally coming down on me, all of it—the blunder I'd made in going to Chew right away, the beating, the liquor—how I couldn't get rid of Federle—and I was about to collapse. Fine enough. The chair would do if I couldn't make it to the bed.

"Get that shirt off and let's have a look," Federle said. "Sit down here. The other way."

He more or less pulled the shirt from my back and set to work. I straddled the kitchen chair and put my teeth together as he pulled tape and dry bloody gauze from my back. The way his hands moved, it reminded me of a squirrel burying a nut in the grass.

"Jesus Christ, Pete," he said. "This shirt is ruined, so I'm gonna use it."

Though my front side and my arms were torn up more thoroughly than my back, it was the pair of slashes from the edge of the board on my back that caused the most trouble. Over my shoulder blades, the cuts were deep and kept moving and opening. Federle splashed hydrogen peroxide over everything and swabbed it away with patches of gauze and the ruined shirt. Then he broke open the small bottle of mercurochrome and used swabs to dab it into the deeper holes.

"You fucker," I said.

"Hey!"

"I don't mean it." The red stuff burned like hell, but I figured it was doing some good.

"Don't worry, don't worry. You need to dry up. You need to stop moving around so you can scab up good."

"You shouldn't be so nice."

"You got anybody else to be nice to you?"

"Jasper Lloyd sent me a car today."

"That's the box down in the alley? The Chrysler?"

"Sure."

"It's got a towing tag on it. They'll come in the night to tow it away."

"You move it for me?"

"I can do that."

"Why don't you take it to work with you?"

"Oh yeah?"

"It don't cost me anything."

"I really can't say how much—"

"You got that thing I asked you for?"

He pressed a patch of gauze down and taped it in place. "I got a line on it," he said.

"You'll need some money."

"They don't give stuff away," he said. "Except cars, I guess. Old Man Lloyd can bear to part with a little."

"Take what you need from the counter there."

"But what's the case? What do you need the gun for? You're working for Lloyd?"

"You're sticking your nose in."

"Well, you're asking me to stick my neck out. I got a family, such as it is. I'm not afraid, but—"

"Lloyd's in some trouble and he asked me to look into it."

"You're going after the boys who roughed you over?"

"Maybe so, maybe no."

"Let me help you," Federle said.

"They strapped me to a board and put me under the water."

By this time he had finished his work on my back, and I could see him stalking restlessly out of the corner of my eye.

"I've seen some of that," he muttered. "Fucking Japs wouldn't take a hint."

I was still straddling the chair with my arms crossed over the top of the ladder-back. Though I was dead tired, I couldn't let myself slump because it pulled at the stitches.

"What happened to you?" I asked him.

The question made him squirm even more. He was at the window, checking the latches and peeking through the shade.

"I got burned up," he said, "by my own guys! Don't that seem funny?"

"Let me think on it a little while."

"You ever seen a guy burned up, Pete? I guess you must have."

"I've seen a little of everything. But mostly the burned ones were really burned down to charcoal."

"You and me—ain't we a pair!"

I had to get up from the chair. Federle skipped over and took my elbow to keep me from falling.

"You'll be all right, Pete. The whiskey will dry you up. I've seen plenty worse than this. I could open up a story that would make your hair stand up like a porcupine! Maybe sometime I'll tell you."

He steadied me where I was and went over to the counter. With one hand he slid the clip off my money and spread the bills out. He picked up the bill he wanted and held it up for me.

"This is what he's asking," he said. "But I haven't had a look at it yet. And if the piece is on a no-payment loan from somebody, I can probably talk him down."

"I don't care about the money," I said. "Keep it for yourself."

"Ain't we friends, Pete? You shouldn't give me money."

"Suit yourself. I said I don't care about it."

He picked up the key to the Chrysler. "Get some sleep," he said. "That's what you need. You should drain off before you lie down. You understand? Latch up this door when I leave."

Some part of my brain sparked with an idea.

"Thanks for the whiskey," I said.

"It was lying up in the cupboard at my place. I figured sooner or later my wife would be at it." He shook his head. "Not so good for me."

I was cold from standing shirtless, and it made my belly clench. Federle let the key and the bill fall into the pocket of his baggy work trousers. Slipping out the door, he glanced around my little place. "Drag something in front of the door here. In case anybody wants to pay you a visit tonight, it'll make a racket for you."

"Sure," I said, "but I think they're done with me."

"Good night then."

"Thanks, Ray."

He pulled on the door until it clicked shut behind him. The last thing I saw of him was his eye. The white showed all around. Though I figured that Ray Federle probably knew how to walk without making any noise, I could feel him waiting on the other side of the door. I secured the dead bolt and pulled the bare telephone stand over to the door.

Federle moved off down the hall. Though it was still early, it had gone dark outside, and I knew that soon the spiders would come to plague him. I was glad at least that he'd have the car so he could get away from things. Against advice and my own sense, I didn't visit the toilet. I turned off all the lights in the place, stepped out of my trousers, and rolled into bed. My head throbbed but not notably, and soon numbness settled over me. As I burrowed into dreamland, I thought I heard the Chrysler's engine jump to life and rumble away down the alley.

CHAPTER
12

Thursday, April 13

It might have been around four in the morning when the pain in my bladder woke me up. My eye, adjusted to the dark, easily made out the way to the toilet. It took so long for me to produce anything that I finally had to sit down to piss like a woman. The chill in the air made me shiver the whole time, and when I finished, I pulled a blanket from the bed and wrapped it around me.

It didn't seem likely that I could make it through the window and up to my seat on the fire escape without a terrible ruckus—if I could manage it at all—so I pulled up the shade just a bit and dragged my living room chair near the window. Without the lights on, it was easy to see out. I didn't have the view I would have had from my seat on the fire escape, but it was comforting to see my old alley.

Federle had been right about the liquor. My hands felt less swollen, and my breathing was a little easier. I was all alone, really, and I realized that there wasn't much keeping me alive. If things kept running toward misery, I figured I'd skip over to the other side some day soon, step in front of a streetcar or a truck or heave my carcass off the top of the Guardian Building. Not to botch it up, that was key. Certainly with a gun I'd have a way to do it reliably. In a second it could be over. In a second I could kill Federle or anyone. That's what a gun's good for. I could run up and kill Federle's woman for the price of a slug or two.

Maybe I had contracted a case of the spiders, too. I was trying to remember what the Catholics said about killing yourself. It wasn't something you could work off with just a spell in Purgatory. Or was it Limbo? It seemed like a pretty good story, and I wondered how the old-timers had ever come to make up such a thing. What was there to live for, really, if you didn't believe in heaven, if you knew that nothing could last forever? My face wasn't whole anymore, and I couldn't tell right then why anyone would want to have anything to do with me. Outside my window I could see how the few feeble lights were swallowed by inky blackness.

Federle's woman was upstairs somewhere with the children. It seemed a lifetime had gone by since she slapped me. Was she happy that her man stayed away at night? What sort of black scheming moved her sleep, her daydreams? Federle had gone off to war—and now at night he had to keep his hands at work or lose himself to the darkness. Though it was not my greatest talent, I tried to move myself to feel for all the poor souls who might be in the same boat as me or Federle. Millions of men had been sent off to war, and they didn't have the luxury of sitting by a window and thinking. They were getting shot up or they were burning or killing someone else, all of them caught up and lost in a wave of darkness like the world had never seen.

I had been in Detroit my whole life. I knew how fast, even in the best of times, I knew how easy it was, for any ordinary man to get shuffled to the bottom rung of the ladder, or to panic on the downward slide. When I was working as a police officer, I knew how many guns could be found under mattresses and in closets when we had to come in and haul some sorry bastard off to the pokey. Some men had to hock their iron to scrape up a few dollars for another week's rent or a meal or to have their child's tooth pulled. We got called over, too, whenever a gun got turned around backward. You don't see it spelled out in the newspaper how many men put their brains out after they've come to the end of their rope, how many make the quick decision to take a hard rest after so many frustrating years.

Even the newspaper men, with skin as thick as bark, however they might thrive on dirt and scandal, know they can't print everything. Just as a way of getting things to keep working at all, it's often necessary to put on a happy face and stay civil during the daytime hours.

But for those who come awake at night, there is no way to escape the thought of it. The human world is a place crawling with fellows who could go bad at any moment, and it's only the daily decision to stay civil that lets us paint our pretty pictures. I knew well what Federle was trying to tell me about the spiders. He had trusted me, on the first day he had ever spoken to me, to understand that he meant to do well but couldn't ever be sure that he would. I played it glum and made no answer then; I kept what I thought to myself. Federle had been to hell, and now he had come back to a place that wasn't much better. Federle wanted to show me, he wanted to let me in on something, but I already knew enough about it, and I had already decided for myself: It's best to keep such things quiet, not to let the words of despair come out of you.

By the time Federle crept up to return the key to the Chrysler, I had put myself together. My tub was rigged with a shower ring and curtains, and I managed to rinse part of the stench off me and to wash my hair. In just the couple days I'd been away, my razor had gone dull, and I would have cut myself up if my cheeks and neck hadn't been puffed out smooth. My clothes were wrinkled from the toss but still clean, and when I finished dressing and combing back my hair, I thought I knew the face looking back at me in the mirror. I threw out the glossy patch from the hospital and used one of my own. Despite myself I felt better, and I hoped that some movement might work away the stiffness and the tightness of my muscles. I was glad not to be hung over. My head seemed clear.

Federle came up and knocked softly at the door, even though it was near ten in the morning. I came over quickly and cleared the door and opened it for him. Though his movement always seemed crabbed, he skipped in my door with the same agility and sense a cat might have coming in from the rain. He held a small paper box in his two hands like a football.

"Pete, you look swell," he said. "Are you heading out?"

"I might step out for a bite," I told him.

"That car runs like a champ," he said. "Don't look like she's ever been run much. You might've thought they kept her in a garage."

"You got something for me?"

He seemed surprised by the question. With his two hands he pushed out the box to show me and then reflexively pulled it back to his belly.

"You ever played with a gun much?"

"Hand it over," I said. "Don't I seem like a serious guy?"

"Sure," he said, passing the box to me. "He wouldn't take no less for it. But I put a couple gallons in the tank from the garage service pump."

There were a few rags wrapped around the piece to keep it from rattling. I pulled the whole mess from the box and began to peel it like a banana.

"That's like an officer's weapon," he said. "Generally we only carried the long stick."

I held the semiautomatic pistol in my hand and pointed it toward the floor. It was half again as heavy as my old Police Positive, and the grip felt too square in my palm. But from the action and the look of it, the gun had been cared for by someone. I wondered who it had been stolen from—and if it had been used in any other crime that would now track back to me.

"This fella wouldn't part with any rounds," said Federle. "I figured you could pick them up somewhere. You know anybody?"

"Don't worry about the shells. He didn't have a shoulder rig to go with it? I should put this in my pocket?"

"You'd wear that on your hip—in a holster. I'm sorry, Pete. I can ask him about it."

"No, no. Don't worry about it. I might have a rig somewhere." I was thinking glumly that I'd have to dig through the standing forest of junk in my mother's garage. I had not been inside it since I found my father's stash of bills in the legs of the workbench.

"So it's all right?" Federle asked.

I turned the gun over in my hand. It was too heavy, too long, and too loud for the job, and automatic guns required too much trust in complicated machinery.

"It's fine," I said. "That's one I owe you."

He smiled and seemed to slack down from his edgy stance a bit.

"You should stay out of trouble," he said.

"I should, but I don't ever listen to reason so well."

"Pete, let me tag along with you."

"Tag along where?"

"Wherever you're going. You're on the case, right? I'm not asking for any favor. I can handle myself. They give me an education in the marines."

"You got a job already."

His deep brown eyes showed hurt. "They got me scrubbing out toilets, Pete. I'm the low man. They got me swabbing up after niggers, Pete, scraping up chewing gum from the floor."

I wrestled with it. He was pent up and quivering, a wiry retriever waiting for me to toss him a stick.

"Come on," he murmured.

"You got a license to drive?"

"Clean and healthy," he said.

"Go on and get cleaned up," I told him. I pulled my lips together and ran the tip of my tongue over my broken teeth.

"Ten minutes," he said.

He was out the door and down the hall before I could say anything to take back my offer. I kicked the oily rags and the box toward the closet where I kept the trash because I didn't care to endure the pain of stooping to pick anything up. Since the gun was only a danger to me without bullets, I stashed it in the bare cupboard. I wondered if it would be possible to sneak into my mother's garage without her noticing. I felt the dread that seeing my vile condition might bring up some motherly feeling in her. And I knew that the garage would reek with my father's presence. My old cleaning kit had weathered a Michigan winter there, but I knew it would contain everything I needed to take care of the piece. It didn't seem likely that the old shoulder rig would do for the bigger pistol, but I thought I might at least try it out—if I could find it at all.

My plan was to go out to the Lloyd main plant just to see if I could actually get in with the pass badge. Beyond that, I thought I might have a look around to see if I could scare anything up by accident—I had that much of a plan. If Whitcomb Lloyd was there and if he would see me, he might be willing to talk. The Old Man had surely sent word to him if he was in town.

Probably Jasper Lloyd couldn't keep himself from sending a steady stream of notes and messages to his boy even though he was supposed to have given up control. I didn't see how Whit Lloyd could possibly keep as tight a grip on things as the Old Man had been able to do with Frank Carter's help. Accountants were running things these days.

Federle came down and rapped at my door. He was dressed in a white shirt and gray flannel slacks. He had passed a dry razor over the thick beard that grew toward his chin. As I stepped out into the hallway, he offered me another bundle.

"My wife Patty baked some bread for you," he said.

"Hell. I get my bread around the corner." I took the package anyway.

"She cooks good."

We struggled down the stairs to the street. I followed along as he continued to gab about his wife's cooking, about the weather. The Chrysler was parked along Heidelberg, and as I squatted to get into it, I tried to see who might be watching. I didn't have as much of the panic I had felt after running away from the hospital. The dope they had been feeding me had trickled away, and my head felt clear but for the railroad spike that had evidently been driven through it. Probably the new car on the block had pricked the interest of the neighbors, and I couldn't shake the feeling that someone or other might try to put a tail on me. But I couldn't actually see anything wrong. Even as a kid, I didn't ever see so very well, and now with the one eye it was hard to pick things out in the bright light. Sensibly I might have picked up some specs to make the vision better in the one eye—or just one lens and a piece of frosted glass over the patch.

Federle wanted to head west on Vernor, and I didn't say anything about it. We drove by the cemetery and kept on Vernor for a time, even though it would have been faster to roll down Mack. But just as we crossed over Grand River, Federle forced the car into a veering left onto Third Street from the right-hand lane, and then turned east again on Cherry. He slowed down almost to a stop and kept his eyes on the rearview mirror.

"I thought you told me you knew how to drive," I said.

"You said to keep an eye out," he said. "I got spooked."

"Go on down to Michigan Avenue, it goes straight out. And don't try any more trick moves. If somebody wants to put a tail on us—"

The whine of a motorcycle cop's siren made me clap my mouth shut. I turned my whole body around so I could see.

"Just the one thing I asked you to do, Federle. Just the one thing."

"The clutch is tight!"

"Just stop the car," I said.

The officer pulled the cycle ahead of us and angled it toward the curb with its lights pulsing weakly in the bright sun. He put the stand down and swung his leg off the machine.

"You didn't lie to me about the operator's license, did you?"

"I got it with me."

The tall officer put his gloved hand at the corner of the windshield and bent low. I could only see his mouth but I thought I recognized his way of talking.

"That's a bad display of driving, sir. Can you explain what you wanted to do back there?"

Before he was asked for it, Federle put out his operator's license for the officer.

"I'm sorry," he said. "I missed a turn."

"Is this how they drive in California?"

"No, sir. I did a wrong thing there. It won't happen again. I'm just getting adjusted to the streets here." Maybe Federle was worried that I had stuffed the piece under my jacket. The tendons on the back of his hand stood out white as he pressed on the steering wheel with his fingertips.

The officer put a foot on the running board and bent down to have a look at me. Though the light was working against us, he could see me well enough. An easy smile came to him.

"Pete Caudill," he said. "I almost called you detective."

"Good to see you, Johnson. They got you down to traffic now?"

"I like the outdoors." He slipped the license card back to Federle. "Sewer gas and diesel fumes, just like back home in Kalkaska."

"You put on a few pounds, Johnson," I said. "You got a girl cooking for you?"

"I get a girl now and again. But listen, Pete, what's with the mug? What happened to you?"

"I got thrown from a horse."

He was talking right over Federle, who had his hands in his lap and his lips pursed.

"That's the story?" he said.

"It's a hard town, Johnson."

"I'd be happy to … You've got a friend or two left, Pete. If it's bad, you should let the regular police in on the deal."

I could see that Johnson was considering a talk with Captain Mitchell of the major crime squad, his natural uncle. "Johnson, I appreciate the concern. But there ain't much to do now, unless you can change a bandage."

"All right, Pete. I know how it goes," he said. He looked down at the pavement for a moment, considering. "I go all over, but I hang my hat at the precinct here if you want to say anything about it later."

"I appreciate it, Johnson. But I ain't in any trouble. I'm just driving around with my friend here."

He looked us over for a bit longer, and then stretched his neck. On his face I could see the worry and cagey concern. It was a face that had lost a great deal of boyishness in the months since I'd seen him last. He and Walker had done well with the bad hand we had been dealt before the riot, and of the three of us, he was the only one who seemed better for it.

"It's good to see you, Pete," he said. "It sure is."

"I feel the same way, Johnson. Good luck to you."

Johnson stepped back and drew himself up to run the kinks from his backbone. He straddled the cycle and looped back the way he had come. Federle and I sat for a stiff moment in the car.

"A police detective, eh? I knew you were on the force, but that's something I might never have figured you for."

"I never figured myself for it either," I said.

Had I ever spoken to him about being on the force? It seemed either that I had lost the knack for remembering what I gave away with small talk or that Federle wasn't playing straight. But for the time I let it pass, and with some difficulty I rolled down my window and tried to enjoy the cool wind and the sunshine. It was good to be out and about in the light of day, while the spiders had all tucked themselves away to wait for darkness to come again.

CHAPTER

13

"Regular army," Federle muttered as we drew close to the administrative gate at the Lloyd plant.

They wore their rifles slung back and didn't seem to have much to do. As always, the entire area was a hive of activity, and with change-of-shift on the way, I was glad we were about to get off the road. There was growing worry about industrial saboteurs, and so security at all critical war production plants had been tightened up. It seemed unlikely on this sunny day that anything might run amiss, but I knew a storm or two had passed over Lloyd's pride and joy, and not so long before.

Federle drove up to the guard shack at the gate. A Lloyd company guard with an oversized cap and a sidearm in a white holster stepped down from his post.

"What can I do for you, gentlemen?"

I passed the badge to Federle, and he gave it to the guard.

"We're here to see Mr. Lloyd," Federle said. "We've got free passage."

The guard peered at the badge, looked us over, and peered at the badge again. He stepped back, looked over the old Chrysler with an odd look on his face, and then came close.

"Mr. Caudill, do you have a specific appointment with Mr. Lloyd?"

"Sure I do," said Federle. "The Old Man sent us."

"Who's this?" the guard said, nodding toward me.

"He's my secretary," Federle said.

"That's right," I said. "Secretary and personal valet." I tried to nod curtly, as I had seen James do.

"How come he don't drive?" asked the guard.

"He's got a bum eye," Federle said. "And a wooden leg. He's a good secretary, though."

"All right. Hold on."

The guard seemed to have been hired mainly for his deliberate slowness. He took the badge back with him to the shack and got on the horn to someone on the inside. As he waited for an answer, he continued to stare hard at the little glittering badge, as if it was a kind of magic trick that demanded an unwavering eye. When he got through on the line he mainly nodded into the phone and muttered answers tersely. It seemed to take an eternity. I tore open the butcher paper and began to pull apart the loaf of bread Federle had given me. I sawed off a bite and worked it around a little. It was good bread, very salty.

"I guess you guys check out," said the guard, handing the badge back to Federle. "Pull on through and park right along the way, you see? Somebody will come out to take you in."

"Thanks, brother," said Federle. He made a derisive salute with two fingers to his forehead.

The whole long gate rolled away on casters after the guard made a signal to the controller. Federle pulled in slowly, leaning forward to get a better look through the windshield.

"Can you believe this?"

"It's a factory," I said. "You didn't have any factories in California?"

"Sure, but still. Guys like us."

"They got you cleaning toilets at a factory, don't they?"

"But over there I don't get to come in the front door."

Somebody's assistant had come out to get us, some flunky, and we stepped toward the building. I brushed a trail of bread crumbs from my jacket and my slacks as I shuffled along. The front of the building was impressive but in a halfhearted way. You could see the grim businesslike hand of the Old Man holding back the designers. Everything worked to shuttle the pencil pushers and the bean counters to their holes inside. Visiting businessmen could be processed, whatever their language, like DPs on Ellis Island.

The brisk assistant walked off ahead of us and stopped to wait at each turn. He used a key to open an elevator, and we stepped inside. There was only an unmarked button inside, and we rode upward to what I guessed was the fourth floor.

It wasn't any different from the ground floor, as far as I could see. A great many doors lined the hall, and through these an assortment of suited and uniformed men streamed quietly to and fro. There were women inside the offices and inside filing rooms. Federle and I caught glimpses of them as we passed, but nobody said anything to us. Something about the design of the place made it hard to bear; we could see people talking but couldn't make out the words. My head was beginning to spin from the walking.

The lackey led us through an unmarked and open door into a round reception area. He stopped dead and jumped back, bumping Federle and bringing our whole train to a halt. By the window stood a stooped man of medium height pinching dead leaves from a potted plant.

"Mr. Lloyd!"

Lloyd turned brightly toward us. He was taller than I had first been able to see.

"Mr. Caudill and his secretary, sir."

Lloyd walked over to Federle with amusement on his face.

"Mr. Caudill?" he said.

"I'm Caudill. He's Federle."

"Whitcomb Lloyd." Lloyd put out his hand eagerly to both of us but shook with a poor grip. He pushed my hand away when he was done, clearly glad to be through with the formality.

The lackey piped up. "But Mr. Lloyd," he said, "where is Mrs. Bates?"

"I've given her the remainder of the day to pursue her leisure."

"Shall I find someone else?"

"Think for yourself, Rogers. Don't we pay you to take care of things?"

Rogers scuttled behind the broad, rounded desk and picked up the telephone there.

"Now, Mr. Caudill, Mr. Caudill. My father has spoken well of you, but I must say—"

"I'm not so easy on the eyes right now."

Lloyd smiled and led us back into his inner office. "I know about your mishap," he said. "But I was going to say that your face is clouded with worry. And also yours, Mr. Federle."

"We weren't born with the silver spoon," Federle said. "Sir."

Lloyd studied Federle for a moment. He drew his posture out and seemed to grow a few more inches. "I was born into a poor mechanic's family," he said. "My father and my poor departed mother worked to impart to me the values of thrift and diligence from the time of my infancy."

"Did the lesson ever sink in?" I asked.

"Certainly not! I should say never! Does my father seem happy to you, Mr. Caudill?"

"No."

"He's never once been satisfied. Every triumph he's made has been attended by a dozen new worries. He's never been the sort of man who can step away from the fray to contemplate and remember what's happened in his lifetime." Whit Lloyd drew himself up to his full height, and I saw that he was as tall as I was.

"So you see, Mr. Caudill, that I've learned from my father how *not* to spend my life. Are you satisfied so far with the course of your own life, Mr. Caudill?"

"I don't say so."

"Follow along, then, and perhaps you'll become enlightened."

He opened the door to what seemed to be a closet and revealed a tiny elevator at the rear of the office. Lloyd waved us in, and I could see that Federle had to bite down on himself to keep from balking. We crowded onto it; it might have held four men if I hadn't been so bloated. Lloyd closed the pocket door and pressed the lowermost button on the panel. When we hit bottom, we stepped out into a broad, well-lit corridor.

"We're perhaps thirty feet below the ground here," Lloyd said. "Have you a fear of enclosed spaces?"

"We've got business, Lloyd."

"Call me Whit. Why shouldn't you? When again will you have the chance to hobnob with a titan of industry?"

"It's about the murders," I said.

"Murders?"

"The Old Man asked me to stop over to look into it, that's all. He seemed to be worried about you."

"You can see, Mr. Caudill, that I'm well secured here. As it is, I can't get a moment's leisure. Presently we'll be joined by a guard and a clerk wielding a clipboard. They appear from every corner of the place. I can't be rid of them. That's why I like to travel whenever I can."

Federle stood apart and regarded the corridor. It ran as far as the eye could see and sloped gently upward in the distance, and it was apparent that it branched off to the various sections of the great plant. There was a little propane-powered cart parked along the wall.

"I come all the way out here," I said. "I don't want to play."

"How much did my father pay you?" Lloyd asked.

"He didn't pay me anything."

"Then you did it for love. I was going to offer you double payment not to trouble me, but I don't trade in such fickle currency." He cocked his ear and listened to the footsteps echoing down the stairwell next to the elevator. "They follow me in case I say something brilliant that needs to be recorded for posterity. We'll outrun them."

He climbed aboard the cart, and Federle and I joined him. The thick metal door of the stairway opened, but Lloyd started the motor and we puttered off down the corridor.

"I'm sympathetic to your position, Mr. Caudill." Lloyd drove eagerly, with his head craned forward and his belly almost touching the wheel. "I know how painfully tedious the workings of such a situation can be, and I'm keen to help. But really I'm of no use. I know nothing about these killings. You've no idea what a grip the legal department has in such a place as this. No one here is even permitted to speak to me personally of any criminal activity. Let's kill all the lawyers! There is a chain of responsibility. You're the only one who's dared to broach the subject with me. But you're an outsider! So I suppose it's all right."

"Can you give me an idea why these murders might be happening just now?"

"Hypothetically, if such a crime were to occur? You mean now, as opposed to any other time in the company's history when we weren't surrounded by the sharks of commerce, when we weren't caught up in a great war?"

"So you think it's possible someone might be doing this—"

"We are beset at every turn and in every arena by men of boundless energy and deadly purpose, Mr. Caudill. Even the subordinates in my own plants, if they're worth their salt, have designs. It's really quite exhausting even to think of it. It's intractable."

Federle said, "Now *you're* unhappy."

Lloyd turned back to look at Federle with delight. "But I have an escape!" he said. He stopped the cart at the end of a side corridor and cut the motor. "I have a life outside this place."

"I've got a wife and kids, too," said Federle. "It ain't all peaches and cream."

"My wife! My wife and I have, you might say, a marriage of conviviality. I haven't seen the woman more than three times in the past year. My children are off to school, well coddled, to be sure." He turned a mocking dour look toward me. "And safe, too, I should say."

Federle muttered something that was lost in the echoing tunnel.

A guard sat on a stiff chair before the door at the end of the corridor. As we approached, he stood and spoke into a grate in the wall.

"Can you manage a few steps?" Lloyd was at least ten years older than me, and though he was sometimes stooped and slack about the jowls, I could see that he had some of the spring and grit of his father. If Federle and I seemed crippled to him, I could let it pass.

"Go on," I said.

We plodded up a couple dozen steps and another guard let us through to the factory floor. Though the din broke partway through to the stairwell as we climbed, the full sound blasted like a wave when the thick door opened. Lloyd stepped aside to let us be awed by the spectacle. Compared to the cramped passageways and elevators, and even to the office building we had been through, the factory was so big as to seem like the outdoors.

Here it was easy to see how a minor god full of purpose had tried to make a world in his own image—and had succeeded as well as any man in history.

Aircraft engines came slowly along on hooks like hogs in a slaughter-house, then came down to the men on the line with air-driven grinders and bolt guns. The great line turned back on itself and crossed over an immense craneway, unused for now. The comforting stench of grease and oil and pneumatic fluid swirled up from the floor and out through an immense bank of sunward windows, thirty feet or more above. So much was happening at once that I knew I would never be able to understand, even if it could be explained to me; but I did not really envy the men who had to understand.

"Twenty-four hours a day," shouted Lloyd close at my ear. "And yet there's talk of default on our military contracts. A great deal of pressure, as they say."

It was hard for me to imagine how they could squeeze more production out of the place than they already had. I looked out on the whole thing through the haze of dust and humidity that hung in the air and the softness of my brain. I had been through any number of smaller plants inside Detroit, but the Lloyd plant was monstrous. I saw that a few of the men on the line had noticed our presence. From the way they stiffened and turned hard to their labor as we came near, I could guess that Whitcomb Lloyd was not much loved, and I wondered why he had no fear for his well-being.

"We are beset on all sides by men in uniform as well," Lloyd said. "You see there the young Hardiman brothers in conference with a colonel and a—a captain? Can you see so far, Mr. Caudill?"

Across the line not far down from us, on a yellow-painted path along the craneway, stood a group of six or seven men. They kept close together to be heard over the din. I could not see well enough to pick out the military rank of the officers, but I thought I could pick out the Hardiman boys. They were stockier than their father, not as tall, but each sported the same head of wavy hair. Because they had to shout, it was hard to tell just how hot their conversation was. But the men in shirtsleeves—shop foremen—seemed to stand nervously outside the square, clutching rolls of blueprints, keeping their faces averted.

"The Hardiman family controls a large portion of our publicly traded stock," said Lloyd. "The boys have inherited all their father's flame and flair for the increase of wealth. Really a formidable duo."

Federle said, "Can we cut out of here? This place drives me nuts."

"Is it the noise? You'll get used to it." Lloyd considered Federle blithely.

"I don't mind the noise. It's the smoke."

"These Hardiman boys got an angle on them?" I said.

"We all have angles, Mr. Caudill. Some are more acute and some more oblique. I would say that the Hardiman boys are certainly better than most at playing their angles to great advantage."

To placate Federle, Lloyd had begun to walk up the line. As we left the grinders, the din grew deeper and less jangling. Here the moving line was high along the ceiling, and the space below was filled with rolling racks and cases of smaller parts, staged for easy delivery to various points along the line. There was a great deal to see, but it tired me. In my mind I brought up the image of Roger Hardiman's face as it had looked after much of it had been splattered away by Barton Rix's shotgun aboard Jasper Lloyd's yacht the previous summer. In my mind it seemed so clear. I wondered if Estelle Hardiman knew enough of the real story to impart it to her sons. *She must have seen the body,* I thought. *She must know everything. She blames me.*

"What's your relationship to this Mr. Chew of *The Detroit News,* Mr. Caudill?"

"Chew?"

"He takes great pains to mention you in his little article in the morning edition," said Lloyd. "Lurid! Sensational! I suppose you haven't read it."

"I never read the papers."

"You might want to pick up a copy," Lloyd said. He turned to face me directly and drew himself up. "If you're to have the run of any Lloyd facility, I'll have to request that you sever any contact with this man. I'm not pleased to be so serious, but you must understand that this company represents my father's legacy."

"I see how it is."

"If it seems your loyalty is wavering, Mr. Caudill, I'd suggest you waver to the better side."

"You're threatening me now?"

"Why should I?" Lloyd asked. "My father trusts you. Why shouldn't

I trust you, too? Jasper Lloyd is a folk hero for the common man, a legend in his own time."

We were joined at a discreet distance by a guard and by a fat man with a clipboard. The fat man looked at first like a lady to me, and I had to look again.

"I'm trying to help you out," I said. "You don't need to think about that bastard Chew."

"I need to think about every little thing," Lloyd said, "but it's a terrific drain on the constitution."

I don't know if it was a show, but he seemed to sag visibly. He waved the guard closer. The fat man came along, too.

"You," said Lloyd, waggling a long finger toward the guard.

"Yes, sir?"

"Why aren't you wearing a name tag?"

"I was never issued one, sir. Just the badge. It has a number—"

"Take my two friends here to the Security Office and have them each issued a gold badge."

"Gold?"

"At my instruction—are you paying attention?—the paperwork is to be left blank. Do you understand?"

"But what about the income tax, sir?"

"My gentlemen friends are volunteering their services in our noble cause. Now, it's a matter of some importance."

"I see, Mr. Lloyd."

"A matter of national security. You'll have to trust that you're doing your part to support special programs quite beyond the scope of your knowledge."

"Yes, sir."

"If you fail in this duty, you'll answer to my father. Can you accept this responsibility?"

"I guess I have to, sir."

"Good. There's a good man. I'll be down later to sign all the papers myself." Lloyd moved his body in such a way as to cut his subordinates off from us. "Now, Caudill," he said, "good luck to you. I can't say if we'll meet again. You might want to begin your quest with a copy of the *News*.

Our Mr. Chew, if I remember correctly, mentions something about another body at our facility in—Illinois? I leave it to you to find the truth of it."

Lloyd turned and took the fat man by his fleshy elbow and walked on up the line. The nameless guard looked after him and then back to us, trying to decide if there was a gag in play or if we were something substantial to trouble him.

"Let's go," I said.

"We're on a schedule," Federle said.

Though he had a badge and a uniform, we were harder than he was.

"Okay," he said.

We walked back toward the stairwell.

"We got your number," said Federle. "Your badge number."

"Just keep quiet," I told him. "Keep your yap shut."

CHAPTER

14

It was a great relief to break out into the open world after the din and the stench of the great plant. I had lately not been in fighting condition at all, but I was surprised by the crushing fatigue that often came upon me in waves since I had been on the mend. Federle was fagged out from the double duty as well, but he was still hot to dig in. I let him drive back to the city.

"What a cookie that Lloyd is. He don't paddle straight."

"He doesn't seem to know what he wants," I told him. "That's the way to trouble."

"We'll pick up a paper somewhere."

"It doesn't matter," I said. "I don't need to worry my eye with it. That weasel Chew knows how it is. If he comes around, he'll get the message quick. You need to get some sleep if you're pulling a shift tonight."

"Sleep now? How can I sleep?"

"You're no good to me if I can't trust your wits."

In part I guess because he was so run-down, he couldn't find any answer for me.

"You get some sleep now," I said, "and leave me to poke around."

"I could quit my job," Federle said. "I'd do it in a minute. Lloyd would cough up some dough if we asked him. It's only pin money for either one of them Lloyds."

"Then we'd be working for him for sure."

"Well, who are we working for exactly?"

"We're just working," I said.

"The Old Man's got something on you?"

"No."

Federle pulled along the curb in front of our building. The day was straggling toward evening and the block was busy with schoolkids and women hurrying home to make supper.

"I feel like you're giving me the boot," said Federle.

"I am. Don't get sentimental."

"We'll go again tomorrow? We should brace those Hardiman boys. They got a hard-on for Lloyd. Rich bastards."

"Sure."

Federle took the car out of gear and cranked the hand brake. As he struggled out the door of the Chrysler, I caught sight of a bit of the scarred flesh over his ankle. It was like melted pink wax.

"All right, Pete."

"You know how to keep your mouth shut, right?"

"Who am I gonna talk to?" He let a flash of irritation get away from him.

"Sooner or later that damn Chew will come around."

"Let him come," he said. He flashed a white smile but his eyes were dull. He drew his finger like a knife across his throat, and then he turned away and went into the building.

I got out of the car and came around to the driver's side. I sat down and tried to shift myself into a comfortable position—an impossible job. It had been a few months since I had sold off my Packard, and I had some worry that I might have lost the trick of driving. But the car was tight enough and had a hot enough motor to keep me moving along. I left Federle behind and drove off the wrong way so he wouldn't know where I was heading. It wasn't because I trusted him any less than anybody else; I knew he had been through some things, and so he'd have an idea about how he would handle himself in a pinch. I didn't want to think of him as a partner but rather as an assistant or something less vital. Federle, I could see from the first time I had met him, would always need to be kept at an appropriate distance.

I picked up a copy of the *News* from a stand just down from police headquarters on Beaubien, and then parked where I could still see the building. Chew's article hadn't even made the front page. I wondered naturally if someone at Lloyd Motors was leaning on the paper to keep the story dull. According to Chew, a set of bones had been found beneath an unused casting mold outside a small stamping plant on the east side of Detroit, one not owned directly by Lloyd but for many years supplying parts exclusively to the company. There had been such a crush for metal that every old slab had been taken for scrap. So they finally moved the old mold, several tons of steel, after it had been put aside for a number of years. It was clear that Chew was struggling to make it out to be more interesting than it was, and no one yet could say how old the bones might be; but he tried hard with his words to make some connection between the bones and the new murders.

He brought me into the story, I guess, to show what he could do to trip me up. "Former Detroit Police Detective Peter Caudill, now employed by Lloyd Motor Company, offered no comment. Mr. Caudill was recently the victim of a vicious assault, about which he offered no comment as well." Although the mention of me was admirably useless for the story itself, it was enough to goad me along, to throw a wrench into the mix. I was sure that the notice would not escape my mother's little scissors. She had saved all the newspaper articles that ran when I shot the black boy years ago. Later, when my eye and fingers had been blown away, she was delighted to find my formal police portrait on the front page. I wasn't the type to be written up for a happy story, and so I suppose she had to take what was offered. Maybe she'd take out the scrapbook filled with the remembrance of dead and maimed relatives and add another page.

The only galling aspect of Chew's story, though, was that the paper had inset the photo of Walker's sister I had given to him. There was a formally posed picture of another woman, also a Negro, with the blank-eyed look of an alcoholic, with the unlikely name of Avis Davis. This was the woman who had been killed in Indiana. She was prettier and more composed than Walker's sister, but it was clear from the photo that she'd done some hard living.

According to Chew, both women had been "horribly mutilated." I guessed that he had not bothered or been allowed to see the bodies for himself, and I wondered if he had even seen any direct evidence of any mutilation, even a crime scene photograph. Probably he had only heard off-the-record rumors from his usual contacts. The regular Lloyd security men were everywhere, and they had the money to buy some quiet wherever they wanted it, but they could not be everywhere at once. Whether or not the old bones at the stamping plant had anything to do with it, I saw that the story would prick up some ears. There was no telling who might now be interested in talking to me. The thugs who had roughed me up, whether or not they were working directly for Estelle Hardiman, would not have to worry about being picked up, because I had given no description of them to the police. The Hardiman boys likely knew my name as well. If it looked like a crime that crossed over state lines, then Hoover's men might well begin sniffing around. Should there be another murder at a Lloyd plant, anyone with half an interest in safeguarding war production would be tripping over themselves to get to the bottom of it.

All the ruckus might work out well for poor Walker, who only wanted to know what had happened to his sister. But it had gotten under my skin—gotten stitched into my skin like a tattoo. I wanted to extract my due share of blood in the ordeal, not only from the thugs but from all the men and women caught up in all the wrangling for money and power. It wasn't sensible or right for me to want to wreck things, but there it was. I could say that I had gone green with envy or black with bitterness. Or it was only that I was more sore and more tired than I had ever been. I thought it was possible in some way that the crush of business and wealth might be for the best, that it might do the most good for the most people. But I knew I was too small ever to be on top of it, too limited in my thinking even to understand anything about how it worked.

The queer duty I felt to the elder Lloyd also pulled me askew. Though I had never been able to pull the details from him, Jasper Lloyd was in some way involved with my father's death. Maybe because I knew that my father had trusted Lloyd enough to work for him, I thought it was my place to carry on in some fashion. Lloyd had built an empire on his own, but it didn't seem likely that the empire could hold together under Whit Lloyd's governance. What possibly could I do to affect such a thing? I figured I owed something to the Old Man and to my old man at least to look into it.

I wheeled over to Hamtramck, where I knew a man who ran an informal shooting range in his long cellar. It would have been possible to get a gun from him, but he was the sort to ask favors in return. I pried a box of shells from him for cash and pried myself out of the cramped basement when it became clear that he wouldn't have anything like a shoulder holster that would fit my new piece. Back in the Chrysler I slipped a few slugs into the clip. The gun felt smooth and well cared for, but I had some worry about carrying around a weapon that I had never fired.

Downriver to the west, where the factories were thick together, a sepia veil of soot hung always in the sky. Now, with the sun low and golden, it was pretty. The day's activity had worked my joints loose a little, but I knew I'd need to take the edge off the pain to get any sleep at all. I didn't want to run into Federle again, so I trolled down to Paradise Valley to see if I could find a quiet place to pick up a few drinks. Alcohol was scarce, but I thought I knew who might be connected enough to fix me up. Since the riots of the previous summer, things had settled back to the usual business in the Valley, the business section that the colored folks maintained, mainly along Hastings Street. After dark, white folks packed in to drink and dance and find the kind of company they couldn't find in their own neighborhoods. Though it couldn't be measured—an outsider wouldn't notice it—one thing had changed. Since the riot, every white man or woman kept a silent count of the number of steps it would take to reach the exit of every joint they entered in Paradise Valley. They all knew how far it was to the nearest taxi stand.

It was still early, hours before any of the jazz combos would start up, which was fine with me. I didn't need noise. I thought I might grab a bite to eat. There were niggers along the Valley who knew how to cook. But it was always just possible that someone would recognize me at a bigger joint, so I drove off to a quieter street and parked. I chewed on the remnant of Federle's wife's bread without anything to drink. I tore off pieces and kept them in my mouth till enough spit gathered to let me chew and swallow. It was relaxing.

There to the left of me was Walker's apartment building. Though it had been poorly used over time, the building was fully occupied. Every light in the place was on, and I could see that for most it was suppertime. But I decided to go up anyway.

Through Walker's door I heard quiet talk and a little radio music. When I rapped, it turned quiet. I heard quick, light footsteps—and I pictured Walker's children scurrying to the back room of the place. The door opened a bit, and Walker's wife Emily peered out at me over the chain.

"Hello," I said.

She said nothing and registered no dismay at my appearance, but closed the door to remove the chain. She opened it up again so I could enter.

"Mr. Caudill," she said, "you look the worse for wear."

"I'm sorry."

"I'll take your hat."

"No, I won't stay long." I pulled off my hat to be polite and couldn't keep from turning partly away from her in shame for my appearance.

"May I offer you anything?"

"I don't want to be a—"

"We've supper left over if you'd like a bite to eat."

"I could have a glass of water."

Walker was there in the tiny front room, slouched in a chair next to the radio, looking tired.

"I'm about to step out to work," he said.

"I can give you a lift."

"No, it's just down to Sunnie Wilson's place, in the skating rink. He don't need the help, but I go down most nights to throw bottles around."

Emily brought the water and then went back to the kitchen to finish cleaning the supper dishes. I took a hard gulp that seemed to make a clog in my throat, and then another.

"That beating you took wasn't for my sake, was it?"

"I don't think so," I said. "I don't know."

He stood up and grabbed a jacket and a cap from the stand by the door. "Let's walk down together," he said.

I put down the glass on the radio table and followed him down to the street.

"My children don't read the newspapers," he said. "But they did see the picture of their auntie this morning. I guess one of the schoolboys thought it was a good joke."

"I'm sorry about that," I said.

"This man Chew came by the other day."

"What did he say?"

"My Emily won't take any guff."

"I can see to Chew," I said. "I'll need to have a hard word with him."

"I don't worry about him," Walker said. "I worry about falling into the same trouble that seems to dog you. I've got children here."

"I think the boys who roughed me over were working for Estelle Hardiman. And you didn't really have anything to do with that whole mess."

"You and I have had some association. And now a white man brings a bundle of money to my home, says it's from you—"

"Jesus, Walker, I'm trying to help you!"

"Why do you feel like you need to help me?"

That stumped me.

"Do you blame yourself for everything that happens?"

"For some things," I mumbled.

"Am I the one Negro you've decided to adopt to ease your conscience? I'm a grown man, Mr. Caudill. I can provide for my family."

We stopped at the corner of Hastings and Canfield. I pushed my lid back on my head and scratched around my hairline.

"Call me Pete," I said.

Somehow it brought up a smile in him.

"All right, Pete," he said. "My name is Jonah. Did you ever know that?"

"I might have known it. But I forget things."

"Now this money—"

"Forget it," I said. "I jewed it from Jasper Lloyd."

"I can't take that money," Walker said. "You know I can't."

"Lloyd's money isn't dirty. That old carcass has done a lot for this city. He's hired plenty of colored folks—making a good living for themselves."

"Don't lecture me about the welfare of my people."

"Just spend the money—and spend it quick. You can't hold on to things."

"It's your money," Walker said. "I don't work for Mr. Lloyd."

It put me back a step. "I've got my own money. Listen, I went to Lloyd to see if I could get anything from him about your sister. Seems he's got an interest, too. So he asked me to look into it, that's all."

We were standing in the middle of the block, facing each other squarely. Tulips and daffodils had lately pushed up in rows along the front porches, and plump robins hopped in the shadows along the grass, watching us.

"Look, Walker," I said, toning my voice to a low growl. "Why don't you shove all this and help me out? You say you're a grown man; why are you doing a boy's job for Sunnie?"

"I've got to feed my family."

"You're talking to the one person"—I stood close and dropped to a hoarse whisper—"I know you've got some dough now. You could feed those little ones for some time with that kind of cash."

"I told you—"

"You don't want to help me figure out who cut the legs and arms off your baby sister?"

The sun had gone, but Walker's eyes glowed with light picked up from Sunnie's place and from the streetlamps along Hastings.

"I got my mind on owning a place like this someday," he said, taking in Sunnie's big Forest Club. "For my children, for my wife, a little piece of something, a place of our own."

"I don't think Sunnie is going to let the place go."

His face seemed haggard and gray, and his shoulders drooped. He was still built pretty well, but I could see how he was settling into an older man's body, brought down by gravity and stiffening joints.

"I ain't gonna get you killed any faster than you're killing yourself," I said.

Maybe he was too worn out to argue. "All right," he said. "How do you think I can help you?"

I grinned to show him the teeth. "I don't know! Can you put on some nice clothes? I'll swing over and pick you up in the morning."

"I've got a shift at four tonight with Charles the baker. I can't leave him dry."

"Well?"

"Those deliveries have to be done by nine o'clock."

"I'll be back here at ten, then," I said.

"I'll be ready. Just lay a tap on the horn and I'll come down."

He turned away and angled across the street to the back entrance of the Forest Club. Already they were bowling inside. I could hear the cracking and rumbling of the pins like a faraway thunderstorm. It was a good long way from Sunnie Wilson's club to the alley that ran behind the row of shops where I'd killed the young colored boy—so many years ago. Dead now, long time. He'd been pilfering a shoe store with his buddy. It dogged me still. The echo of that bad shot came back to me as I stood alone, a white man in the middle of the colored district. Not so much of a man anymore, either, after all.

As Walker slipped into Sunnie's place, I thought I heard him mumble, "Don't get me killed."

CHAPTER
15

Sometime after midnight I was lying in my bed. The soup and sandwich I had eaten for supper sat gurgling on my stomach, keeping me from sleep. The old pipes in the building clanged whenever the boiler let out a belch and bubbly water gurgled through the cast-iron drainpipes in the walls. Now and again the wind would brush hard enough over the treetops to make a sound like a waterfall. There were mice in the walls, too, but they didn't plague me much because they knew I didn't keep anything to make them fat. They scratched along their trails through the building's skeleton, freed by darkness. In a pitch that was barely audible, the damage done to my skull tuned in and out like a station on the shortwave, and I was tempted to try to make out a message in the chatter.

Out of that chorus I began to hear a tip-tapping that came in the rhythm of someone sneaking down a flight of stairs. This was followed directly by the click and rattle of a doorway being carefully opened and closed, and more steps, now creaking softly down the carpeted hall toward my door. Still, the low knock startled me when it came.

The gun was close to the bed. I picked it up and rolled out and threw a robe over my shoulders. There was no bullet in the chamber, and I tried to decide quickly whether I should rack the action back to set the first slug.

But then another low knock came at the door, and I decided against it. I went over and listened for a moment. There was no peephole in the door, but I had fastened the chain, and so I was able to open the door a crack. I expected to see Lloyd's secretary with my penicillin, but there in a white gown with her hair tied up stood Federle's wife.

Because I had taken off my eye patch for the night, I had to keep the hole shut tight to keep it from gaping. I knew it made me look like I was winking furiously.

"Can I come in?"

"Why?"

"I have to talk to you about Ray."

"Go on and talk."

"But I can't stand here in the hall."

"Sure you can. You are."

"Please," she said.

I was afraid she'd make a ruckus if I closed her out. Or maybe my judgment was reliably bad. I let her in, stepped to the nightstand, and wrapped my patch quickly over my eye. I put the gun down and got all the way into the robe.

"Well?"

"I'm sorry I smacked you," she said.

"I been hurt worse."

"I can see," she said. She wore a regular nightie that reached to her ankles and leather slippers on her tiny feet. Her hair was thick and almost black. She had brushed it out for the night and gathered it up in a pile that wanted to spill out from the back of her head.

"Well?"

She stood with her fingertips just touching together before her and kept her wide eyes on me. Her face had been wiped clean of any makeup, and I could see that she hadn't a line on her pale skin. Her lips looked soft.

"I'm worried about Ray," she said.

"Your man is out to work scrubbing toilets, and you're down here in your nightie."

"You don't think that I—my two girls—"

"He ought to be worried about *you*."

She was looking at me too much with her awful eyes. I fixed my robe and tightened up the belt.

"Can't I sit down and tell you?"

"No," I said. "Make it short and get out."

"They've really worked you over."

"That's all done with."

"Did you like the bread I made?"

"I ate it."

"Don't you want to talk about Ray?"

"What about him?"

"I don't think he's really going out to work at night. Sometimes he comes home and his clothes aren't even dirty."

"So what? My clothes don't get dirty if I can help it."

"He's a janitor! He doesn't sleep. I'm afraid he's just out roaming the streets at night. He can't stand to be cooped up." She was stepping forward in such a way that I didn't notice her feet moving.

"Well, how's his shoe leather?" I had my hands in the pockets of my robe and a scowl screwed down onto my face. "If he was out walking all night, sooner or later he'd get picked up."

"I don't know what he's doing."

"You think he's with some woman?"

"Oh, no," she said. She looked like her eyes might get wet. "I don't know what to think. When he wanted so much to move out here, I thought it would be different."

She was right next to me, so close that I could smell her hair and the light perfume of her skin. I didn't move when her hand snaked inside my robe, didn't even take my hands from my pockets. She found her way into my shorts and wrapped her slim fingers around my prick.

"That's nothing to play with," I said.

She tipped her head forward under my chin and brought her free hand over my heart.

"So sad it all seems," she breathed on my chest. "So sad."

She stroked gently until my prick was good and stiff and poking out the front of my robe. Her breathing was deep and hot on my chest. I knew it wasn't right but I let her go on. It was a hell of a thing to get so stirred up so easily. At the back of my mind flashed a thought about the baby crying, the older girl lying awake and wondering where her mother and father had gone.

I made fists in my pockets. I knew that soon Federle's wife would coax the juice out of me if I let her go on. She brought her other hand down and cradled my balls with surprising warmth and gentleness. The stroking came in a deep rhythm, and I could feel her hips moving too, her thigh turned out and rubbing along my leg.

"My name's Patty," she panted. Her forehead pressed hard into my chest.

It brought up a flash of anger in me that was brushed aside by fatigue and the dreamy thrill of it. I wanted to put my fingers around her neck, to feel her pulse under my thumb. Despite the two children, she was young enough and small enough and pretty enough to dredge up the powerful memory of the backseat struggles of my teenaged years. It was sharply painful to think of how far I'd come, how much of a heel and a black spot I'd become. All the sore muscles, the torn skin, and the damaged joints of my body had blurred together into a generalized pain—but as I felt how close my balls were to riding up and letting go, I felt a growing pain deep in my bowels, too. *I should have stayed at the hospital,* I thought. *A pipe got knocked loose on the inside.*

Finally I pulled my hands from my pockets and took hold of her shoulders.

"I hadn't ought to do it," I said.

"But he's no good to me!" She didn't turn her face up to look at me. She grabbed my prick with both hands, squeezed hard, and slowed the stroking. She said again, "He's no good to me."

"Neither am I. I know that much."

"I'm sorry, Pete," she said, loosening her hands and rolling slowly away.

At once I regretted it. *What's the difference?* I thought. *Why shouldn't we?* My prick felt the chill in an instant but stayed stubbornly alert. I looked sharply at Patty's fine ear and the curve of her jaw, the nape of her neck. Her light gown flounced up as she hurried to the door, and I had a glimpse of her slender ankle.

"I'm sorry," she said. "Please don't tell Ray." She did not turn to look at me as the door closed behind her.

Again it seemed I was made of trouble. There was a tickle in my throat that made me want to cough and the pain at the lower end of my spine throbbed horribly. My stitches, which had been healing well, now seemed to itch and burn. Heat rose up over my chest and from my scalp, making me think of infection. The only light in the place came from a bulb kept low with a rheostat. I made sure the door was latched and chained securely and then hobbled over to the toilet to finish the job Federle's wife had started.

CHAPTER
16

Friday, April 14

Though it wasn't much of a night for sleeping, I got up early, put on some decent clothes, cleaned myself up, and went out for a quick bite. I bought a paper down on the street and opened it up on a bench along Mack with my collar up against the chill.

It was too early for any of the retail places to be open, but everyone was in a rush to get somewhere. I was right along the street, and I got my toes stomped and my hat tipped by gangs getting on and off the streetcars and swarming back and forth across the wide avenue. The noise was incredible. Electricity snapped and popped from the grid as the downtown cars rolled by. Up and down Mack and Gratiot, and all across town, you could hear streetcar drivers ringing their gongs and fanning their air brakes at pushy motorists and tardy pedestrians. Everybody was gabbling—a turkey farm before Thanksgiving.

I didn't see anything more from Chew in the newspaper, but that only meant he was out scrounging for something else, something new. I folded my paper and left it on the bench, and then I ambled back to my place. The hash and the two cups of coffee I'd put in me felt light on my belly, and the weather seemed promising, so I wasn't as worried as I might have been about seeing Federle. There was no telling what kind of life he had with his wife. She might have told him everything, blabbed it all as he shuffled in the door. He might not have cared about any of it either; or he might have. I didn't have the gun with me since I didn't yet have a good way to carry it.

He wasn't waiting at the car, at the front of the building, or at my door, so I went inside my room and turned on the radio. It was getting so you'd have to hear an announcer bleat out a pitch to buy war bonds after every number, which drove me buggy. I didn't own any records or anything to play them on, so I sat waiting in my chair with my thumb on the tuning dial, changing to another station when I heard any kind of spiel start up. It was in the middle of a pretty Dinah Shore tune, "You'd Be So Nice to Come Home To," that Federle finally knocked on my door. I think it was already half past nine.

Federle came in looking sheepish and tired, dressed in slacks that were almost white and a pale yellowish jacket. He held a white straw hat in his hand.

"That's how they dress out in Hollywood?"

"I never was from Hollywood," he said. "It's the nicest suit of clothes I have."

"Don't worry about it. We don't make up the glamour squad exactly."

"I can get some other duds."

From the way he hung his head and avoided my eye, I could see that the wife had been talking.

"You don't want to go out?" I asked him.

"Sure I do," he said. "What's the plan?"

"Game for a ruckus?"

"I don't know," he said. "What sort of ruckus?"

"Any kind of ruckus. I guess I'm feeling pretty good today."

"That's good, Pete." He didn't show any smile. He worked the brim of his hat and kept his head down.

"What's eating you?"

"Did my wife come down here last night?"

"She was knocking, but I didn't let her in."

"I'm sorry," he said.

It didn't seem likely that he was going to throw a poke at me, but I kept myself sideways anyway.

"You're always apologizing to me for what your woman does," I said.

He looked up and smiled thinly. "I can't do anything about it, Pete. Next time she comes down, you might as well let her in."

"Like hell."

Federle was shifting back and forth. "Listen, Pete. Can I trust you?"

"I wouldn't if I was you."

He smiled more strangely, and his black eyes lit up. "When I got burned up over there, my pecker got fried like a sausage, too. Ain't that funny? What good am I with half a prick?"

"That seems funny to you?"

"Not at first it didn't! No sir! But after I worked it over for a while, it got to seem funny. Har-de-har funny, no, but you can see what I'm saying. You got that same type of humor like I do. I knew it the first time I saw that mug of yours."

"All right, Federle, I don't want—"

"It's okay, Pete," he said. He furrowed his brow and looked hard at me. "I don't want to dump all this on you. But I want things to be straight between us. I want you to be able to trust me so we can get to work on this case."

The inside of my lip was raw from working it over my jagged teeth. He was standing between me and the door.

"If you want me out," he said, "just give me the word."

"Don't try to pawn off your woman on me," I said.

"You can see how it is. She's still a young woman. I can't keep her chained up."

"You can keep some kind of a line on her."

"Sure."

"I got my own problems."

"Then we're settled up?"

He wasn't going to quit until I gave him the word. Besides the lack of sleep, it didn't seem that Federle had been taking any food either. The light seemed to sink right into the skin of his face, forming bags and blue shadows.

"It don't look like either one of us is ever going to be settled," I said. "It'll have to do. Let's go, now, before we lose the whole day."

I picked up the gun and slipped it into my pocket, thinking to leave it in the car so it would be handy. We went down to the street and I tossed Federle the keys. It wasn't a pleasure to do it, but I was able to tip the front seat forward and slink into the back without going to pieces. There was plenty of room to sit up straight, but it seemed more comfortable to angle my legs. It was a bit easier on my lower back.

Federle eyed me in the rearview. "I'm a chauffeur now?"

"We're going to pick up a little help."

"Yeah?"

"Just pull on out."

He kept glancing back to me. "Where to?"

"Keep your eyes on the road."

"All right," he said.

"Head up McDougall to Forest," I said. "You don't need to keep looking at me. I told you I never let her in the door."

"It isn't that," he said. He looked back at me in the mirror again and then looked away. "The baby isn't mine," he muttered.

"What?"

"Sophia isn't mine. She couldn't be. When I came home, it was some surprise! But I treat her just fine, like she was my own. I change her diaper sometimes. I never had to do that with my first one, with Isabelle. What do you think of that?"

I looked at his reflection grimly for a time. He was smiling a little, cruising slowly out toward the big street.

"Head on over to Paradise Valley," I said. "And don't spill any more on me till I'm done thinking on all of this truck so far."

He seemed to like driving. Despite the streetcars and the foot traffic, it took just a few minutes to cut over from our place to the dark side of town.

"You know Sunnie Wilson's place?"

"Sure."

"Head over that way."

"Who are we picking up, some nigger?"

"You don't like niggers?"

"I got no preference," he said. "But my wife goes a bad way just at the idea. She don't like birds either—makes her blood run cold." He shrugged. "I've known plenty of niggers."

"If it's going to be a problem—"

"Pete, I told you, I won't let you down. You can count on me to watch your back no matter what happens."

"Don't get sore," I said, watching him closely in the mirror.

"I'm not sore. I'm a little jumpy is all. You know I got a case of nerves." He glanced sorrowfully at me in the mirror. "After I told you all that stuff."

"Ray, I never asked you—"

"I know it," he said quickly. "I'm just yanking your dick a little." He turned to get a real look at me.

I felt like I was on ice with him, and so I pursed my lips. I could taste blood in my mouth from the places where the jagged teeth were wearing down the inside of my cheek. I asked him, "You know this part of town?"

"They don't know me by name at any of these places, that's for sure."

"You're going to turn up here. There it is," I said. "He's up there waiting on the porch."

Walker stood on the narrow porch in front of his apartment. He wore a hat that kept the sun from his eyes and held his big hands over the bullet-chipped rail.

"Lay on the horn," I said. "He doesn't know the car."

Federle tried the horn but there was no sound. He tried it again, and I noticed that the button had somehow thrown a latch in the panel opposite me in the back seat. There was a space made out of molded binderboard under the armrest where you might stash a gun or a sap, and Federle had opened it with the horn button. I thought with a smile that the old Chrysler must have been used by Frank Carter and his goons in the old days when they were still trying to bust up the unions. I moved my shoe to nudge the cover of the stash; it was held in place by two pegs that swiveled to let it open when the horn button was pressed. My eye scanned the rest of the interior, and I realized that there were a number of places where the parts were funny.

By this time Walker was looking us over very carefully.

"Roll down your window and wave him over," I said.

Walker had put on his better shoes, a shirt so white it looked blue, and a pair of wool pants with a strong pattern woven into them. He also wore a light jacket. Though he was stocky in build and roughened by circumstance, he made a nice figure. Certainly he fared better coming down the steps than Federle or I would have done.

"Hah," said Federle, "think of that. He's coming."

I could see Walker assessing the situation as he approached the car. I put my face against the glass so he could see me. The Chrysler coupe was too low for him to get a good look at the driver without stooping, so he opened the suicide door and flopped down onto the seat. He reached over and pulled the door shut.

Federle craned his head to get a better look at Walker, and Walker turned to look around inside the car. He pulled off his hat and rubbed his palm over his near-bald head.

"What's the story, Walker?" I said.

"I wasn't sure you were coming."

"Hey, Walker, don't you know me?" Federle sat with a goofy grin across the seat from Walker. He bobbed his head to try to find a place with good enough light to show his face.

Walker turned and eyed him with some reserve. Then recognition flickered in his eyes, and he let his mouth move into a sour smile.

"Well," he said. "Ray Federle. I didn't think I'd run into you again."

CHAPTER

17

Federle's open grin was too much for me. I felt like I needed to get out of the backseat to stretch my legs, to clear my head of all that he had spilled to me. It seemed to ease his worry, and his happiness at seeing Walker upset me somehow.

"Now, hell," I said, "why would you two know each other?"

"Before I got my executive position swabbing floors I did some jobs around town," Federle said.

"He drove a forklift on the dock for a time—"

"About a week!"

"—until he got fired from Palmer's," said Walker.

"You got fired from Palmer's?" I asked. "How in hell does a guy get fired from a job like that when they're scraping up cadavers to work these days?"

"That's a funny story," said Federle.

"Never mind," I said. "I don't want to hear it. Drive over to the Lloyd plant before all the shooters head out to lunch."

"What about Walker?"

"What about him?"

"Well, he don't have a badge like we do, eh? They'll put up a front, you know that."

"We'll see what swings when we get there."

Federle pulled away from Walker's place, and I chewed my lips and kept quiet. Here Federle had just now offered his wife to me, confessed that his dick had been burned off, and made a point to let me know that he was changing the diapers of some other man's baby. He was humming to himself now because the radio didn't work on the car either. Whatever foul mood anyone else might have been in, Federle seemed happy just to move along. Walker, I guess, was used to sitting still and waiting. He stared out ahead, and I could see the nicks and little scars at the back of his neck and head.

I wondered about my own mood and my own intentions. Only a day or two earlier I had been so miserable that I would have eaten a bullet. Looking forward, I knew that mood would fall on me again—and again and again until my light finally went out. What a miserable life it was! Such a botch of everything, such a span of years wasted. For myself I would not have gone on. But slumped as I was in the back seat, driving off to Lloyd's noisy, fiery, reeking pit without a clue what I wanted to do there, I could at least see the truth about myself. For my own sake I wouldn't do anything, because I hated what I had become—scarred, mean, and unhappy as a pit dog. It seemed I was ready, though, to latch on to anyone else's need. Walker had asked for my help, as had Jasper Lloyd. Eileen had a young son out roaming somewhere in the world, and Federle—Federle was as much of a wreck as I was. I had let myself get soft toward him because I had the pathetic idea that I could do something for him.

The more I found out about him, the more I realized that it was beyond me to help him. Either he would get me killed in the whole mess or I would see him drop away entirely, as it had been with Alex. But curiously, the grisly expectations didn't weigh on me like the months of doing nothing had. My wounds and bruises were healing up nicely, and though my back still dogged me, I thought I might crack a head or two if the need arose. We were heading to the Lloyd plant, one of the largest industrial complexes in the world, and I knew well that I'd be ineffective, even lost, inside it. But the lack of any plan or strategy could not deter me. As much as anyone, I didn't have anything better to do.

There were three of us now. We couldn't match up in any way but bluster to the four musclemen who had worked me over. But I was always looking out, hoping to meet up with them again in the daylight. I wanted to know where they had come from, why they had almost killed me, why they had let me live. Any idiot could have seen I knew nothing of value. I wanted to put my face close to the Hardiman boys, to see if they'd flinch, if they knew all of what happened to their father, if they knew what kind of man he really was. More and more, I was driven by thoughts of my father, and I wanted to see how Whit Lloyd could possibly walk straight with the Old Man towering over him. I wanted to know, just for the sake of knowing, who had taken Walker's sister and Miss Avis Davis apart.

It was after eleven when we rolled up to the Lloyd plant. I had Federle circle around the place, trying to get a sense of where everything was located. You couldn't even get close to the parts along the river, and the rail yard was a vast tangle of tracks and sidings where an auto couldn't go. Even with the extra security, I could see it would be easy for someone who knew the place to skip in or out. There were fences and gates and walls, but it was such a sprawling monstrosity that you could only hope to control it or tamp down on it enough to keep everything from bursting into flames. Tens of thousands of men—and now women—slipped in and out every day, over three main shift changes. And I knew that with so many men and women thrown together in such a trying time, some would find a way to pair off in a nook or a cranny or between stacks of lumber or pig iron. Though the Old Man had made it his personal mission to stamp out the dope, I knew that there would be a supply of marijuana and heroin and opium working through the plant. Plenty of the men took whiskey before they clocked in, and they stole sips from flasks during their bone-tiring shifts when they could manage it, if the Lloyd plant was anything like the thousand other shops in Detroit. Workingmen were hard by nature. I knew that Walker could handle himself, and I had to believe that Federle had training and experience; but it seemed ridiculous to think that we could ferret anything out in that jungle or prevent any crime from happening.

"Pull around to the security department," I said. "We'll see if we can get Walker some credentials."

Federle worked the car around the long, circular drive. There was no marking or sign to tell the location of the security offices; we knew where to go only because we had been taken there the previous day. The security men, it appeared, wouldn't stand for any extra army guards to cover them as the administration people had. There was nothing blocking the drive, and the only person we saw outside the building was a bandy-legged old man who came out to take the car to the inside lot.

We all got out, and Federle handed the key to the old man. Walker strolled toward the building, and Federle went after him. The old man squinted at me for a moment until I fished a dollar from my pocket and held it out for him.

"I can't take it," he said. "Mr. Lloyd pays my wage." He hobbled and swiveled himself over to the fender of the Chrysler and propped himself with a ragged hand. "See how the paint don't match?"

"So what?" I said.

"That's one of Frank Carter's old cars. They patched up the bullet holes here, you see? They had to replace the whole door, so it was easier to get the paint to match." He peered at me. The sagging flesh of his aged palate caused him to snort as took in a big breath through his nose. He said, "How'd you come to own this vehicle?"

"We stole it off the lot in the back," I said. "You security guys got your thumbs up your ass."

He turned his head and looked sourly over the brick-heavy facade of the building. "They don't let me on the inside anymore now that Frank Carter's gone. I'm just parking cars now, I guess. Greasy bastards can go suck." He turned back to me, and it was a moment before his lazy eye came even with the other one. Both eyes searched over my damaged face, considered my build and height. "Fred Caudill's boy, are you?"

"Sure."

He chewed it over and decided not to say anything more about it. Bracing himself along the fender and the roof, he got into the car. He had to help his last leg along with both hands. I came over to help him with the door, but he stopped me from closing it.

"These doors are bulletproof, see? The side panels, too. But not the windows. You got to duck down." He hunched himself a bit to show the technique but didn't really move much. "There's a steel plate covering the gas tank."

"You think we'll need all that?" I asked him.

He smiled up at me, showing both racks of worn-down choppers. "It ain't like the old days," he said, "but it don't ever hurt to have a little extra in the hole." The old-timer jerked his stubby thumb toward Federle, who was standing with his hands on his hips in his bright suit, and said, "Is he a friend of Dorothy?"

"I don't really think so," I said.

"Better watch him anyway."

"All right, I will."

"The Negro?"

"He's fair to middling, maybe better," I said. "I don't worry about him." Then I bent over to speak closely, in part because I knew it would appeal to him to be a part of any action. "Listen," I said. "I got a piece squirreled away in one of the holes back there, and I'd appreciate it if it didn't get found out."

"Don't worry," he muttered, turning shifty and squinty, "I got my eye on it."

"I appreciate it."

"My name's Pickett."

"Okay, Pickett," I said.

He grunted, and I pulled the door shut for him. Then he turned the engine over and let his hand work the shifter all around till he remembered how to drive the setup. Time had shortened him so that he had to crane up to see over the dash and hood. Federle and Walker hot-stepped out of the way as the old man careened toward a gated lot off the end of the building.

"An old man is a nasty thing," Federle said. "He ought to think about staying home."

"You're not from here, Federle," I said. "You don't know what things are worth." Whenever I spoke to Federle, I tried to use the kind of tone that wouldn't bite. He had a bad habit of shooting off his mouth, but I didn't want to discourage him entirely because it let me know what he was thinking.

"I know an old man when I see one," he said. "Maybe I'm just thinking that I'll be getting old, too."

"You have children, Mr. Federle?" asked Walker.

"Call me Ray. I got two at home."

"Well, it's been my experience that worry about your children will make you old before your time."

"Why's Pete look so bad then? He don't have no kids that he knows of."

"I guess the detective has had his share of worry in his time."

"We're like private dicks now," Federle said. "Me and Pete anyhow. We got badges. Walker needs a badge."

"Listen, Walker. We'll go in and see about getting you a badge. But if it doesn't pan out, see if you can find somebody to talk to out here."

"Some jobs you got a man on the inside," said Federle; "some jobs you got a man on the outside."

"You follow me, Walker?"

"I got you."

The three of us went inside. Federle and I had pinned the badges on the pockets of our jackets, as the Lloyd security men liked to do. You could feel right away that it wasn't a place to bring a Negro. There wasn't a woman on the inside, either. The security house was run entirely by white men, and they were all either dressed in gray suits or in medium-blue uniforms that looked something like police outfits and something like work clothes. All wore badges; there was an elaborate system of shapes and colors of metal to show who had pull and who was a flunky, but I didn't care to put much time into figuring it out. Federle and I had the good kind of badge and Walker was plain out of luck. I could see by the mug of the counterman, another old-timer, that Walker wasn't likely to have an easy time getting a leg up.

"We'd like to see about getting Walker here a badge," I said.

The counterman puckered his face and looked us over shrewdly. I could see just a bare glint of his eyes through the droops and wrinkled bags that surrounded them.

"We don't just give out badges without authorization," he said.

"We got badges," said Federle.

"I don't have any say about that."

"Gold badges."

"I can see that."

"Who's got the big say around here?" I asked. "Can't we talk to somebody worthwhile?"

The counterman was already burning. "It's a whole procedure. First you got to get hired in. Then—"

"Hand me up your telephone," I said.

He choked down his irritation and opened his filmy eyes a little wider. Very slowly, he lifted the phone up onto the higher counter of the desk and set it down with a ding.

"How do you get hold of Whitcomb Lloyd on this thing?"

"I can't say if Mr. Lloyd is anywhere on the premises."

"I mean how do you work it?"

He thought for a moment before he answered. I knew that he was angry and a little afraid that Federle and I—outsiders—had possibly been brought in just to look into the security system itself.

"Pick it up and dial zero for the switchboard," he said. "But you'll need something more than luck to reach Mr. Lloyd directly."

"What's your badge number?" I asked him.

"Zero-one-one," he said, drawing his flaccid cheeks back in a lizard smile. "I been here a while. What's yours?"

I knew that my own had a five-digit number but I didn't bother to look it up for him.

"Only got silver after all these years?" Federle said. He had pushed his hands down into his pockets and muscled up his neck to show how little he cared for the desk monkey.

I picked up the handset and dialed the phone with my littlest finger. Though I knew it wouldn't put me out of earshot, I turned away and let the angry counterman stare at the back of my neck.

"This is Pete Caudill at the security house. Can you get me Mr. Lloyd's secretary on the line?"

"Mrs. Bates is not in today. I'll connect you to Mr. Merriweather. It may take a moment."

While the line was quiet I gave Federle the eye. He broke away from the desk and made like he was scanning the place for problems. If I had been worth my salt, I would have secured a couple of clipboards or a little notepad like Hank Chew used so we could pretend to write things down. In a shop of any kind, it's the one thing that provokes the most anxiety in the men. It fouls them up; they have to put on a show of disdain with the other men, but only if they have a spotless conscience can they really afford not to worry. Walker stood close by with his hands at his sides and his face angled politely away. He was smoother by far than any of us. His social graces were the better part of him. It had always taken effort for me to work my way around people, to slip in and do my business without attracting too much bad attention, but it came naturally to Walker. I was glad that he agreed to come along with us.

The crackle of the telephone line brought me to attention.

"Yes? This is Mr. Merriweather."

"This is Pete Caudill. You remember me from yesterday?"

"Yes, sir, I do."

"I got a fella down here at the security house with me who needs a badge like the one I got yesterday."

"I'm afraid I have no authority to order such a thing myself. There are channels—"

"Can you get word to Whit Lloyd that we're down here?"

"Mr. Lloyd is—possibly en route between facilities. If I am in contact with him at all today, I can broach the subject. I'm afraid that's the best I can promise, sir. If you had given me some sort of advance—"

"That's all right. We're coming in. We'll leave Walker here for now. If Lloyd shows up, have him come down and take care of it."

I did my best to imagine the look on Merriweather's face.

He said, "I'll be certain to give him the directive, sir."

I put the handset down in the cradle.

"No dice on the badge for now, Walker. You'll have to hang fire here while Federle and I take care of our business."

"I can do that," said Walker. "I'm a patient man."

"He can't wait in here," the counterman said. He seemed to be immensely pleased with himself.

I leaned my elbows on the counter. "You saying you don't want my man in here?"

"Oh," he said, feeling in charge of his domain again, "that's just counter to SOP. We can't have an unknown man lurking about the building, the center of security for the whole complex. You want to see the manual?"

"Does Walker make you nervous, Zero-one-one?"

He met my eye calmly and let his lips curl up in a nasty smile. "There's a bench outside the door," he said.

I turned to look mildly down on him, and then put the telephone down on the lower desk. He could not have known anything of Walker's character, or that Walker had a personal interest in the situation. From my experience with my colored friend, I knew that he'd likely find out more than Federle and I would, even though he might be shut out of the plant itself. Walker could draw people along—something I could not hope to do. And what's more, I knew I could trust him. I couldn't say what I thought of Federle.

"Zero-one-one," I whispered, as if I were trying to memorize the number.

"That's right," the counterman said. "You want me to write it down for you?"

Federle and I went back into the guts of the plant through the red metal door that had disgorged us the previous day. It was foolish to come; it was stupid, even. But I had to admit to myself that there was a bit of a thrill to be wearing a gold badge, to have some sway in such a place. It was just a small bauble of plated gold, but in my degraded state it let me feel some of the pride I had felt when I first put on my police cadet's badge so many years ago. I knew it couldn't last. I knew all of it would fall to pieces soon enough and that they could take away the sense of privilege Federle and I enjoyed as easily as they had handed it out. You could make your way in the world, but I had come to understand that there was nothing so solid that time and fortune could not wipe it away. I'd try to enjoy the trip if I could. I had been a Detroit boy all my life; I had grown up and become strong surrounded by brick and steel and concrete, and just then it felt right to let the red door close behind us and to walk down the corridor into the heart of Jasper Lloyd's industrial monster.

CHAPTER

18

Federle and I rode a tram underground to the stamping plant because I wanted to get more of a feel for the layout of the place. If there had been time, I might have wanted to watch the tankers dumping coal and coke and iron ore along the river. I could have seen it all, how they brought lumber into the rail yard, how they fired up the great furnaces and made steel and shaped it into flat ribbons and coiled it up. They twisted and stamped and cut the steel and then welded or brazed or bolted the parts together. They even made glass in one of the buildings. In the foundry they poured liquid metal into molds until the sprue holes filled up and dribbled over and splashed sparks down the leather chaps of the foundrymen. There was a paint building and even a small paper mill. We might have followed the course of the plant to its end, where in better times automobiles poured off the end of the line and were stacked on railcars or great ships bound for all parts of the world.

But despair loomed over me even as I considered it. It would take a month to properly survey the place. We'd do well enough if we could ignore the mechanical ruckus and work our way down through the people involved. Maybe Federle was thinking the same thing. As the tram rolled down the corridor, I could see him chewing at the inside of his cheeks.

"Listen, bub," I asked the driver, "who could tell me if the Hardiman brothers are anywhere in one of the buildings?"

"That's hard to say. They want to prowl around all day and night." He was a fat uniformed guard, and he didn't seem happy in his work.

"Well, if they were prowling today, where might they be?"

"That's hard to say. It's like saying, 'Where's the mayor of Detroit?' They got their offices, they got their business to attend to, but they got the run of the place, too."

"It don't seem responsible," Federle said.

"I just guard this tunnel here. Next week it'll be something else. You could call Cappy Blackwell back at the house desk if you want."

"Zero-one-one," I said.

"That's right," said the driver. "That's the lowest number except Pickett. They only let him park cars anymore since—"

He stopped himself from saying any more. He took us to the end of the route, and Federle flipped him a nickel for a tip. The fat guard let the coin bounce off the tight cloth of his trousers and onto the concrete floor of the tunnel. We got out of the tram and clomped up the stairs toward the open floor of the stamping plant.

"He'll drive right back to Zero-one-one and report everything we said to him," Federle said. "It's a rat's nest in here."

"We make 'em nervous. That's good. It doesn't seem they know what we're up to."

"What *are* we up to exactly, Pete?"

"I don't know, to tell you the truth. These Hardiman boys are trouble if it runs in the family."

"They got it in for you?"

"It's hard to figure. Maybe they ought to. I never spoke to them, but—" I thought that the stairwell might be wired with microphones, but the noise was getting bad as we approached the top. I leaned close to Federle's ear. "Their father came to a bad end last year."

"You were mixed up in it?"

I opened the metal door and winced as the noise battered my ears. The place echoed with racket from hydraulic and pneumatic presses, chains, power hammers, hollering, and warning bells. A couple dozen Bliss presses, each big enough to drive a car through, were lined up the length of the building, and eight or ten men manned each one. Scores more swarmed around to perform little steps in the process, stacking, toting, and driving away racks of finished parts. From the look of it, they were stamping panels for a small military truck design, square and plain and boxy.

Federle and I stood dumb for a moment. I fought the urge to cover my ears with my palms, and gradually my hearing became numb enough to stand it. A long, narrow metal staircase went up in stages along the wall closest to us and led to a catwalk that ran over the top of the space, close to the roof of the building. I yanked Federle's arm to move him along with me. By the time we made it to the top of the stairs, we were panting and sweating. I stopped to catch my breath along the wall, and Federle pushed past me and out toward the center of the catwalk. In truth, I wasn't steady on my feet for a number of reasons; my lonely eye could not sort out the lacework of steel cables and girders that made up the catwalk and the roof. But I followed Federle out.

From the top the view was hazy, but it was clear enough to see that there was too much going on, too much traffic, for any mayhem to pass unnoticed. I thought I could see in general how we might pick our way through the factory floor, since it only made sense that there would be a system set up for the men to get around as need be. But it was hard work to keep my attention in the heat and the moisture from all the men and the panting machinery. Sweat oozed out of me, and I knew I'd have to go down before I could get a full map of the place into my head. Federle, who stood only a few feet away from me, seemed impossibly distant. He pointed toward the east end of the building. I moved toward him and peered down through the murky air.

"Something's doing," he yelled.

I squinted my eye and blinked trying to make out something, anything more than a smear.

"It's a whole gang coming in."

"I can't see."

"It looks like…" Federle stood straight up and stared for a moment more. "They're pushing somebody in a chair."

"It's Old Man Lloyd," I said, not loud enough to reach Federle's ear. I pulled him along again and we made our way down to the floor. It was necessary to climb again over a bridge to get inside the light rails that ran all along one side of the building.

I was like a horse run ragged and wrapped in a blanket, and I knew that I would keep sweating until we could get out of the plant and into the fresh air. At least the noise seemed more bearable toward the center of the floor; or else my hearing had been damaged permanently. It took a long time for the parade to reach us, but we let it come and tried to catch our wits and our breath. As they came near, I could see that Lloyd's secretary, James, was pushing the Old Man along very slowly. A group of suited lackeys fanned out behind them, a pack of jackals reduced to waiting for scraps. Near the front of the pack, I soon made out the two Hardiman brothers, bent together and warily watching the route ahead.

The secretary saw me first, and he couldn't help showing a look of dismay. He bent down close enough to Lloyd to say something in his ear.

Lloyd had gone so old as to be beyond making expression with his face. He rolled his eyes toward me and lifted a hand to summon me closer.

"Pursuing justice, Mr. Caudill. That's your task." Lloyd's thin, reedy voice cut better through the air than I thought it would. "Walk along with us. The work must continue."

"This is my man Federle," I said.

Lloyd turned a sharp eye toward him, but did not have the energy to make a long assessment. "You've spoken to my son?"

"Yes," I said. "He wasn't any help."

"He can be difficult. But you shouldn't underestimate him."

"Where is he now?"

Lloyd pursed his mouth sourly, and his dry, gray tongue darted over his lips. "You've met the Hardiman boys, then?"

The whole procession crawled awkwardly forward, and it put me at a disadvantage to have the Hardimans to the left of me, to the blind side.

The larger and older of the pair spoke. "We know you by reputation, Mr. Caudill. It's said you're quite a rough character." He spoke leisurely, with his hands in his pockets and an amused look on his face. "I'm Charles Hardiman, and this is my younger brother, Elliot."

He didn't put out his hand to me. Elliot wouldn't even meet my eye. He only stared ahead angrily.

"Our mother does not speak well of you," said Charles. "There's some bad blood, apparently."

"I never did anything to her," I said.

"You knew our father, though, didn't you?"

"He shot me once," I said, showing the place where the bullet went into my shoulder. "That whole thing didn't work out so well."

"I ought to spit in your face," blurted Elliot.

I walked in front of him and stopped, and the whole gaggle began to turn like a wheel around us.

"Why don't you go ahead and spit on me," I said.

I could see that he was thinking about it. Color rushed up into his face. Though he was a grown man, he held himself like a child going into a tantrum. There had been no trace of the outsized goons who had dipped me in the water, but I knew that the regular Lloyd security men would quickly side against me if any fracas broke out with the Hardiman boys.

"Mr. Caudill!" Lloyd bleated. He raised a withered hand toward us, but I felt no magic from it.

"C'mon, Pete," murmured Federle, close at my shoulder.

Charles Hardiman took my sleeve and tugged me to a forward position again.

"Be civilized, Caudill," he said. "Elliot nurses feelings of resentment. It's a matter of disposition. You can allow for that, can't you?"

He kept hold of my elbow and we broke off from Lloyd's procession. Federle ambled along with us, as did a couple of lackeys and a thin, pock-marked man with a gun inside his jacket. We kept walking, passed the guard stationed at the door to the tunnel, and finally turned off into the long hall leading toward the swing rooms and the cafeteria. It was heavily traveled and noisy, but much quieter than the factory floor.

"Now, Mr. Caudill, what's your business here?" Charles Hardiman asked. "Do you aim to ramble about the plant disrupting operations?"

"I work for Old Man Lloyd," I said. "I don't answer to you."

"You're aware that Mr. Lloyd has resigned all his duties toward the company, then. Control has passed to his son Whitcomb."

"Who do you think got us these badges?" I said.

"Which is it? Do you work for Jasper Lloyd or Whitcomb Lloyd?"

I shrugged. "I don't work for you."

"You're investigating these murders," Elliot said. "Is that it?"

"Lower your voice, Elliot."

"Is that it?"

"Till you get the balls or the blow to kick me out, I'll investigate whatever I want to," I said. "What have you got to hide?"

"You go to hell," Elliot said.

The pockmarked man sidled a little closer, hoping to be able to try out his piece. I could tell that Federle was thinking about this, too, from the way he held himself. He was wishing for the gun I had stashed in the Chrysler.

"You piece of shit," Elliot said, trembling now.

"This isn't like you, brother," said Charles.

Reason got the better of Elliot, and he clamped his lips shut.

"Mr. Caudill, will you introduce me to your sharp-eyed friend here?"

"He's Federle."

"Mr. Federle, have you anything to say?"

Federle looked hard at Charles Hardiman and shook his head.

"He's dumb as a post."

"Elliot, for God's sake, shut up."

"Let him alone," I said. "He wants to have a poke at me."

"In fact, Elliot and I are rather accomplished boxers. Father insisted on an education in the manly arts."

This time reason got the better of me, and I made no comment about their father's manliness.

"Look here," I said. "I didn't come to roust you. We're just looking around."

"The men on the floor don't like strangers nosing around. Just now there's an acute paranoia regarding Axis spies lurking about, bent on sabotage. You've seen the lovely posters placed around the complex by our diligent security personnel?" Charles's eyes were sparkling now. "Certainly this paranoia could be stoked—by a sophisticated party—to ill effect for any interloper on the premises. It could cause any kind of trouble."

"Maybe you should worry about what the men on the floor think of you," I said.

"That's a keen point, Mr. Caudill. But as I am intimately familiar with the workings of the plant, I feel I can trust my judgment here. I have no worry for my own safety or that of my brother."

I took a moment to go over what he had said. Charles was as smart as his father but not as rash. If he said he meant to make trouble for me, I could take him at his word.

"You'd be willing to risk wrecking the place to get rid of me?"

"Wreck the place, Mr. Caudill!" He laughed. "Some day we hope to own it!"

Now Elliot had found a way to control his anger toward me, to see himself as the better man again. He gazed coolly at me and said, "We *will* own it."

"Federle thinks the two of you know something about the dead women," I said.

Charles Hardiman lifted his eyebrows and looked back and forth between me and Federle. Then he said, "There's an interesting angle. I'd be interested to see how that could work." He glanced up and down the long corridor. "We'd be better off to talk about this privately."

"He's just goading us, Charles," Elliot said, squinting now. "He's out of place here, and he knows it."

"Is it true, Mr. Federle? Why would you harbor such an odd prejudice against us?"

Federle said nothing, but his demeanor cooled, and he looked flatly at Charles Hardiman.

"Nothing to say? A hard man?" He met Federle's gaze for a time, and then looked to me. "Caudill, what's the gist of all this? If you've anything substantial to discuss with us, you can make an appointment."

"Probably in another week the FBI will be crawling all over this place," I said. "That doesn't bother you?"

"Why should it?"

"It'll be bad for business, maybe."

Charles mulled it over for a moment and then smiled. "I don't see why it should be. Half the commanders of the armed services have been through here already. We've had visitors here who are so critical to the war effort that they can't be named. It's beyond you, Mr. Caudill."

"The way things are," said Elliot, "business can't very well slow down for us, wouldn't you say, Caudill? The nation can't afford to do without us, can it?"

The pocky hood was getting itchy. He turned away and tried to find something more interesting than our conversation.

Charles said, "As I see it, we're more valuable to the good of the nation than the pair of you could ever hope to be. You see it, don't you?"

"You two nancies," Federle said. "Cowards. All your money saves you from having to stick out your neck—"

"You're out of place here," said Elliot.

"How many men went out and did their duty while you two sat back here piddling with each other? How many died to keep you in the pink? This one's a little funny, Pete. You can tell by the way his pants fit."

Elliot drifted toward Federle, who had never taken his hands out of his pockets. Charles moved to brace his brother back with his arm, but it wasn't necessary. The younger Hardiman smiled and seemed to slither away carelessly from Federle, brushing past him.

"There's no reason to stand for such abuse, Charles," Elliot said. "I can see what drives this man, and it isn't patriotism or love of country." He sauntered off toward the plant floor, and one of the lackeys broke off to follow after him.

Charles watched his brother go with a look of resignation. "I can't see how any of this is useful, Caudill."

"I'll tell you the truth. I'm not seeing it myself. But at least now I know what your little brother's made of."

Charles furrowed his brow. Even before the lackey caught up to him, Elliot was talking and waving his hands. He had a peculiar way of walking, as if he'd injured his lower back. I could see the pockmarked gunsel staring after him with disdain.

"You shouldn't think lightly of Elliot," said Charles. "He does have a few limitations, but he's really an extraordinary man."

"You're both no more than leeches," Federle said. "Born into it. Never earned a thing on your own."

"I struggle to see any moral truth in what you're saying, Mr. Federle. I'm trying to be patient. I'm trying to understand, but honestly I can't see how you've developed this feeling toward us. Elliot and I have worked without respite our entire lives, and we expect to continue doing so until the end."

"Federle," I said. "Ray—"

"You can't just talk it away," said Federle. "You can't. I can see what that little shit is up to."

Charles looked intently at Federle, hoping I guess to penetrate to the core of the puzzle. He kept a perfect unflinching composure, an elaborate calm, that unmanned Federle's fuming rant. His suit fit perfectly and seemed to give him a boxy and solid gravity.

"It's getting us nowhere, Ray."

"I agree, Mr. Caudill," said Charles. "But I'm committed to hashing things out here and now if it will keep you from having to come back again to harass my brother and me. If you've anything productive or compelling to add, I ask that you do it now."

"Ray?"

Federle worked his hands in the pockets of his pale trousers. He glanced at me apologetically and shook his head.

"If you have any serious notion that Elliot and I might have had a part in any crime, it would be simple enough to trace our movements backward for several months, I should think. I'm afraid our time is so closely managed that we couldn't possibly find the time to engage in such a fruitless leisure activity."

By this time I had grown tired of talk. I stood for a few more seconds regarding young Charles Hardiman, and he did not flinch under my bleary gaze.

"Satisfied at last?"

"As much as I'll ever be," I said.

"Then I won't have to see you again?"

"It wasn't me that killed your father," I said. "I didn't want any of that to happen."

"I know that, you fool." Charles set his jaw again. He muttered, "I know more than you do."

I turned away from Charles and took Federle's elbow. He was trembling weakly, as if he had burned all his energy keeping still for so long. We walked slowly into the bowels of the factory, and I did not flatter myself to think that Charles Hardiman watched us as we went.

CHAPTER

19

Despite the frailty I had felt in him after the encounter with the Hardiman boys, Federle seemed keen to examine the whole complex of mills and factories. But I felt the familiar healing fatigue setting in, and I found myself worn out more thoroughly because I was still half-thinking about everything he'd blurted out to me about himself in the morning. I was thinking about Walker, too. It had been a couple of long hours since we had to leave him. It was hard not to be a rube inside any of the massive buildings; it was hard to keep from gawking at the machinery, to keep from working out how power was transferred along belts and chains and cranes, how electric cars and light railcars came in and out with loads of raw or finished parts, assemblies, or gangs of men. There were blowers to move air and pumps to move water and other fluids, along with all the hoses and pipes and valves necessary to keep it all under control.

Federle seemed to want to explore the whole plant like a kid, but I dragged him back to the security house. He had the sense or was dumbstruck enough not to say anything more until we had left the place. We picked up Walker, and Pickett brought the car around for us.

"We're on the track with those Hardiman bastards," Federle said, sitting behind the wheel. "We ought to stick a knife in the both of them and be done with it."

"Have you ever put a knife in a man?" Walker asked, riding now in the back seat of the Chrysler.

Federle's muscles twitched from his jaw all the way up to his temple. "Sometimes you got to," he said.

"Have you ever done it yourself?"

"I've seen plenty of Japs run through, if that's what you mean."

"No, I mean have you ever—"

"Walker," I said.

"Have you ever yourself—"

"It don't mean I'm proud, Walker! We all did some things." Federle's hands were splayed out, palms pressed to the steering wheel. "Sometimes I can't sleep when I want to. I dream too much. Is that what you want me to say?"

"Federle," I said.

"I see the face of some skinny cave rat right up close to mine, like our eyeballs were almost touching. You know how a bayonet can go right through a man?" He made the fingers of one hand into a point and jabbed his arm through the wheel. "Then I can see his face—I can't help but to see right through to his bones, his skull—"

"Federle," I said, "keep your eye on the road."

"—I got my hand right through his ribs—see? And I can put my hand right through that stinking Jap and out the other side. I can see it plain as day. Only I'm not sure anymore if it was a dream or if it was something I really did. How would you like to carry that around, Walker?"

"How would you like to see your mother raped by a gang of white men?"

"Ahh," groaned Federle. "Jesus Christ."

"He's going to crash us, Walker," I said. "What's got into you?"

"Mr. Federle, I don't mean to be hurtful. I don't mean just to bring up bad feeling in you. But I've already seen more killing than I wanted to in this world. Can't we find a way to work out a case like this without thinking of killing anybody?"

"We don't know what-for about the Hardiman boys yet," I said. "We don't know a thing."

"It's only a way of talking, Walker. I didn't mean it."

"You all got the freedom to talk that way," Walker said.

"I talk too much, I know."

"What we're trying to do—leastways as I've been led along by Detective Caudill—is to find the man or men who killed my little sister. And to the length we're working for Mr. Lloyd—"

"Them Hardimans are nasty fish," Federle said. "They want to wreck Lloyd."

Walker said, "They want to sniff after their fortune. That I can see. But I don't see those fancy boys dirtying themselves up in such a way as to murder women in cold blood."

"It's the queer blood, you can't say anything about it," said Federle. "That Elliot, if you had seen—"

"Listen," I said. "I can see your angle on this, Federle. But if there's any chance that it could be the Hardiman boys—or if they've hired out the job—it won't help us any to have you going off."

"I'm sorry, Pete. I'm sorry about it. I get carried away. I got a case of nerves, I guess." Federle lit up a smoke and it fluttered in his hands as he drove.

"I'll tell you something," I said. "You could write a book about what's wrong with the Hardiman family. But we're not set up for anything like that right now."

"I'll keep a lid on it, Pete. You don't have to worry about me."

"I'll tell you something else," I said. "This ain't something Hank Chew needs to know anything about. Walker, you remember the girl—Jane Hardiman?"

"Well, of course."

"You never met her, though. You never met any of them, did you?"

"I sure didn't," Walker said.

"Well, I'll tell you now," I said. "It was Roger Hardiman that sent young Jane over to Willard Frye and the gymnasium boys." I remembered Frye well—he had taken my eye, my fingers, the life of my partner Bobby, and young Jane. Living in my own mind, I had never really considered that Walker and Federle had never set eyes on the man.

Walker said, "You think Roger Hardiman would send his own little girl to that Frye? What kind of a man..."

"That ain't the half of it," I said. "That's a queer household, you know that. Jane came along late, some years after Charles and Elliot. I don't think she could quite fit into the family entirely."

"You think she—you think the mother—" Federle's brain was working. The fire had gone from his eyes, and he slumped forward, leaning on the wheel. "If the father—"

Walker said, "Roger Hardiman didn't care much for Jane because she was another man's daughter."

"We couldn't prove any of that now," I said. "That's the kind of thing that gets lost from the evidence room. But as far as Hank Chew is concerned, it would make a story to kill for."

"I see now," muttered Federle. "I see."

"Those boys aren't entirely soft, you can see," I said. "And the woman—" I choked off what I might have said and watched Federle carefully. "Estelle Hardiman isn't as pristine as the papers make her out to be."

"I guess so," said Federle. He was wrung out. When he was tired and off in dreams, his fingers and hands worked and writhed like he had an itch in all his knuckles that he couldn't ever scratch away.

"If those Hardiman boys have the run of the Lloyd plant here," Walker said, "they might just as well have that same privilege at the other plants."

"How can we know where they've been?" I said. "We aren't the police anymore. We aren't private dicks, either, really. How can we put up such a big investigation?"

Federle looked pale and thirsty at the wheel, and he didn't seem to hear us talking.

"You probably still have some friends on the police force, Detective. Though you aren't so friendly as you ought to be."

"If we could put a tail on them now— You think they always stick together?"

"Pardon my saying so, Detective, but I don't think you could follow anybody without being noticed. Do you still keep that glass eye?"

I turned to face him and let loose the ragged grin. "You think I ain't a regular guy?"

"You aren't regular, if there's one thing you aren't."

"Go on," I said. "You ever done any tailing?"

"I never got so far into law enforcement, if you'll remember."

"What about you, Federle?"

He gave no response. His face was slack except for his pursed lips.

"He likes to drive," Walker said.

"Listen, Walker, I was thinking of something else. I know that Estelle Hardiman has some Negro help staying at the place. Maybe those two boys—"

"All the colored folks in the city are friendly with one another. Is that what you want to say, Detective?"

"Okay, Walker. Don't start in on it."

"We all have a secret society. We call it 'The Secret Society of Colored Folks.' Only I ought not to be so free with you about it."

"I'm only saying, if I was in your place, if everything was stacked against me like it is around here—"

"Matter of fact," said Walker, "I think my wife knows the maid at the Hardiman place in Grosse Pointe. She knows her people anyway."

"Then why do you have to prop me up when I only asked you a simple question?"

"Well, when everything is stacked up against you, as you say, it can bring a little pleasure to be able to throw some grief around yourself."

Federle was smiling vaguely at this or at some part of his dream life.

"Okay, Walker, I can take a joke," I said. "Can you at least see what you can find out on that end?"

"The Secret Society meets every Sunday."

Federle drifted to the curb near Walker's place. It was toward supper-time, and there was a sort of lull over the area. I stepped out to allow Walker passage from the rear seat, and then leaned back in to grab my hat.

"Take the car back and get some sleep," I told Federle. "I'm going to grab something to eat here."

"Yeah?"

Inside my pocket I peeled off two bills from the folded money.

"Here's forty dollars. Buy something nice for your wife."

"Yeah? I'll get something for the kids."

"Don't wreck the car."

I pulled the door forward to close it, and Federle drove slowly away.

"I got some doubts about that man," I muttered.

"Every man can do right or wrong," Walker said.

"Some people get plumb crazy. They can't help what they do."

"Do you believe that?"

"You know it's true."

"Do you think Mr. Federle will fall onto that path?"

"Honestly, Walker, I'm not even sure about myself."

"Heaven help us all, then."

"You were starting to tell how Federle got fired from his work at Palmer's."

"You want to hear that story?"

"Sure."

"I was there on the dock, lifting and pulling with a hand jack, you know. They needed a forklift driver, and they couldn't see letting me do it, even though I had done some of that work in the past. So they hired Federle, though it was clear he hadn't ever learned to drive one. He hadn't been there even a week, I don't think. He was the type of man that wanted too much to be chummy right off.

"One of the drivers—a great big roly-poly one—came in every day at the same time with his rig and went into the bathroom while we loaded up the trailer. He used to shut himself up in the stall and smoke a cigar and read the paper. Every day it was like this.

"So the one day—probably it was a Friday, payday—Mr. Federle filled up a toy balloon with oxygen and acetylene—they do a bit of welding over to Palmer's. You can guess. He went into the bathroom and lofted the balloon into the stall, knowing that the driver would pop it with the cigar."

"Popped it with the stogie!"

"Blew the door right off the stall. Shattered some of the lights in there. The driver came out with his pants around his ankles. He started crying after a while, like he just couldn't figure out what had gone on."

"That's a good one," I said.

"He wasn't hurt except for his hearing. But that was the end of Federle."

Thinking it over, I started to laugh. Even Walker let loose a low chuckle. I coughed only a little.

"It doesn't seem so bad," I said.

"It's a rough crowd. That sort of joshing can get ugly pretty quick."

"Sure." Walker meant that it could get especially ugly for a colored man when a joke turned bad. I was wondering if he'd found out anything while he was cooling his heels at the Lloyd plant, and I was about to ask him about it.

"I'm going to show you something, Detective," he said.

We walked a couple blocks east without any talk between us. It was a pretty nice district, filled to the brim with colored families. Because of the war, everybody was either signed up or holding decent jobs, and some real money was working its way through the neighborhood. It wasn't anything like Indian Village or Boston-Edison or Palmer Park, but I could remember how the colored folks lived in past times. The children now had shoes and trousers in good repair, and the old ladies had cushioned chairs to rock in on their porches. Maybe some of them had lost their men, but it was funny to me to think how much good the war had brought to that neighborhood and to Detroit in general.

Walker led the way up to the porch of a nicely kept house on Russell. He rapped politely at the door and stood with his hands clasped behind his back.

"You're not carrying that weapon?" he whispered.

I had to pat myself down to check. "It's in the car."

"All right then."

The door opened inward and a tall Negro woman smiled out at us. She was very dark, almost black, and it was hard to tell how old she was.

"Jonah Walker! Why don't I see you on my doorstep more often than this? And why don't I see you in church on Sunday? I see that pretty wife of yours."

"Auntie Lu," said Walker. He took her two hands and leaned in to kiss her cheek. "Auntie Lu, I brought someone to see you. This is Mr. Caudill."

She looked at me very seriously and appraised my ugly mug.

"I'm Lu Ella Marker, Mr. Caudill. I'm so pleased to meet you."

She reached out her hand to me, and I clasped it for a moment, though not as easily as Walker had.

"Ma'am." I couldn't think what Walker had in mind. I was sure I had never met the woman before. My mind raced to bring up a picture of all

the dark faces I had seen years before when I had been through the trouble
after killing the black boy as a patrolman. There had been so many faces
over the years, dark and light.

"Come right in, now. I'm just in the middle of supper."

Walker and I stepped through the door and into the small room at the
front of the house.

"Set yourselves down while I check on my soup," Auntie Lu said.

There were two chairs and a wooden bench with a cushion and carved
rails at the back. I sat on the bench, and Walker continued to stand.

"What's it all about, Walker?"

"Auntie Lu can cook."

"I can smell it. But I didn't mean in the car that I wanted you to set me
up with any chow. I can feed myself."

Walker looked down at me sadly. "Have a little patience, Detective."

There was an enormous leather-covered Bible, worn to tatters with use,
on the table next to the most frayed chair. The low light of evening angled
in the front window and glinted in Auntie Lu's eyes as she stepped toward
us again.

"Now, Jonah. We'll have to see about you missing the service every
Sunday."

"I've got to work, Auntie."

"Work!"

"You know I have to feed my family."

"We'll talk about this later, Jonah Walker. Now, Mr. Caudill, what can I
do for you?"

"Ma'am, I don't know."

"I think you know Mr. Caudill, Auntie. He used to be a detective with
the police."

"No," she said. She peered more closely at me, wiping down her hands
on her apron. There was a shrewdness to her that held back almost all the
reaction that came when the light clicked on for her. She craned her head
toward the staircase and barked, "Boy! Come down here!"

"Auntie?"

"Visitor!"

"All right, Auntie."

I heard papers rustling and the sound of clumsy footsteps across the floor above us.

"Mr. Caudill, would you care for something to drink?"

"No. Thank you, ma'am."

The boy's footsteps were wrong—one soft, one loud, a tap and then a quick thump. It was clear as his feet and legs appeared that he was gangly and spastic, and still I could not guess who it was. When his face came into view, I could see that he was smiling broadly—too broadly. He wore smoked glasses over his eyes.

"Is it a white man here, Auntie?" he asked.

"Joshua!"

"I'm sorry, Auntie. But is it?"

I knew him. A slicing pain across my chest and also in the lower part of my left leg throbbed together.

"Is it a white man? Is it the police, Auntie?"

Walker had brought me here so I could see what my work had done. I had rescued him from a mob of white boys during the riot of the previous year, and now he stood before me: as tall as I was, though slighter by sixty pounds; and spastic, and blind.

"I don't think Mr. Caudill is a policeman anymore, Joshua."

CHAPTER

20

What could have made me want to abuse myself so thoroughly? I could not explain it because it made no actual sense. Was it the example of the boy, who was blind and a cripple, but who faced the world with good humor and optimism? Joshua had been beaten near to death, and I had managed to rescue him from a pack of white boys just as the riot broke out. It was also the last time I had seen my nephew Alex, crouched in the shadows with the Devil in his eyes. I had in one moment saved the Negro boy and lost the last bit of blood kin I had, save my mother.

Joshua should have been bitter. He had lost more than I had, and might now live another sixty years as a cripple. But he never stopped smiling as we sat talking in Auntie Lu's front room.

He knew it was me even before Auntie Lu introduced me to him.

"Mr. Caudill? I don't believe I've ever been able to thank you properly."

He advanced across the room, keeping his balance on his back foot with each step. He nudged each foot forward in a practiced way, feeling his way across the floor, and held both arms before him like they were wrapped formally around a dance partner. It looked like he could map out the room by sensing where things were with the skin of his face.

I grabbed his hand as he put it out to me.

"I knew it was you as I came down," he said. "Auntie thinks I'm being rude, but it's true: I remember the smell of you from that night. And from the cell you kept me in at the station. Do you remember, Mr. Caudill?"

"I remember everything."

"I only remember running," he said. "I was never athletic that way! I've been told how you saved my life."

"I couldn't help myself. It seemed—"

"But I have to thank you! It would have been the end of my time here on earth."

"I'm sorry how it turned out for you," I said.

"You can't blame yourself for any of it. Better to be alive than dead, sir!" He smiled openly as he spoke. In fact, he seemed much happier and more confident than he had been the year before, as if a burden had been taken from him.

"Is that you, Mr. Walker?"

"Yes, it is, son."

"Thank you for bringing Mr. Caudill to see me."

Walker said. "I thought it might do Mr. Caudill some good."

Joshua's smile grew even broader. "Do you remember, Mr. Caudill, how you made me pee my pants down in that cell?"

"Joshua!"

"Beg pardon, Auntie."

"I remember, boy."

"I want you to know I don't bear a grudge. You were doing what you thought best. I was so afraid! But what do I have to be afraid of now? Every extra moment I get to spend now is a gift. I want you to know I'll always be grateful to you, sir."

"Well," I said, "that's all right."

Probably I was inside the house for only a few minutes. But when I did manage to quit the place, it was like I had been underwater. I couldn't seem to get enough air. I left Walker to his family and walked away as fast as my legs could carry me toward a good drink. There wasn't any good excuse for it.

Joshua had grown like a sprout in the time since I had seen him last. If not for the crookedness, he would have been a bit taller than me, and he was still young, with a few more years to grow. He was a smart boy, I could see, and now he had some confidence. Despite the blindness, or because of it, he now had some sense of purpose. It made him better than me, and someday it would make him stronger than me. I could not really say if he counted me as an enemy or if he was truly grateful that I had put off his dying. Probably both things were true, which was too much to think through.

All the people I had known—those who were still living—were changing and growing, making their way in the world. Hank Chew was out there somewhere in the city, scouting for dirt and playing the angles. I imagined that the Hardiman boys were together glowering over a map of the world in the smoky den of a big mansion somewhere. Federle—God knows what Federle was up to or where he was. Alex, in the months since he had disappeared, might have grown into a man. Would I recognize him if I saw him? Walker probably was bussing with his wife and laughing with his children, settling down to a good supper. Eileen and her new beau might have been walking into a movie palace downtown. Everyone in Detroit and across the whole world was wrangling to get ahead, to make a better life. Everyone but me. I was still struggling to figure out where I had gone wrong. Why didn't I just run off?

I put some grub down my sorry gullet and then found a quiet place to get filthy drunk. Over the course of the evening I put away twelve or fifteen shots of whiskey and a couple mugs of beer. I can't say where else I might have gone that night or how I got around. Sometime during the long evening I picked up a little pint bottle of whiskey and put it in the pocket of my jacket.

The city at night was a circus of lights. In the tall towers downtown, even toward midnight, I could see people moving inside the offices and in the hotel rooms, bustling in and out of lobbies and theaters and nightspots. I thought it must have been a Friday or Saturday night because of all the hollering and horn blowing. Teenagers packed ten to a car trolled up and down Woodward looking for thrills. There were a great many pretty women, too, or so it seemed to my drunken eye, with their hair done up, their teeth smiling and white, their hips pressed and nicely rounded in tight skirts. I must have been staggering, and I know I was ugly, but nobody seemed to notice me. Everything just flowed around me. The liquor blotted away all my aches, and for a time I just wandered, hopping streetcars back and forth, walking around Grand Circus Park and Campus Martius.

That's all I want to remember. Some time later in the night, after I had I dozed off for a moment on a bench in a park somewhere, a beat cop poked me in the ribs with his billy club.

"Go on home," he said.

"I will," I told him, and staggered off into the night.

It must have been after midnight when I wandered off Joseph Campau and onto Dearing. Around the corner the theater lights were dark, and even the neighborhood dogs were asleep. A few stray cars came by on Campau, rumbling up and fading away now and then as I stood staring at Eileen's dark house. For a long while I kept still, lost in a kind of drunken dream. My fingertips and toes were as cold as ice, and water dripped from my nose and my eye. I wanted to sleep with Eileen in her bed, to draw off some of her warmth. I needed it—I needed healing, and I knew I couldn't find it in any other place. She was lost to me, though, and I could offer nothing but trouble. I should not have come.

I was startled to attention by a slight rustle and the faint sound of chewing in the sprouting tulips next to Eileen's porch steps. I walked a bit closer across the grass and saw a good-sized opossum crouched there like a primitive demon. When he saw me, he pulled in on himself, and then as I drew closer he tried to make himself bigger. He opened his mouth and hissed at me, showing the foul inside of his gaping mouth. I came close enough to kick at him with my shoe. He clamped down with his needle teeth on the leather and held on until I managed to shake him loose. I was taken by a great shudder as I watched him waddle away. He stopped behind the neighbor's little shrub and watched me. His close-set eyes smoldered green.

The opossum had been messing with something on the ground behind the tulips, up against the brick of the porch. I thought it might have been a badly thrown newspaper. Then, too, I thought of Alex's worn baseball glove, and I wondered if it might still be lying there forgotten. The way the streetlights cast shadows along the porch, it was impossible to see anything. So I got down to one knee and felt along the ground with my left hand.

I grabbed something solid and brought it up to the light, knocking the heads off a few tulips.

It was a severed human forearm.

Drained of blood, the skin was like hairy wax. The fingers were curled to the palm like a dead spider's legs. But I could see from the ink staining the thumb and forefinger that Hank Chew wouldn't be stuffing any more notes into the pockets of his little vest.

CHAPTER

21

You can flounder through a dream sometimes when you know it's a dream and you ought to wake up. You want to wake up, but your whole body is caught stiff, like a panther is on top of you, smothering the life out of you. You're sure your heart is going to thrash itself loose from all the pipes and cords that hold it in place. That's when you might let out a little groan—if you can catch enough breath for it. You want to swim up out of that under-world but you can't. It's a lot like drowning.

Only I wasn't inside any dream. I knew—as bad as things were—that it wasn't so common to find sawed-off body parts lying about. Chew's arm was heavier or lighter than I expected it to be, and I could not seem to manage it with the faulty grip of my bad hand. I turned it round until I saw the gristle and the round cap of the bone at the severed end. Years had gone by since I had misplaced my eye and my fingers. *Where are they now?* I thought. The liquor fog ran straight out of me.

I leapt up onto Eileen's porch, tossed Chew's arm to the side, and tried the door. It was bolted, so I put the shoulder to it. Nothing doing. I slammed my forearm close to the bolt a few times, and I thought that thirty or forty more whacks might begin to splinter the oaken door or the reinforced frame I had put in. The window was too high in the door to let me reach down to the inside latch.

I stepped back on the porch and had a run at it. I bounced back and into a heap on the planked porch, and in frustration rose up and stomped my foot near the door handle. By this time all the dogs in the neighborhood were yodeling, and a few lights began to pop on in the windows up and down the street.

I ran around to the back door and found it unlocked. Armed only with my stupid rage, I stumbled in and blundered through the house. Eileen's bed was made up primly, and, excepting what I had knocked over myself, nothing in the house seemed out of place. I went up the angling stairway to the attic and found nothing; the basement was quiet, too.

All my strength had deserted me. I walked back out to the formal dining room, little used since Alex had gone, and slumped down in the chair in the corner next to the telephone. I picked up the handset and dialed the operator. "I'd like the police. The police. Yes, thank you." I could hear blood squirting weakly inside my temples. "Yes—Kibbie, is that you? It's Pete Caudill. I'd like to report a murder."

Through the lacy curtains over the front windows, I could see the scout car arriving before I hung up the phone. The neighbors had summoned them. I got up weakly to meet the officers at the front door.

They let me hang fire in cuffs in the back of the scout car while they staked out the scene. Despite the late hour, pretty soon a crowd of neighbors in their bedclothes gathered across the street, and all the houses had at least one light on. I kept myself slumped down out of sight on the long seat, and might have been able to sleep except for the acid vomit that threatened to come up if I relaxed my clenched throat.

Two dicks from the homicide squad finally arrived in a long, gray, unmarked car and parked in front of the scout car so that their lamps lit up my hiding place. It was Dilley and Foulard, two old-timers who lived right next door to each other in identical houses right up close to the Sojourner Truth Homes, where a passel of Negroes had been moved in by the National Guard a couple years before.

They knew me, and from the way they tipped their heads together toward the scout car after conferring with the patrolman, I could see they weren't too happy about having to deal with me. They took charge of the scene, grunting and pointing. Two other patrolmen had arrived, and Dilley and Foulard sent them with their notepads to brace the onlookers and knock on doors.

The detectives shuffled onto the porch with slack faces to have a look at Chew's wing, their hats tipped back over their shiny foreheads. It was another half an hour before they turned their attention toward me. They came out together along the narrow walk that led to the backyard and leaned down to give me the hard eye through the window of the scout car.

Right then a little coupe pulled in off Campau and slowed to a crawl when the driver saw the ruckus. Dilley and Foulard left me and strolled across the street. My hands had lost all feeling, and it pained me to push myself up in the seat. The driver was a small man with a thin mustache, a sparse head of hair, and round glasses. Dilley motioned for him to roll down the window.

I could only see the lower part of her face as she leaned toward the open window of the auto. Her white chin and the bright red of her lower lip, but I knew it was Eileen, and I knew she was safe. All the air went out of me, and I let myself go against the door next to the curb. The glass felt cool on my forehead.

Saturday, April 15

"Well, why didn't you say anything about these goons to us when they worked you over?" Dilley's tiny eyes seemed cruel, but he was all right.

"We might've picked 'em up," Foulard said.

"I don't know," I said. "I keep a tight lip."

"We heard you were in a state," said Dilley. "But if you don't talk, what can we do?"

For effect, they had carted me all the way down to the headquarters on Beaubien. It didn't look like they were planning to charge me with anything, but I wasn't clear in my thinking.

Dilley said, "Suppose you tell us where we can find the rest of Chew."

"You guys must know him better than I do."

"So you know him, then?" Foulard's face was like a patty of ground meat, fat, with lines and creases where his jowls and lips hung down. His eyes were lost behind baggy folds of skin and heavy lids. But like Dilley, he was all right.

"I wonder how you knew Chew," said Foulard. "You were chummy?"

"No," I said. I knew I had to tell them something. "I only rang him up to ask a favor, and I regretted that right away."

"I wonder what kind of favor it was."

"A colored fella I know had a sister in Cleveland—"

"You're talking about Walker," Dilley said.

"Sure."

"So you called up Chew to see if he could dig anything up, is that so?" Dilley's little eyes seemed very watery, and he had to press at them with the handkerchief he kept wrapped around his mitt. "Why you like Chew so much?"

"I never liked Chew."

"Why not call us?" asked Dilley. "You don't want to see us no more?"

"You coulda come down to see us. We ain't strangers," said Foulard.

"Well," I said, "I get some bad ideas."

Dilley sat down and leaned his bulk on the table over a meaty forearm. "Your father liked to drink, Pete. But he never let it get the best of him."

"He was a good Joe," Foulard said.

"I know it."

"You don't need to be as good as him," Dilley said. "But you could at least stay out of the gutter."

I didn't have any way to respond. There was a glass of water near me on the table, and I wanted it, but I knew how it would taste on my swollen tongue. My belly felt hard and stuffed.

"What about this Lloyd business? What about this badge?" Foulard put his thumb in the corner of the box with my belongings and rattled it a bit.

I couldn't come up with any reason not to spill a little. Besides I was dead tired.

"Chew got me thinking about the Old Man. Walker's sister was found outside the Lloyd plant—"

"Inside, you mean," said Dilley. "Right?"

"Indiana, too," Foulard said.

"So I went to see Lloyd."

"You just went to see him, just like that?"

Foulard chuckled. "You got some friends."

"A family friend, I guess," Dilley said. "Your old man was chummy with Frank Carter, wasn't he?"

"That's the story." In some ways, these two knew more about my father than I did.

"What's Lloyd want with you?"

I shrugged. "He wants me to poke around, I guess."

"So you didn't have use anymore for Chew? How'd that sit with him? Was he getting on your nerve, making a pester?"

"He came to see me in the hospital. I gave him the send-off."

"That's another thing," Foulard said. "You say these goons picked you up right after you saw Lloyd?"

"They pulled me out of my bed late that night."

"Uh-huh," said Dilley. "And they just dumped you over to the Hardiman place?"

"Did they?"

"You told us they did," Foulard said.

"I never told you that," I said. "I might have told them at the hospital. I have to think. I wasn't really in the picture then."

"The meat-wagon boys confirm they picked you up there," said Dilley.

"I wonder how the Hardimans might be involved in all this."

"Go on wondering," I said. "I don't know."

"You'd like to find out, though, wouldn't you, Pete?" Dilley was leaning in on me now. "You'd like to kill those goons if you could get your mitts on them, wouldn't you?"

"I'd like to do a lot of things," I said. "But I don't seem to get anywhere."

"Maybe those goons have been traveling," Foulard said. "Cleveland, Indianapolis..."

"Now Chew's gone," I said.

"We haven't decided yet if it's Chew's arm," said Dilley.

"You know it is," I said.

"It oughta be," he said. "But we haven't decided."

"I can see four big guys working you over, Pete," said Foulard. "No offense. But four guys working together, chopping up women? And now we find an arm, just an arm?"

Dilley said, "Right there in the daffodils at Pete Caudill's sister-in-law's house. Don't it seem personal somehow, Pete?"

I worked my lower lip over my saw-blade teeth.

"You've got an aspect that makes people dislike you," Dilley said.

"You're telling me."

"You didn't get that from your pop," said Foulard. "No offense to your mother."

I looked up at him with some affection. The pair of them had stayed at it longer than they should have.

"We'll look after Tommy's girl," Dilley said.

"You can leave it to us."

"Sure enough," I said.

"It's been a rough time for you."

"I wonder if you need to get away," Foulard said. "But you shouldn't cut out just now."

"How could I?"

They took me down to the basement and left me alone in one of the empty cells so I could get some sleep. It was close to the cell Johnson had used to hold Joshua before the riot. Dilley and Foulard must have known me better than I knew myself, because they never took away my leather belt.

CHAPTER

22

Whatever I had swallowed during the previous night's carouse rolled through my belly like thunder through the sky. Dilley and Foulard had the daytime crew hold me halfway through the afternoon before they turned me loose. I had not been able to sleep during the night, of course, and though there was a fair mattress on the cot in the basement cell, I couldn't get any use from it. I suppose I might have nodded off for a few minutes in the cab I took to get uptown to Eileen's place. Even on a Saturday, the roads were jammed and the streetcars were packed with bodies. These were workingmen—and women, too—dressed in their rough clothes and heavy shoes, looking dumb and blinking from fatigue.

I was thinking about work, too, but I knew I'd be no good without sleep. I worried that I might do something stupid if I tried to get over to the Lloyd plant. I had swallowed too much alcohol, and without sleep to wash it away, I felt chewed up inside. My gut was like a swollen worm. My eye, too, and all my sinuses ached. If Walker had waited for me to swing by for him in the morning, he'd be done with that by now. I thought that maybe he'd have picked up a driving shift somewhere when he saw I wasn't coming. I had wasted so many days in my life that one more didn't seem important.

Federle I tried not to think about. He had the car, and he was probably sick with worry about where I had gone. Maybe he had spent the morning checking hospitals and the morgue for my dead carcass. It didn't seem possible that either Federle or Walker could know much about what had happened during the night.

What sorry excuse could I have had for showing up at Eileen's door? My own tainted presence had drawn Chew's murderer to her. By rights I should have left off all hope of knowing her any longer. I could feel the acid of my gut pressing upward, one long, gnarled tube of bile that would never be clear again. Stupidly I sent the cab away, and he puttered off down Campau as I stood on the walk surveying Eileen's place in the light of day.

Nothing was sealed off, though it was obvious that there had been a blundering and thorough search of the scene. The flowers that had been struggling to bloom in front of the porch had been scratched aside, and dry soil had been scattered across the walk and pressed down into thin cakes by dozens of flat feet. The curtains were all closed, the door was shut, and an unmistakable feeling of emptiness sat upon me. My mouth was as foul as the river downstream from the factories, as metallic and sharp as the water the thugs had dunked me under. My tongue was raw and cracked.

My shoulders weighed down on me. I was on the porch, but I could not bring myself to knock at the door.

"She's not there," a voice growled not far off. "She won't be there."

I turned dully but saw no one. Over the long porch I dragged my feet, until I could see the hazy figure of Eileen's old neighbor surveying me through his thatch of shrubbery.

"Patterson," I said.

"I don't know where she's gone," he said.

He was trimming back the feral strands of some bushes that had not been cut in the fall. His knuckles were so twisted from arthritis that it was hard to see how his little pruner could work in his hand without nipping away parts of his fingers. He wore boots that seemed twice too large for him, that rose over his bowed legs almost up to his sagging crotch.

I didn't know if he could see my weary nod or if he cared about it. It took a long time to make up my mind that it would be best not to press him about Eileen. Another wave of shame worked over me: I should have been able to guess where she'd go; I should have known her better than I did. It was too late to do anything about all of that. Despite what I might have told myself about loving her, I could not honestly say that I deserved any part of her attention or regard. To judge only from what had happened during the time I had been closest to her, she would be right to forget me if she could.

Patterson left off his clipping to watch me carefully while I stood on the porch. After I came down from the porch and meandered away toward Campau, I could hear him begin to cut again. The gentle sound was rattled away by an air hammer buzzing in the body shop alongside the alley.

When I came up the back stairs at my apartment building, I was careful not to slap my shoe leather on the treads, and I was easy with the key in the door. I sat down right away to take off my shoes. It was all for fear of alerting Federle to my presence. He would know the creak of every floorboard. I was powerfully thirsty, and so I had to pull a glass of water from the kitchen faucet. It would have been best to open the tap at once and blast the glass full. But trying to be a sneak I turned the knob only slightly, which drew a rattle and an echoing groan from the depths of the plumbing. The water was good, but I couldn't enjoy it because my mouth was bad. It seemed to me that I could feel the water dribbling around a solid mass of undigested something in my gut.

Wherever I turned, I expected to find some bloody part of Hank Chew poking out. I had an idea that whoever had chopped him up had planned a little game for me, like an Easter egg hunt. Maybe his pecker and balls were in a jar in my cupboard. If I opened my icebox, I might see his head wrapped in tinfoil like an Easter ham. If I looked in my closet, would I find his clothes hanging up, spotless and neatly pressed? Maybe all his little paper notes were tacked up in a row on the ceiling over my bed.

I had to think. I had to figure out the whole game, but I wasn't in the condition to do it. Even if I had not been short of sleep and hungover but good, I'd still have been a half-wit. Clearly Eileen was in some danger, the kind that might flash at any time—*but probably most when darkness falls,* I thought. *And darkness is falling all around.* For all I knew, she might have gone to stay with my mother for a few days. I played with the thought that she might have arranged to stay at her new beau's place, though it seemed unlikely that her character could change so much.

They'll know how to find her. He will.

Whoever had separated Chew would be able to get to Eileen; I believed it without really considering it. I guess I had become so sick of my own self that I had come to believe in such magic, that there could be a criminal so slick and ruthless that I couldn't do anything to stop him from his work. It wasn't so, or at least I could try to tell it to myself. In my mind I could think about it straight: If it was only one man, he was just gristle and bone like anybody else. Even if it was a proper gang like the thugs that had worked me over, they could be put to rest as any other thing with blood to spill could be put to rest. But it wasn't a matter where thinking could make an end of it. I had lost a portion of my nerve, and I thought of myself as a danger to anything I cared about. It clawed at my heart the way superstition had wracked me as a child.

I knew it would be selfish to track down Eileen. I could do nothing to help her now except keep away. At least as far as Jasper or Whitcomb Lloyd was concerned, my lack of personal concern might let me work to some kind of effect. I vowed to quit Eileen altogether, to swallow any feeling if I could, to cut myself away.

Nobody on the force would believe I had done anything to Chew, but maybe there would be some who would be glad to smear me with it anyway. Dilley and Foulard hadn't even grilled me much about it. If anything more turned up, they'd pull me back in for a proper squeeze. I could line up a lawyer. How would they like that? I could scrounge up the dough.

The main problem was that I knew I had it in me to kill that lousy Chew. It's the sort of thing that crossed my mind whenever I got a troublesome fellow alone in a secluded spot, like a way of playing with ideas. It would take a powerful reason to get me to chop somebody to pieces, for sure—if it was a matter that couldn't be finished any other way. But I was reasonably certain I wouldn't ever cut somebody up and leave the parts around like a kind of game. I wouldn't *do* it, no, but I couldn't keep from *thinking* about it. Ever since the goons had made me tell them everything, I knew that the inside of my brain wasn't safe from the light. It was always possible that I'd flap my gooms again and the world would know what nasty ideas I had. If I could just leave off thinking altogether, maybe I'd be better off.

It comes from being murderous. Though I had not so far done it casually, I had killed a few men. Most of them clearly deserved it. I had busted up a few dozen more in my time, and from the look of things, it wouldn't be long before I'd have to spatter myself with mud again. It wasn't the guilt that bothered me so much. Every time you do a bad thing, your mind changes because of it, your way of thinking. You get to be a little darker, and you can't help thinking the bad way. The brain can get sick like a liver that goes bad from all the poison it has to suck up.

I pulled off all my smelly clothes and crawled into bed. Despite the worry, it wasn't long before I settled in. I remember thinking about how regular my breathing was getting, and then I went out like a light.

Sure enough, as time is lost in sleep, there came a timid rapping to wake me up. I was flat on my back and my mouth was dry and sticky like tar. My eyelid would slide open only with some effort, snapping loose from the crust at the bottom lid and dragging over the dry ball until I could see my cracked ceiling—no notes from Chew.

The rapping came again: three slow, polite raps. I imagined Federle squirming in the hall.

"Come in," I croaked, though not loud enough to be clear.

The knocking came again.

I rolled and let my legs fall over the edge of the bed. There was numbness and tingling in both; this came and went. I stood up and croaked again. "Come in!"

I should feel better than this, I thought. *A good night's sleep.*

When my eye began to see, a seated figure seemed to draw itself out of the darkness at my little table. It was Ray Federle, tapping a folded pocketknife gently on the cheap wood.

"The stitches should come out," he said softly.

"You should have knocked on the door," I said.

"I could hear you snoring," he said. "The door was open."

"Well," I said, "why couldn't you let me sleep out the night?"

"It's getting toward time for me to go out," he said. "I should have let you go on dreaming."

"I wasn't dreaming."

He seemed fully at ease, slumped lightly in my chair with one elbow on the table. His breathing was deep and relaxed, as if he had been sleeping himself. The knife was long and slender and gently shaped in a double curve. The handle was made of pearl or bone worn smooth from use. He let it slip down between his thumb and first finger until it tapped the table, flipped it, and slipped it down again, over and over in a steady rhythm.

"Where have you been, Pete? It seemed like we'd go out again today."

"I got hung up last night."

"You should stay at home. You always get in trouble when you go out."

"I got one mother already," I said. There was only one chair at the table, so I put myself down in the stuffed chair.

Federle didn't say anything for a time, and I eased myself back and rubbed at my legs to get the feeling into them again. I couldn't say what time it was, but the world outside my window was dark except for the glow the full moon made through the thin clouds.

It was no comfort to know that he had not cut my throat as I lay sleeping.

"You don't want to say anything about how the case is going?"

"I'm ready to be done with all of it," I said. "It's enough to put me under."

"Maybe Walker scared up something about the Hardimans."

"Maybe he did. Maybe— What day is it?"

"You didn't talk to him today?"

"Listen," I said, pushing myself up from the easy chair. "I was in the clink most of the day." I went over to the window and made the shade go down, and then I walked across to switch on the light. The brightness made the apartment seem even more cramped.

"What did they put you in the can for?"

"I was— It wasn't for anything that I did."

"They got you with your pants down?"

"What's that?"

"It's nothing but trouble being out late," Federle said. "You should know that by now."

In the light he seemed weaker, less comfortable. There was a green canvas bag on the table with the long carrying strap neatly coiled up beside it.

"Living alone," he said, "it's hard on a fella. I was on my own—" He broke off and took up the knife between his strikingly slender fingers. "Before I settled in with Patty, I was a rambler, all right. Pete, it's good to be a part of something, I want to tell you. You should try to keep in at night if you can."

"I'll stay in. I'll listen to the radio. That seems right."

"Don't be sore at me."

"Come on in while I'm sleeping and sit down at my table. Wake me up with your tap-tap-tapping little knife. It makes me feel like everything is safe on the home front."

Federle's blank eyes rolled away. I could see how many ideas he might have had blustering inside him, how he had to be on the alert all the time to keep the wrong ones from coming out.

"I'm saying that the best way to be safe is to belong, to be connected to things."

I didn't make a ready answer.

"If things were different—if you'd met Patty—or a girl like her—if you can get past that awful first impression you had—"

"It's pretty late to think of that, Ray."

"Sure." He sat up in the chair as if he were waking. "Do you want me to pull out those stitches or not? You can't leave them in or—"

"All right," I said. "Why not?"

He opened up the square green bag on the table. Over the buckle someone had used ink to scribe a perfect circle on the canvas. Inside the circle the letters RE had been neatly written.

"My friend Reno didn't make it," Federle said. "So I brought home his kit."

There were only a few things inside the bag: forceps like a big pair of tweezers, a couple of rolls of gauze wrapped in paper turned a little brown from heat and salty water, white tape, a little turkey baster with a rubber bulb on the end, a few tattered stick bands. Federle arranged everything on the table and seemed sad that there wasn't more.

"You've still got that alcohol in the head?"

"It's not good for drinking," I said.

He got up stiffly and said, "Sit down here." Then he went off to fetch the rubbing alcohol.

I slumped down into the hard chair in just my shorts. The air in the room was dead, and I had not enough hope or energy to get up to crack open the window. There was a fan in my mother's garage, I knew, a desk fan, but I had not brought it to my place.

"You're done with the pain, mostly, eh?" Federle said. "It could look better, but you're healing, anyway, not festering."

He set to work methodically. First he broke open the cleanest roll of gauze and used his knife to slice off a few square pieces. Then he opened the bottle of alcohol, soaked one square, and used it to strip the germs off the tip of his little blade. He wiped the forceps, too, and a corner of the tabletop, and then set all his truck there while he used his hands to judge how the stitches had set. He pressed his fingertips all along the jagged lines of stitches front and back like you'd test a steak to see if it was cooked right. His fingers were deft enough to lull me into a stupor like a barber would.

"See here, on the back, it's not done setting. It's deep, yah. But they can still come out. The scars will flatten out better if we leave it a little wet. You just have to take it easy, Pete."

He soaked a few more squares of gauze and scrubbed over the lines of stitches across my chest. The alcohol felt at first like it burned and then like it was turning the flesh to ice. The silk sutures were dry and stiff like a row of caterpillars. One by one he gripped each stitch with the forceps and snipped it with the very tip of his blade. There was no pain. He dropped the bits onto the floor. At first I watched, but there were so many, and the process was so soothing, that eventually I closed my eye and let him work. It was only the thought of the sharp little blade that kept me from falling off to sleep entirely.

"When you're on the landing craft, Pete, you can't believe you'll be able to jump out when the time comes. You can't believe it. You can see up ahead on the beach some guys getting ground to hell already, and you don't see how you could throw yourself into it. But then you have to. You do."

I could feel the heat radiating from Federle. His breathing got deeper and deeper as he became absorbed in fixing me up.

"You've never been—it's like *black sand*—I bet you never saw such a thing. Brother, I can tell you, it gets hot here, but you don't know what heat is. You can't drink enough water to make up for the sweat that comes out of you, and you're covered in sand, like dust, really, turned to black like the dingiest darkie you ever saw. Well—all they told us was that we had to get to the airstrip, we had to break in to get to the airstrip in advance of the regular army boys—"

He broke off, and I opened my eye to see him mopping the sweat from his brow with his rolled-up shirtsleeve. His face had gone slack, his eyes wide and staring. But then he broke into a heated smile that seemed off-kilter.

"You want to hear about it?" he said.

I shrugged and kept my eye on him for a moment more, and then I settled down again.

"If you're on the beach like that and *everybody* is shooting, everybody on every side of you, it doesn't sound like rifle pops anymore. It's like a roar. Listen. Nobody would believe it, but in a case like that, you can *see* the bullets while they're flying. It's the God's truth, sometimes you can set your head to the side a few inches to dodge a bullet if you can see it coming at you. But you can't keep your eyes on everything, Pete.

"Always on the little islands there's the beach and then a line of trees that starts some way up from the shore. If you can make it to the trees—from the ships they're half the time lobbing shells into the trees while you're trying to get up in there. If there are more guys coming off the boats behind you, they're shooting, too, shooting from behind you. Plenty of guys go down this way. Maybe—"

He stopped talking for a while as he thought about it. I could feel sweat easing out of my whole body from the stillness of the air, but there was nothing to be done about it. Federle's hands seemed strikingly hot whenever his knuckles or fingertips pressed against my skin, and I thought that there must have been a coal fire burning inside him.

"Those stupid Japs—can you imagine? Why wouldn't they just give up? We would've given them food to eat, clean water. They were all starving, even the kids. I can see how you wouldn't—if you were a soldier, and the enemy was coming along, you could see that it was all over for you, you might still want to fight rather than let them take you—if you were a soldier. But there were *women and children* all over the place. Hundred-year-old grannies hunkering down, hiding in caves or in holes in the ground. Why wouldn't they come out? I can't tell you—the flamers—we'd clear out the caves all right, whenever we got to them, the bunkers, pill boxes."

"You had to do it, Ray."

"I had to? Some of the guys—I don't want to put a shadow on them—but some of the guys wouldn't go. Some guys put the gun on themselves. What do you think of that?"

"I don't know," I said.

"How it was, we couldn't blame them. We didn't say anything about it. Sometimes—every day—I thought of eating a bullet myself. You can't help from thinking, can you?"

"But there must be a reason to go on, right?"

"You'd think there must be," he said. "Anyway, for you, Pete, you ain't in such bad shape after all."

Finally it was time for Federle to work on my back. He prodded me forward until I was resting my head on my forearms on the table. Federle scrubbed hard with the gauze and alcohol because the stitches in my back had broken in places and there were partly healed grooves where the stitches had become covered too much with flesh. From the stinging I could feel where the skin would still have to work at closing over. But the pain was nothing.

"We were finished up, more or less. So I was catching a breath, we were packing in some grub along the shore, up at the top of a short rocky bluff. A breeze was blowing over us, the waves were breaking over the rocks, and the army had come in behind us to mop up. We weren't really finished. We'd have to go on to another island, we knew, but we were taking it easy, you know? And I saw down in the water the plumpest little baby, the healthiest little Jap baby after all the tiny skeleton babies we had been seeing—and the sight of it made me happy for just that second before I realized that he was just swollen up from being dead. He was dead, somebody's baby, floating in the water. Probably his own mother had thrown him in to keep him away from us."

"Come on, Ray."

"It wasn't too long after that I got burned up. You'd think it would make you crazy. It does make you crazy. While you're there, while you're in the middle of it and the whole earth is cracking up around you, you have to forget about all that stuff you thought about yourself before that time. You have to forget about your mother, your sisters, what you learned in school. You get scrambled up. You only think about moving up the next hill, moving up to get behind the next tree if you're thinking at all.

"When I got put afire I kept running. I kept running. Finally I fell down, and while I was lying there, it was a dream. All those layers sliding back and forth—I was looking up at the clouds, it was all I could see. But somehow I thought I was facing down. I was looking down into hell, Pete. The ground had opened up to take me, and I could see straight down into it, all the way down to the pit. After everything, it was a relief."

He had to dig into the skin between my shoulder blades to excavate a few stitches that had been covered over. He kept one hot palm pressing me down to the table while he worked the knife's needle tip into me. Then he set the knife down across the back of my neck and worked with the forceps, alternating tools until he was satisfied that he had pulled out everything that needed to go. The alcohol jerked me to attention with the sharp burning along the two torn lines, and the rough swabbing and scrubbing Federle did afterward made me clench my fists and jaw.

"Listen, Pete. Sometimes now when I'm not pulling a shift, I walk the floor of the little place up there, when everyone is asleep. You know how it is. I told you. Sometimes I think of picking up a knife and killing them all in their beds. That's what it does to you. After you've killed somebody else's wife, some other poor sap's kids, really everything he had to show from his life in this world, you can't leave it all behind you. Every day you've just got to make sure you hold on. When you give up, then it's over. You see what I mean?"

I pushed myself up from the table and felt how the position had made my hands fall to sleep. Though I was slick with sweat, my fingers were cold. I had to look at Ray Federle.

"You know I could just keep my mouth shut about all this, Pete. I know you think you're not a lucky guy."

"Ray, I'm sorry about all of it."

"You're older than me, Pete. I hadn't ought to talk at you like this, but—"

"I don't mind you talking."

"I want to explain. When I see those Hardiman boys getting rich, prancing around while boys are getting slaughtered— You see how it is? Don't you see what they're made of?"

"I can see all right," I said.

"Don't you think I can see something about them? Could I be wrong about it?"

"Listen, Ray, we'll look into it together. That's what we're supposed to be doing, right?"

He began to tuck his kit back into the canvas bag. He seemed resolved not to say anything more to me about the Hardiman boys. He slipped his slender knife back into the front pocket of his work trousers.

"I wouldn't ever hurt Patty or the girls, Pete. You know I wouldn't. But I thought it might help you to see—"

"It helps me out."

He pulled the flap through the buckle of his kit and gathered up the carrying strap. A shadow crossed his face, and he glanced around for a clock.

"You should get some rest yourself," I said. "Thanks for the work on the stitches."

"What I need to do is get to work," he said. "I'm set to be late. Do you mind if I take the car?"

"It's fine."

"Listen, Pete. If something happens to me, will you see if you can get a little money from Lloyd so Patty can take care of the girls?"

"You shouldn't talk like that."

"You're right. But just the same."

"If you want them to be taken care of, make sure you can take care of them yourself."

He broke toward the door. "I will," he said. "We'll go out tomorrow, won't we?"

"We'll have to," I said.

"You'll be able to get some sleep now."

"That's what I always hope for."

After he left, I sat in the soft chair for a long time before I put myself to bed. I sipped a little whiskey and thought of my old partner, Bobby Swope, who had made me promise to look after his own wife and bastard child as he lay dying—just as the blood was running out of him. They all wanted to make me promise, and I had not been able yet to stay true to any promise I had ever made. The liquor ran up into my head quickly, and though I had ample cause to worry about Ray Federle, about the car he drove, the gun he had bought for me, and about the razor-sharp knife he carried with him, I did nothing to go after him.

CHAPTER
13

Sunday, April 16

It might have been a dream that made me angry before I ever woke up, but the timid knocking at my door made me see red. It seemed that the outside world was always knocking. I tossed away the sheet that had been tangled around me and struggled toward the apartment door. I heard the handle rattling and the whole door shaking gently against the frame. To judge from the light on the window shade, Sunday morning had started without me.

"All right!" I said.

Lloyd's secretary, James, stood close to the door with a few beads of sweat sprouting along his hairline. He seemed to go a shade paler when he saw me, and his eyes widened as if a puff of air had hit him.

"What?"

"I should come in," he said.

I stepped aside to let him in. He stood stiffly, partly turned away.

"I wanted to tell you I'm sorry, but I was unable to procure any penicillin."

"I keep myself pickled," I said. "It keeps away the germs."

He seemed to be bursting out of his tight collar. An anemic vein snaked across his temple, throbbing, and another swelled along the front of his neck.

I came a little closer to him, took his shoulder, and turned him toward me. "What is it?"

"Did you want to— You might put on a robe."

My pecker, fluffed up erratically from bad sleep, drooped out the front of my shorts like it wanted to shake hands. Without stepping back, I tucked myself in and stood a bit nearer.

"Mr. Lloyd has asked— There's been a problem."

"You mean there's been a murder."

He let his eyes loose to glance around the place.

"Are we alone?" he said.

"I got a girl in the back," I said. "Parts of her, anyway."

He took a big step back and finally met my eye. He had trouble holding the look because I was not wearing my patch, and the eyehole put him off.

"I'm allowed to make a joke, ain't I?"

"It would be lost on me, sir," he said. "There's been some trouble at young Whitcomb's house."

"You mean they found Chew's carcass."

"Hank Chew? It's a young woman, sir."

The throbbing at the center of my sinuses ratcheted up like someone was inflating a rubber bladder inside my head.

"They found a girl at the house?"

"On the grounds. It's shielded from view—"

"You haven't called the police?"

"It was thought that you might—"

"Listen," I said, "you'd better— What's the time?"

"Half past nine," he said without checking his fancy wristwatch.

"You'd better call it in. But give me half an hour. Where is the Old Man?"

"Mr. Lloyd has been removed from the premises."

"Can I see him later?"

"Given the circumstances—"

"And Whit Lloyd?"

"I believe Mr. Lloyd is in California."

"Jesus Christ," I said. "You people."

"I'd better go."

"I'll find you if I want you," I said. "Don't think you can just cut out on me."

"Just as you say, sir."

He slipped out the door and made his way quietly off. I tried to gauge the time it would take to get to the Lloyd place. There wasn't enough time—never enough time. I couldn't say if Federle had managed to make it home with the Chrysler and the key, and I was not in any mood to speak to his woman. But there was no other way. I went to the bathroom and swabbed my face in the sink. My hair looked dead, so I ran a comb through it to put it straight back. *I'm as good as dead, to judge from that mug,* I told myself. *A hell of a way to start the morning.* I found clothes to wear, slipped into my hat and jacket, and stepped out the door.

I thought I could find Federle's room by judging how the fire escape ran upward, but there were two floors above mine. I walked as quietly as I could down the hall of the first floor and found the layout of the rooms all wrong. I got turned around, and there was nothing to tell me which door to knock on. When I reached the stairs, I was able to get myself straight, and I went on up to the top floor. It was clear to me then where the fire escape was, and I stumbled along until I found a door with half a dozen tiny handprints smudged onto the lower part of it. I knocked softly.

Patty Federle pulled the door open as if she had been expecting me to stop in for tea. She said nothing but stepped back curtly to let me in. The apartment was full of light. Her expression was blank, but my own cloud of guilt made it seem that she was not pleased to see me. There was no sign of the children.

"Has Ray come in yet?"

"He's dead asleep," she whispered. "He's been running himself into the ground lately."

"I'm sorry."

"He's a grown man. I can tell how much he cares for you, Mr. Caudill."

Patty Federle kept herself as well as any woman I'd ever known. Her eyes were too strong, but everything else was set in place just like a picture.

She had already made up her hair and dressed for the day, with just a touch of powder on her face. I could not take the time to think about how she had managed to stay with her husband after everything. A woman will carry her worry by pressing her lips together or by tightening around her eyes, but as I saw her that morning I couldn't see any of it.

A slight movement took my eye from her. The littlest girl was stuck in a kind of chair that kept her from moving around, and she had been sitting there in plain sight the whole time. I noticed that the older girl was there, too, sitting at a small table near the window, staring dully at me. Her eyes were almost perfectly round, and circled by thick black lashes. Her brows were full, too, for such a young girl, and the effect was like a bird staring.

"He means well," Patty said. "He's been through so much."

"I'm sorry," I said, "but I'm short of time."

"Do you want me to wake him?"

"No. It's all right. Do you know where he put the key to my car?"

She turned and walked to the end of her kitchen counter. The key hung from the last hook in a row of four, next to a shoehorn on a little chain. Patty brought the key to me, dangling the ring from her thumb. When I brought up my palm to take it, I could see that she felt at least a little something, because her eyes had grown dark.

"I hope you can see how it is," she said.

"Sure, I can see it exactly." If there had been anything right to say, I might have said it. "I'd better go. Tell Ray— Tell him I'll swing by later to pick him up."

"I'll tell him."

I slipped out and hurried down the hall with the desperate feeling that Ray Federle might come bounding after me. There was another girl dead, and if she was at the Lloyd place, it would have been best for me to take the car and any money I could scrounge and cut out of town right away. I thought of the time, but since I did now own a wristwatch, I could only try to put off thinking of it while I bowled down the stairs to the street.

It wasn't sensible, but I drove over to pick up Walker. He was sitting forward on a folding chair outside his door, holding his hat in his hands and hanging his head. When I pulled up, he stood and began to walk toward the stairs. I pushed on the horn to get him to hurry, and I heard the secret panel pop open and the heavy gun tumbling out to the floor in back.

"Where's the other one?" Walker asked as he slipped into the car.

"Well, he's asleep, or so the story goes." The Chrysler's tires left a little rubber on the pavement as I pulled away.

"I was looking for you yesterday."

He knew where I had been, but I spelled it out for him anyway.

"I spent most of the day in the clink."

Walker nodded.

"You know why they threw me in the clink?"

Walker shook his head somberly.

"I come across Hank Chew Friday night."

"Did you take care of him?"

"I mean I came across a part of him. His right arm from the elbow down. The dicks took me down to talk about it."

"How do you know it was Chew's arm?"

"You can take my word for it."

"I thought you might want to have a day of rest today," Walker said. "Emily's off to church with the children."

"Listen, Walker, I'm trying the best I can."

"You'll get us killed if you don't begin to drive a little better."

"There's another woman been found dead. She's out on the grass at Lloyd's place."

Walker sat quietly for a moment. He shook his head. "That should be the end of it," he said.

"How's that figure?"

"Can you imagine the ruckus this will cause? Mr. Lloyd won't have any need for us now. Mr. Hoover will come out himself to have a look at this."

"We're trying to get over there to have a look before the dicks can make it."

Walker didn't have much more to say.

"So far they haven't found the rest of Chew," I said. "Or I don't think they have. So far as I know, he might still be walking along."

Since he made no reply, I shrugged and looked out the window. Lake St. Clair glittered in the sun. There was a fair chop to the water, and only a few larger yachts were out. Maybe it was too early in the season for the boats. A freighter crept along out in the channel, moving down toward the Detroit River.

At the gatehouse, two security men came out, one on either side of the car. They were two-suiters, dressed up nicely for their duty but brought up the hard way, from the look of them. They might have been brothers; both had the flattened noses and battered brows of pugs and the genial nature of men who can handle themselves. They were not the same pair who had allowed me in to see the Old Man when I had strolled up on foot the first time. They knew us on sight—they were expecting us—but still they looked us over well before they let back the gate.

One said, "You're Caudill."

I nodded.

"All right," he said.

"I'm Walker."

"Go down the path over there to the circle of ash trees." The pug looked out to the road. "They'll be coming pretty soon," he said.

Walker and I looked across the broad lawn and saw how the open space was broken by stands of trees and rock walls made to look older than they were. I pulled the Chrysler through the gate; the brick arch seemed like the entrance to a tunnel.

I said, "We'll come around the circle and set up the car to go out in a hurry. We'll walk down."

We were outside Detroit, and so any call to the police would bring Grosse Pointe public safety men. They'd be a little softer toward the Lloyd family and would have an interest in keeping a lid on things. But it was an even bet that they'd have been talking to the Detroit boys, and they'd surely know me if they saw me.

Walker and I walked down the path across an open meadow and into a grove of trees. I thought I could see flashes of an odd whiteness inside the blooming greenery.

"Step right behind me," I said. "Watch what you do. Don't drop anything. Don't pick anything up. Watch where you put your feet."

I stepped a few yards closer to the ring of trees and looked closely at the ground. The dew had burned off the grass already, and I couldn't see much in the way of tracks. The trees weren't far from the water. The Lloyd property swung out at either end to form a calm little bay, and in the middle of it they had built a long pier jutting out. Because of the budding and blooming ground cover, the lake was mainly out of view, but I could smell it. We stepped into the circle carefully.

"What a place," Walker said, looking out toward the main house.

As I drew closer, I could clearly see the whiteness of the girl's dress against the darkness of her skin.

Another colored woman, I thought. *How does Chew fit in to all this?*

I took a few more steps and held out my arm to bar Walker from moving closer.

She was propped up against the bole of a big ash, her legs spread. Her dress had been pulled up, and from the bloody mess there, I could guess how it had gone. Though we never went closer than ten steps from her, I could see that someone had gone to the trouble of opening her eyes. Her lips were pulled back, showing the teeth like a sneer. On the side I could see, her elbow cocked stiffly upward a bit to show how her arm ended in a dainty stump. On the grass beside her I saw what I took to be her hand.

Walker said nothing. He stared over my shoulder, and I could smell the trace of coffee on his breath and the oil in his hair. When he saw that it was a colored woman, I swear I could feel how his heart skipped. He wanted to rush past me. *He thinks it's his sister,* I thought. *He feels so much for her still.*

Maybe it wasn't more than a few seconds, but I took in all the details before I finally recognized her. My gut sank when it hit me, and I had to grit down the white panic: She was not a stranger to me. It was too clear just how personal it had become. From the way the girl had been arranged—facing the big house, with her dress pulled up, fouled down below and bloodied everywhere—I knew that the killer or killers had a mean sense of humor. The whole scene was set up to match Jane Hardiman's murder, and there was no mistaking it. I had seen it firsthand, and I had burned the crime scene photographs into my skull. This girl was set up to match that scene, point for point, except for the severed hand. *I knew her.*

Who could know about this? I thought. *What did I tell them?*

"She isn't on her way to church," said Walker.

I turned angrily toward him.

"You should have some respect," I said.

"Detective, you can't tell me anything about respect."

"What does that mean?"

"I don't know," said Walker. "But we can't help her now."

I looked again at the scene. Death made her look younger than I knew she was. In the bright light of day I could see that her tattered dress was something a younger woman would wear—she might have kept it all through the hard years of the war.

She had been dragged up from the lake. Even if she had not been brought in from a boat along the pier, the Lloyd property had hundreds of feet of shoreline where a little boat might be brought up in the night. I could see clearly how the old leaves and dirt of the ash circle had been disturbed by her body dragging. Doubtless she had been wrapped in a tarpaulin or a carpet just as Jane Hardiman had. My chest was seizing up, and it might have been fitting if I had just dropped dead of a broken ticker right inside the circle of trees. I wanted to get rid of Walker somehow and grab the girl and make every trace of her disappear. Ideas went reeling through my head in a panic. We could drag her into the water, into one of the smaller boats that Lloyd kept along the shore for his rich paddling friends. The guards, the secretary, James, the household help, Old Man Lloyd—

"Step back out the way you came," I said.

"Here they come, Detective," Walker murmured.

"We're covered," I said hastily. "We've got badges, haven't we? This qualifies as Lloyd security business, am I right?"

In fact, I was not certain that I had brought my own badge, and of course Walker had been forced to do without.

"Let's go on up to the house. They can come and find us if they want us."

It was a walk to the main entrance, and I supposed that the Lloyds would have a driver take them to the various areas of the property. It was uphill, too, set along rolling hills unusual for flat Michigan, and both Walker and I were panting when we stepped up to the entrance. There was a buzzer to the side, and a pair of ornamental knockers—brought over from Switzerland or England, I supposed—in the center of each great door. I picked up one heavy brass knocker and let it thud down a few times.

Whitcomb Lloyd swept back the door.

"Mr. Caudill, you've arrived too late!" He was smiling with dark humor, but I could see in his eyes that he knew what a mess it would be.

"I thought you were in California," I said.

"I was, indeed, until yesterday. I arrived late last night. And now this."

"I'm Walker. Jonas Walker."

"Hello, sir. And Mr. Federle?"

"He couldn't make it," I said. "How was California?"

"Beautiful, as always. My wife sends her regards, Mr. Caudill."

"She never met me."

"Nevertheless, she's certain she'll be charmed to make your acquaintance. You've a reputation for a sort of impish charm for the ladies. Do you believe that?" He was still holding the doors open with his long arms. He let one go and swept an arm inward. "You must come in," he said. "I expect there will be quite a crowd today."

"You should put some men out there to keep the shutterbugs away," I said.

"I like the way you think, Mr. Caudill," said Lloyd. "That's a critical appraisal of the situation. You'd make a good businessman."

The butler appeared and stepped neatly toward us. The strain of keeping his distress below the surface made his eyes red, his mouth sour. "Your hats, gentlemen?"

"We'll keep 'em," I said.

"Some refreshments? Coffee? Tea?"

"No," I said. "We won't be long."

"I think I'd like a cup," said Walker. "Just plain black, if it's no trouble."

"Why don't you bring a pot," said Lloyd. "We'll be in the library."

Like the rest of the house, the library was covered with paneling, carved along the edges and around the fireplace with old designs of flowers and knots, heads of ladies in profile, birds in flight, and even tiny reliefs of German cottages and farmhouses. The furniture was a mess of too-fancy chairs and sofas from different periods and heavy wooden tables, some inlaid with patterns of veneer or with mother-of-pearl. Strewn along the walls and atop flat places, precious art pieces made it hard for the servants to dust the place. There were a number of books as well, arranged carefully in the built-in shelves. They looked as if they might have been read, but I supposed that they, too, had been purchased from some formerly wealthy estate on the Continent.

"I can offer you a pipe, gentlemen, or a cigar," Lloyd said. "My old father has no vices, but I could spin tales about the men who have gathered in this room. Charlie Chaplin once sat in that chair, Mr. Walker."

"Fatty Arbuckle gave me an apple one time," said Walker. "He had a bushel of apples, and he was tossing them from his open car out front of the Opera House."

"That's a tragic story," said Lloyd. "A man done in by his appetites."

"Listen," I broke in, "what's the story here? You have any idea who might be doing this?"

Lloyd seemed to relish the attention, the chance to put on a show of how smart he could make his words. He began, "Mr. Caudill, I know you have an idea what comes inevitably with the sort of vast fortune the Lloyd family has accumulated. Any man excepting the Buddha himself wants to nibble or tear away a chunk of it. There might be, in Detroit alone, a million men who'd like to live in such fashion as we do here. You might include yourself and Mr. Walker in that tally."

"I wouldn't live this way," I said. "All this moldy old stuff."

"Too many ghosts, Mr. Caudill? You're a sensitive man."

Walker said, "I couldn't ever rest easy in a place like this."

"How many of those million or so men you talk about are homicidal maniacs?" I asked.

Lloyd turned sour. He paced around us. "You've killed, haven't you, Mr. Caudill? What about Mr. Federle? I except you, Mr. Walker, as we've only just met. For all I know with any certainty, my own butler might slice my throat as I lie sleeping."

"I couldn't ever rest," Walker said very quietly.

"Your friend Chew will be delirious when he gets a whiff of this." Lloyd eyed me pointedly, hoping to draw anger or some sharp response. His nerves made him thrust out all his words like jabs.

"He will," I said.

"It's a disaster in the making. From my point of view, it's positively biblical in scale—a plague of locusts, a flood. Rivers flowing with blood! Fire raining down from the sky! But we are not yet lost. Did you ever learn anything about the principle of supply and demand in school, Mr. Walker?"

"I believe I've forgotten any of that, sir. I apologize."

"Let me ask, when was the last time you purchased a new automobile?"

"Never, sir."

"Well," Lloyd said, "when was the last time *anyone* purchased a new car?"

"Before the war," I said.

"Exactly right! I should lower my voice. Do you know what all the pent-up demand for automobiles will cause when this war is won?"

"More money for you," I said. "If you're not sunk by then."

Lloyd seemed glad that I was speaking sharply, as it gave him the excuse to make his own speech more extravagant. "This war is like a long winter. Everywhere"—he was swinging his long arms broadly—"open commerce lies dormant beneath the snow. When peace comes at last, you'll see a great flowering—mark me now. What a century it's been so far! But the past is nothing to compare with what will follow. If you've money to invest, you could make yourself a wealthy man. Anyone could."

"The problem you ought to consider," I said, "is that the dicks will be hot for you in this case. And the papers, once they get hold of it, will be crawling up your ass in a flash."

"The police act in the public interest," said Lloyd coolly. "I trust they'll behave appropriately."

They'll want to talk to me, too, I thought. *Dilley and Foulard don't seem to move too fast, but—*

"Something troubles you, Mr. Caudill?"

"Can you tell me again about your little trip to California?"

"I arrived in the area by plane at perhaps half past ten in the evening, and then I drove myself here. This is all easily verified. May I ask, Mr. Caudill, why you're so worried that the police will suspect me? Does the guilt from all your past missteps plague you with worry? For myself, I trust that these dedicated men will see the truth plainly from the evidence. I've nothing to hide."

"You don't consider all the maniacs who might be after your money," I said. "You don't worry about a frame-up?"

"Mr. Federle suspects the Hardiman brothers," Walker said. "If it's all right to say so."

"Their mother, too, is a magnificent piece of work," Lloyd said, showing an undertaker's smile. "Aunt Estelle, I used to call her. Do you believe that?"

"No," I said.

"You're too keen, Mr. Caudill. You don't believe in anything."

"That doesn't get me anywhere," I said. "These boys— Can you tell me anything about Elliot?"

Walker started to say something, but he seemed just then to realize that he had been talking too much.

"You'll find the young Hardiman men haunting the big plant tirelessly," said Lloyd. "Even on a Sunday, the formal day of rest, I'd say they'll both be nursing some plot, scheming together in that Machiavellian way they seem to have been born to. If you find them there, they won't be friendly."

"Do you think this place is as safe as you might want it?" I asked him.

"The house itself is secure. The grounds...well, you can see how expansive the estate is. Would you like to come and stay here to coordinate all the security matters? Would it make you happy to follow in Frank Carter's footsteps? After all, it's my father's fondest wish."

"You make me want to pop you in the nose," I said.

Lloyd laughed with such gusto that a fleck of spittle flew in a long arc from his mouth and landed on the shoulder of a terra-cotta statue of Hercules. Walker started to chuckle.

"Mr. Carter never spoke to me that way!" he said.

"You ought to be more serious," I said.

"Mr. Caudill, I'm fully aware of the gravity of our situation. In the past week I've spoken to representatives of perhaps a dozen foreign countries, scores of suppliers, competitors, accountants, lawyers, foremen, security men, engineers, architects—imagine it! In the past week! Try to conceive of it—a young woman is murdered—or two or three—with everything going on in the world, Mr. Caudill, how much attention shall I give to these women? How important can it be, really, compared to the welfare of our fighting forces all across the wide world? Make no mistake; the Lloyd Motor Company is critically important to the war effort. I trust that the police will do their duty as far as these murders are concerned."

"If it's clear that the murders in these different states are connected, and especially if it seems they're making a target of Lloyd Motors in particular, then they're going to bring in the FBI. That doesn't bother you?"

All his nervous energy drained away as we watched him. He took on the same drooping posture I had witnessed at the big plant, and his eyelids and jowls began to sag as if the life had been let out of them.

"You'd perhaps ask my father about the FBI," he said.

"Where is he?"

"I've had him taken to his place behind the plant. It's along the river."

"Could any of this wreck the company?" I asked.

"If we could make a study of the relationship between reputation and economic activity—"

"I'm just asking a simple question."

"Things do get wrecked, Mr. Caudill. Empires crumble."

"I don't see how it could happen," Walker said.

"If we could see the future," said Lloyd, "it would be easy to stave off ruin."

"You just said we'd all get richer after the war," I said.

"If the war can be won, and I think it must be, then I believe it's inevitable that there will be a flourishing of enterprise. And so you see I'm always torn between optimism and pessimism. If I focus on the trouble at hand . . . it's necessary to press forward as if one believed in the future."

"He still hasn't brought the coffee," said Walker. "I feel like I've troubled him."

"Perhaps the butler really is our culprit," said Lloyd. He had turned to look out the bay window toward the grove of trees. "If that's the case, maybe all this will be wrapped up by suppertime."

I stood up and looked down the gentle hill. Probably at least half the safety officers from the Pointes had swarmed to the property. All the way down to the water, the cops were strolling and pointing. A few portly suited inspectors were now making their way toward the house.

I tapped Walker on the shoulder and he rose as well. We stepped quickly out of the library and I led him down the long dark hall, past the servants' quarters and out the little door at the west end of the big house.

"All of this comes down to me," Walker muttered. "I should not have intruded on you like I did."

"You can step out if you want to," I said.

"No," he said. "Now we're just about coming to the end of it, I think."

"I guess you're right about that." I knew that the pieces would soon begin to fall. They'd string me up for all of it soon enough, no matter if it was the Grosse Pointe men, or Hoover, or Dilley and Foulard. I thought of the wrinkles that came up around Eileen's eyes when she smiled, and tried to consider the best way to keep Walker and Federle away when everything came crashing down.

CHAPTER

24

She always told me her name was Bessie Love, and I wondered if she was even old enough to have seen any of the pictures that actress had made before they began to add the noise to the movies. Had she made up the name on her own, thinking that it gave her a worldly flair? Had she been named Bessie by her mother and added the Love on her own? Anyway, I always thought of her that way, as Bessie, and if we had the need to speak I would use that for a name.

I had been seeing her—I had been putting the sex to her—for some months, ever since I had fouled things with Eileen. Maybe it wasn't more than a dozen times. At first it was because I was plain crazy, and then it became easy after I settled into it. There was never any other woman. I had been with her the night the thugs pulled me off the street, and I had been with her the night I found Hank Chew's arm outside Eileen's house. I guess I should have known that my sorry life was an open book because I was too stupid to keep an eye out for trouble. It would have been easy for the thugs or for Ray Federle or anyone else to know my business; and now young Bessie was dead as dead gets. No mistake, either: whoever took her to pieces did it because of me, and they laid her out on Lloyd's lawn because they knew I'd be one of the first to have a look at her.

I wasn't a drunk, ordinarily. The last time I saw her alive, though, I was lit up to the gills. Walker had made me look at the blind boy Joshua, and I wanted to blot out any thought of him for a while. I hopped the crosstown line to get over to Black Bottom and I staggered into the house where she kept herself. You went in the front and came out the back; that was how it worked. I expected the place to be busier than it was, and in my addled mind it was because of the holiday—because of Good Friday—but then I realized that I had missed it by a week. It seemed like a joke, and so I chuckled to myself.

I didn't have to wait long in the foyer. On some signal from upstairs I didn't catch, the two leathery brown pugs at the bottom of the staircase gave me the nod. I stood up and hoped I hadn't sucked up too much juice. My feet felt cold.

They must have known me from the first time they laid eyes on me. The whole neighborhood must have known me. Pete Caudill, the nigger-hater, the nigger-killing cop, son of a cop. Maybe they knew that Walker had taken me to visit the blind boy earlier in the day. Maybe they knew everything about me, and they were keeping notes about it, all my failings. The Negroes were organized, they had some intent and purpose that was far enough outside my reach as to be impossible to see—for a one-eyed whore-chasing thug. If they talked about me, it was never to my face. Walker was the only colored man that ever took the trouble to try and reach me.

There was a whole set of courtesies to be followed in such a circumstance. I had to knock at Bessie Love's door, but I didn't have to wait for any reply before I went in. She was seated at a little dressing table, turning over a wooden brush in her hands. Nothing in her face betrayed any surprise or concern over my ragged appearance.

"Mr. Caudill," she said, "sit right down. Would you like something to drink?"

"No," I said. "That would put me over." I let myself down onto the battered couch and sat back to wait for her. The liquor had filled me up, and the tight room pressed me and made me feel stuffed after the walking I had done in the cool evening.

Bessie came and began to take down my trousers. She slipped off my

shoes and put them neatly to the side of the couch. By that time she knew
what to do, and it was a great relief to let her do it.

She took my coat and thumbed down the buttons of my shirt. I let her
take it off me but I stopped her hands when she tried to peel off my Clark
Gable. If she felt any disgust toward my mottled skin or the scabs or
stitches, she kept it inside of her. She put everything off to the side neatly .
and let me watch her with her own things.

Bessie was an ordinary colored woman. She wasn't pretty, but she kept
herself clean. On her hands and arms and legs she used a kind of butter to
make the skin shine. When she moved around the room before me, she did
it slowly and deliberately, so I could watch her hips and her fanny and
bosom turning and pressing inside her dress. Her eyes did not meet mine,
but I could see that she was thinking of me; she knew how I watched her.
Carefully she began to take down her dress, pulling the cloth flat and
smoothing it over a padded hanger. While she hung up the dress, she lin-
gered and tightened up her back so my eye could take it in properly. Then
she turned and stepped close to me. She stooped to drop her half-slip,
bringing her shoulders forward so that her breasts could swell up over the
top of her brassiere. She wore nothing under the slip but her garters and
stockings.

Shame and guilt and alcohol burned through me. My face was hot and
my hands and scars throbbed with blood. I watched her plump rear as she
turned to hang up the slip, and my prick swelled up and flopped over my
thigh.

I had never been able to decide if it was wrong. I had the money and she
had the sex to sell, but I could have bought relief from any number of white
whores throughout the city. There was the usual bad feeling that I carried
in my gut regardless of circumstance. But then, too, there was the shadowy
thought that I had decided to smear my shame over this poor Negro
woman only because I knew how I was hated in the community. In the beginning maybe it was true; but by that night I might have sworn that I never
meant to hurt her—I had begun to think of her tenderly. Maybe everything was true.

She was careful with her precious stockings. She never removed her
low-heeled shoes or went to her knees on the tattered wool rug. After she

hung up the slip, she came over and sat next to me on the couch. The way her legs were turned, I saw how odd her woolly bush and the warm glowing flesh of her thighs looked against the ghostly white of the silk stockings. With one soft hand she pulled my leg toward her, then went up my thigh to cradle my balls gently. She took up my prick with the other hand and worked it to a proper stiffness, and then produced a rubber from inside her brassiere. She rolled it down over me.

Then she threw her thick leg over the top of me. Her shoes rubbed against the outsides of my thighs as she squatted with her belly close to my face. Then she lowered herself down and kept still for a moment.

Even if I had not been through such a beating—even without the sharpness of how it reminded me of the night the thugs had taken me away—it was the kind of plunging, intense feeling that could bring water to my eye. And I was grateful that my prick at least could feel connected in some human way. I wasn't crying, but water came to my nose and mouth and my scalp was prickling with sweat as if my body was rising up to meet with her hot wetness.

She leaned forward against me and reached back to unfasten the brassiere. When she got both swinging breasts free of the thing, I drew in my breath against the thrill of it. She put one hand tenderly around the back of my neck and braced herself on the back of the couch with the other, and then began to stroke her whole body up and down over me. I had my arms over her thighs and my hands gripped the fat cheeks of her ass.

I knew that later I would wonder if anyone else in the building could hear the noises we made or if they could feel our movement along the beams of the floor. I would worry that behind some mirror or through a peephole a camera might have snapped photos of this colored woman riding ex-detective Pete Caudill like a horse. I would think of Eileen, I would feel the sting of hard regret. But all the while as I was inside Bessie Love, I didn't think of anything. And especially as I felt that last flush of wetness balling up, I didn't think of how brown her skin was or what revulsion she might feel at my touch. When I closed my eye and let go, for just that moment, the world was right again. Nature or God had made it that way so we could go on living even as we killed ourselves and made a hell of the world.

There was the courtesy and the skill of long practice. After I was done, she waited for the proper moment to slip off of me, and then she pulled a clean rag from the table beside the sofa. Probably with every man she was different, but she knew how I liked for her to take off the rubber and squeeze the last juice out of me with her hand. She wiped me up with the rag and turned away to put herself together again for the rest of the night.

I got up quickly and pulled on my shorts. I put on my shirt and my trousers and sat back down to tie my shoes onto my feet.

"If you go on like this, Mr. Caudill," she said, speaking from behind her dressing screen, "you'll get yourself killed before your time."

"You think my time is set already?"

She was quiet for a moment. I could hear the gentle splash of water in a basin.

"No," she said.

"Maybe my time already went by, and I'm living on past when I'm supposed to."

"That could be so," she said. "But I've never heard of it."

There was a piece of glass the size of a baseball on her dressing table, flat on one side. Pearly swirls of violet rose like smoke from the bottom of the globe. I put money under the glass, not more or less than the customary amount. The bills were rough and wrinkled, and it made me ashamed. I wanted to stay. I put my jacket on and walked to the door.

"If I got killed tonight," I said, "would you miss me?"

Because I had stepped across a certain line of manners, I was sure that she would make no answer for me. She knew I had to leave.

"I might think of you from time to time," she said. "If ever a thing came along to put me in mind of you"—she paused a moment—"I wouldn't try to forget."

I pressed my welcome for a few seconds more, and then I put my hand to the doorknob.

"I don't want you to get killed, Mr. Caudill. I don't want anyone to get killed. There's been enough of that."

I leaned against the door and listened. I listened for the whisper of her slip or the rustle of her dress, for water to splash in the basin. But it seemed that she had stilled herself behind the screen, waiting to see how I might answer her. Quietly I turned the knob and opened the door enough to let myself out. The clicking of the latch as I closed the door seemed to echo in the hall.

There was a little toilet and a sink at the end of the hall, but I didn't stop to clean myself. As I walked down the back stairs, I did not know that Bessie had already spoken the last words she would ever say to me. I didn't know that I would see her soon enough, cold and cut up and twisted into a mockery on the Lloyd estate. I *should* have known, I should have been able to *feel* the malice that my presence had turned toward her. But I remember what I was thinking, I remember it very clearly—I was wondering where I could get another pint of whiskey to rejuvenate my faded liquor high. I was keen to press on into the darkness before me.

Now, sitting inside the old Chrysler with Walker outside the Lloyd estate, my impulse was to put the brakes to it. It was only a matter of time before some lawman put me together with Bessie Love. How could anyone fail to recognize a mug like mine? Whit Lloyd was so full of worms that he didn't know who he was. With all the mortar shells raining in on him, I knew there wasn't much I could do to save him. There was something of the Old Man in him yet; if he could stall and weave long enough for the war to be over, he might come out all roses. But it was too much for me to juggle. The only thing I thought I might do is figure out who had cut up the girls—before they pinned the whole deal on me.

Walker and I were just outside the gate at Lloyd's place. They had brought in a meat wagon to take the girl away.

"Walker, do you remember that boy I killed?"

"You haven't killed anybody, Detective."

"You remember it, Walker. I'm not talking about Joshua."

He let his eyes go out of focus. His hands were on his knees. "I remember," he said.

"Do you remember his name?"

"His name was Davis."

"Sure it was. Do you remember anything about his family?"

"Why do you bring this up just now?"

"The dead woman they found at the Lloyd plant in Indiana was named Davis."

"I'll ask you once again, Detective, if it might not be best for us to go right to the police with all of this."

"I'm falling to pieces all over again, Walker. I shouldn't put any of it on you. But it's my skin they're after this time, whoever it is. They're trying to pin it all on me somehow."

"Maybe it's just a coincidence after all. Davis isn't an unusual name."

"I don't believe it."

"Well," he said, "it's far enough along now so that the story will play itself out no matter what we do."

It was a philosophical way of looking at things, but it offered me no comfort. I took the car out onto Jefferson and wondered where I thought I could go.

CHAPTER
25

I pulled up to the alley alongside my apartment building and waited out-side to see if Federle would pop out on his own. Soon enough, he came down, wearing the same loud suit he had worn when we braced the Hardi-man boys at the Lloyd plant. Without a word, Walker slipped out of the Chrysler and got into the rear seat.

"What's the situation, Pete? Where have you been?"

"Why don't we let Walker drive?" I said. "What do you think?"

"Sure," Federle said. "But what gives?"

"Come on, Walker. Let me get in the back."

"You can be our driver," said Federle, "if we can't get him inside the plant. He can drive, can't he? And listen—I been waiting for you all this time—I haven't had a bite to eat since four o'clock yesterday afternoon."

"Walker can drive."

We shifted ourselves around and headed out vaguely toward the Lloyd plant. To put off making any kind of real decision, I steered Walker along what amounted to a backdoor passage to the great plant. I managed to pick up the pistol and put it back into its hiding place. Once we were out on the road, Federle turned around to see what I would say.

"Come on, Pete. Patty told me about the rush you were in this morning."

Settling in for the drive, Walker said, "The detective keeps losing his friends."

"What's that supposed to mean?"

"Walker means that Hank Chew went to pieces."

"That so?"

Walker said, "I keep my ear to the ground, Detective. They have Mr. Chew's arm on ice in the morgue—so I hear—with a tag on his finger reading 'Chew, Henry James.' "

"What else have you heard, Walker?" I asked him.

"You never asked me if I found out anything while I was waiting for you outside the Lloyd plant on Friday."

"You find out anything about the Hardiman boys?" Federle asked.

"Listen, Federle. There's this other thing. Walker and I just came from Whit Lloyd's place. A girl got left on the grass last night."

"Like the others?"

"Like the others. Set up to remind me of Jane Hardiman, specifically. You know what I'm talking about?"

Federle shook his head. "I never met the girl."

"I thought those men were gone," Walker said softly.

"As far as I know. But somebody sure knows my name," I said.

"Did you learn anything about the Hardimans at the plant, Walker?" Federle piped.

"That old man who parked the car for us took me around some."

"That old guy!" said Federle.

"He's been froze out, so he says. They have to let him stay on because Jasper Lloyd puts the word in for him. I heard the whole story about how he has to keep working because his wife is sick and a tree fell on his roof, the whole thing."

"Well, you were passing the time of day with him," I said.

"I wasn't occupied any other way."

"Pull up over here, Walker, so Federle can get a sandwich. There's a lunch counter there, see?"

Walker hung along for a moment until it was clear, and then turned the car around to park at the curb on the east side of Junction Street. I slipped Federle a few bills, and he stepped out toward the counter.

"Just a sandwich," I said. "We're in a pinch."

"Okay," he said. "What do you want?"

"Nothing messy," I said. "Ham and cheese."

"Walker?"

"No, thank you."

I considered getting out of the backseat, but it seemed like an effort that wouldn't pay. Walker and I waited in silence while Federle fetched the grub. When he returned, he put a paper cup of coffee on the dash and handed my sandwich back to me. I realized I couldn't eat it.

"Now, how about this old geezer, Walker?" Federle said. "Did he have any ideas about the Hardiman boys?"

"I don't think he knows anything about the murders. I'm certain he would have told me if he knew anything about my sister's murder. He told me every other thing that crossed his mind."

"Where's this taking us?" I said.

"He was talking to me about rumors is all. You can't really put your faith in any of it. But according to what he's heard, the Hardiman family is buying up stock in the Lloyd Company."

"Well, that's only sensible," I said.

"They aim to push young Whitcomb out once old Mr. Lloyd is gone."

"They told me as much themselves."

"According to the old timer, the Hardiman boys have been in some trouble. The younger one had been sent away for a while."

"I told you," Federle said.

"What's that mean?" I said. "He went away to school?"

"He was trying to work it up into a real mystery for me," said Walker. "I can't say what he was trying to tell me. He was hinting that there had been some bad behavior, but I don't think he really had any details to tell me. However you look at it, the Hardiman family doesn't seem to want to lie low in the background."

It made me think of Jane Hardiman. I knew that she had been a handful. For a teenage girl to step out with colored men—a seventeen-year-old girl—but nothing was regular about them. It wouldn't ever make good sense, no matter how much I worried it over.

"It's Elliot all along," Federle said. "The pair of them are working together."

"Come on, Ray. Be sensible."

"Well, what about this girl over at Lloyd's place? You said—you said that Chew was dead, too? The two of them are working together. It's the only way."

"I wish we could find those goons," I said. "Maybe they know a thing or two."

"They're at the plant. Don't you think so?"

"I mean the thugs who pulled me from my room."

He turned his face away from me like I had slapped him. He chewed at his lips and pattered his fingers on the dashboard.

"Jesus Christ, Pete, that's enough of that," he said.

"What?"

"Of all the people in the world, why would you try to talk to me like that?"

"What's so special about you?"

"You know goddamn well those punks didn't take you out of your room, Pete. Of all the guys in the world—you think I don't understand what a man needs?"

"They took me out of my room."

"You can say it as many times as you want to, Pete. It don't change anything. I know what you were doing that night. And I don't think bad on you for it. I've done worse."

When he looked back at me, I saw that his eyes squinted and tears were running in a solid stream down his face and into his collar. He began to work his arms and hands like he was caught in a dream of being buried alive. Walker sat behind the wheel, his eyes wide.

"I know, Pete. I know how it is. I'm trying to be a friend to you. I'm trying to help you out."

"I'm not worth helping out," I said weakly. The wind had been crushed out of me.

"Don't you believe it," Federle said. "I've been to whores. Ain't we all been? That's one time too many for you, that's all."

He knew I had not been in my room that night. Of course he knew. He knew how it shamed me. Federle had the human sense to see why I hadn't wanted to admit it to myself, and he was trying to see me through it. Though I hadn't ever told him, he could guess that the thugs had just picked me up on the street, drunk and filthy as I was from being with the girl.

"I'm no good," I said. "That much is true."

"Don't say that, Pete. Don't say it. Somebody in this world has to be good." I thought he would climb into the backseat with me. "I'm counting on you to be good, Pete."

It made me look over to Walker.

"That girl up there at Lloyd's house, Ray, that's the one I've been going to see."

Federle didn't show much of a reaction. His face was slack and rubbery. He swabbed the water from his face with the meat at the base of his thumb.

"You might have told me that, Detective," said Walker soberly.

"So I knew all three of those women. Or at least I can draw the connection, you see?"

Walker said, "And Chew as well."

"As far as I know, Chew is still walking around. They never found the rest of him."

Beneath the sleeves of his cheap jacket, I could see how Federle's arms writhed. He kept his lips pressed tight together. Walker tapped the wheel with his wedding band and stared out through the windshield.

It took the wind out of me, and it sapped me of my natural strength. I felt like I had been sick for a long time, like I was empty of nourishment. But I was glad that Federle had forced me out into the open. I wondered what Walker thought of it. It seemed doubtful that he had ever contracted a loose woman, steadfast as he was. But after all, he was a man, and there is something in nature that makes men do bad things.

Thoughts of Eileen pressed at the edge of my mind. I wanted badly to be able to talk to her, and I wondered how I could keep her safe at all. Whoever had killed Chew and placed his wing knew what scared me. It was clear, too, that the whore had been killed to show me something; it might as easily have been Eileen, and maybe the next time...My heart quailed in my chest, and I wondered if it was too much feeling or the tremor of a heart attack. I wasn't in any condition even to help myself, much less Eileen or Jasper Lloyd.

"Is that gun still in the car, Pete?"

"It's in the back."

"Maybe we'd better just head over to the plant."

"We'll try to find the Old Man. What do you think, Walker?"

Walker had his eyes on a small truck moving toward us at a leisurely pace. As it drew closer, we all watched. I pulled myself forward to crane over the seat, and Walker and Federle leaned toward the windshield. Junction was not such a wide avenue, and the truck had to pass close to us. I gripped the seat and let out a snort because—despite my poor vision—I could spot the truck's twenty-year-old design from some distance.

We all watched as the truck passed us by like a vivid ghost from another time. Whitcomb Lloyd's pale eyes looked back at us calmly as we felt the rumble of the old truck's engine. Though he showed no reaction, it was clear that he could not have failed to recognize us.

Walker smoothly turned the key in the ignition and started up the Chrysler. He squealed the tires and made the Chrysler buck as he turned us around. The coffee slid hard to the right on the dash and splattered on the windshield and the vent and on Federle's lap.

"Go after him, Walker. Go after him!"

Walker veered wildly as he tried to complete the U-turn. He managed to get the car pretty quickly off the sidewalk and back onto the street.

Lloyd had opened up some distance, but there wasn't anywhere he could go. It was a part of town I had known since my boyhood days, and there wasn't any way to run such an old truck faster than our little coupe.

"Jesus, Pete," Federle said, "what's he doing? Why would he be driving a truck down here?"

"We'll ask him," I said.

Walker muttered, "I don't want to lose my license over this." He yanked the gear stick in and out as he closed on the truck, knocking me around on the big backseat.

"He'll have to turn up ahead where the tracks come in," I said. "And then he'll have to turn again."

"Why is he running from us?" Federle was bracing himself against the dash and the seat.

"Push down on the horn, Walker, so I can get the gun."

"Mr. Caudill," Walker said.

"He'll flip that truck if he doesn't slow down," Federle said. He slithered over the seat and into the back with me, kicking me in the head as he went.

Lloyd saw how the road was going, and the truck wavered and slid in front of us as it slowed for the turn. Walker had closed up the distance and now held half a block back. Because of the time and the day of the week, there wasn't much traffic, but it was clear that soon enough someone's luck would run out.

"Just let him go, Walker, before we kill someone," I said.

As we made the turn at the railroad tracks, we saw Lloyd struggle to make the sharp turn at the next street. He had to swing wide to keep from slowing too much, and this brought the big tire of the truck right over the front end of a motorcycle angled out from the curb. The box end of the truck bucked up and back down, and Lloyd could only drive straight into the brick front of the printing shop along Campbell. The front wheels jounced up over the curb and came down, and the rear end of the crashing truck went slowly up, hung in the air, and then came down with some finality.

Walker stopped the car and hopped out. He went out ahead of me loping heavily toward the crash. I spilled out of the backseat and started after him, wanting to shout at him to stop. But I saw the driver of the truck come down from the passenger side of the vehicle and run off to the east in a flash. He threw a sheaf of white papers into the air, and they fluttered down to the pavement and swept off down the street. *Chew's notes,* I thought. *Chew's precious papers.* Lloyd—if it was Lloyd—moved remarkably well for a man pushing fifty. Out of the three of us, Walker had to be the fastest, but there wasn't any chance of him catching Lloyd if he could move like that.

Walker and I got to the truck first.

"Don't put your hands on anything," I said.

"He's gone," said Walker.

"Did you see him?"

"I saw him run."

"I mean—it was Lloyd, wasn't it?" I glanced over the truck to make sure I wasn't mistaken: It was the same Lloyd Cargo Van I had seen in the garage at the big house. By this time I had worked my way around the truck to the open door of the passenger side. Walker looked through at me from the driver's side window with a somber expression.

"Listen, Walker," I said quietly. "We were just passing through, right? We didn't know who it was."

Walker nodded.

I looked back to see Federle closing the car door. In plain view he held the pistol in his other hand. When the motorcycle cop stepped out of the building ahead of him, Federle whirled around and stashed the gun somewhere in his baggy clothes.

The cop saw his wrecked cycle and spread his gloved hands in dismay. Then his eyes followed the trail up the street to the smashed truck and he saw us. Even though his helmet was on, I could recognize the lanky figure of Johnson as he moved toward us. It was clear that he recognized us, too, or at least he knew my unlucky mug. From the way he held his palm over the holster on his belt, I could see that he was thinking he ought to pull his weapon free.

Federle walked toward us, buttoning up his jacket, careful not to come too close to Johnson.

"Listen, Walker," I said, "this guy ran us off the road. We're just on our way to the Lloyd plant."

"I don't think that's the way to work it," he said.

Johnson was too close for me to make an answer for Walker.

"For God's sake, Pete! Is anyone hurt?"

"The driver's gone," I said.

"What's in the back?" Johnson asked, working around me to peek inside the green door.

"Who knows?" For all I knew, the truck was rigged with a bomb. My inclination was to step away.

"Did you see what happened?"

"Sure. It was a crash."

"Is that Walker? Did you see what happened, Walker?"

"I sure did."

"We're working on a security detail for Jasper Lloyd," I said. "We're on our way over to the plant."

Johnson pulled off his helmet and scratched his sweaty scalp furiously. By this time the whole street had come out to view the ruckus. Even the folks in the print shop stepped timidly through their door. The truck had not been moving fast enough to cause much damage, but the sight of it on the sidewalk made a spectacle.

Walker made his way around to us. "We ought to tell him who the driver looked like."

He was right, of course, and so I took Johnson by the elbow and drew him toward the back of the truck.

"What else are the police good for?" said Walker.

I got close enough to put my words to Johnson only. "I want to say it was Whitcomb Lloyd driving that rig."

Johnson's eyes went out of focus, staring down at the pavement while he thought.

"You were following him, then?"

"We were stopped at the lunch counter back there. He came up the street and I spotted him."

"I got the coffee on my pants to prove it," said Federle, who stood with us now.

"You're sure it was him?" Johnson said.

"I'm not so sure. But he ran that truck away like fire. I think he spotted Federle."

"How can I call this in if I'm not sure? What kind of stink will it make?"

"You can be casual, can't you? I bet some witness in the rabble here saw something. Tell the boys to roll up nice and easy."

"You'll swear it was him," Johnson said.

I looked warily at all the faces in our little huddle. "We're leaving," I said.

Johnson said, "No, no, no."

I turned away, and Walker and Federle fell in with me.

"Pete!"

"Give me the key, Walker. I better drive."

"It's in the ignition, I think."

"Jesus, Pete," said Federle.

We kept walking tight together toward the Chrysler.

"Halt!" barked Johnson. "I order you to halt!"

Just as we reached the car, we all flinched as a shot cracked behind us. Johnson had fired his service revolver into the air.

"Get in," I said.

Federle muttered, "Jesus, Jesus," as he ducked into the backseat.

I looked long and hard at Johnson before I sat down behind the wheel. He had dropped his helmet and held his weapon at his side.

"We'll all get arrested for this," Walker said.

I fired up the engine and squealed back out of there.

"That's a bad spot to leave Johnson in," said Walker. "It's not right."

"He'll figure something out," I said, but I was only hoping.

CHAPTER

26

Federle was ghostly white in the backseat.

"What's wrong with Lloyd?" Walker said.

"I think plenty."

"He couldn't kill those girls," said Federle. "How could he?"

"You talked to him, didn't you?" I said.

Walker kept still on the seat beside me. He almost looked sleepy.

"Why would he? Lloyd's got everything. Why would he? Those Hardiman boys—"

"So far, we don't know," I said. "We don't know anything. But if the coppers find something on that truck, will it be enough for you to lay off the Hardiman boys?"

"S-sure."

He was fairly trembling. I couldn't tell what was shaking him up. Maybe it had been the first gunshot he had heard since he had been home from the islands.

"Put that gun away in the cubbyhole," I said. "And get hold of yourself."

We hadn't ever talked too much about it, but I thought his combat jitters might be coming over him. He had seen some real action down in the

Solomons, and it wasn't only hula girls. He was almost lying across the backseat.

"Johnson will set the police after us," Walker said. "They'll round us all up and sort things out their own way."

"He won't set for that kind of trouble until he needs to. So far we ain't done anything to hang for," I said. "We saw somebody crack up a truck, but we didn't hang around. So what?"

"He fired his weapon."

I had to smile. "I bet that's the first time he ever had to do that outside the range."

"If it was Mr. Lloyd we saw there," Walker asked, "what can we do now?"

"He'll be long gone," said Federle weakly. "He's got the dough to go anywhere."

There were two places, or three or four, that he'd be likely to go. The bottom dropped out of my belly when I thought of Eileen. Now that Whit Lloyd's game had come open, maybe he'd go after her to get to me. *She wouldn't be home.* She'd be at work, and that plant was on the far east side, down along the river off Jefferson. If Lloyd knew where she worked— Eileen was too smart, and had been through too much. It was too far for Lloyd to think of sneaking to.

He could go to his big house, but that was as far to the east as you could go without falling into Lake St. Clair. It would take an hour to get there. And of course he could expect that the coppers there might want a word with him.

Now I regretted that I had put so much in Johnson's lap. He might well decide to dodge trouble by keeping quiet, reporting the crash as a possible drunk or a stolen vehicle. We hadn't said anything to Johnson about what we suspected Lloyd had done with the girls. What a dope I'd become! Why would Johnson risk so much heat by reporting what I'd said to him?

But Lloyd wouldn't know anything about it. He'd have to expect that the cops were now looking for him. Wouldn't he? And he had chosen to run.

"We'd better see if we can get to Old Man Lloyd," I said. "We're not but two miles from the plant here."

Walker said, "Can we believe he was telling us the truth about where Mr. Lloyd is?"

Federle looked sick, like he had just been slammed by influenza.

"He could run to the plant from here," said Walker, "or take the streetcar. But I don't see how he could mingle in without somebody knowing him."

"Brother, they got the army guarding that place," Federle muttered. "It ain't the marines, but—"

"He'll find a way in," I said. "Sure he will."

"So you think he'll head for the plant," said Walker.

"He'll have to," I said. "Where else could he go?"

"He could go anywhere," Federle said bitterly. "If you got the dough, you can go anywhere."

"I'm wondering if Johnson will even call this in," said Walker. "We never spoke to him about my sister or any of the other things. If he's been on the motorcycle all day, it may be that he's ignorant of the trouble."

"There needs to be ten of us, Pete," said Federle. "We can't cover any ground with just the three."

There was a swelling mess of traffic and men coming off the streetcars on the Lloyd spur because change of shift was coming. If Whit Lloyd was going anywhere, he'd skirt the mess.

Gathering up all around was a storm of shit. What if I had been wrong about Whit Lloyd? If it was a frame-up, and a good one, maybe he had only cracked up because of it. Maybe he had realized that someone was using the truck; maybe it was a part of the whole scheme, and he was trying in desperation to ditch it somewhere.

Whitcomb Lloyd had no one to trust. Money had deranged him. Though I never had real money, I could feel what he was feeling. I had a father who had been a good man, done some good things. I knew the shame that came from failing to meet the measure. For Whitcomb Lloyd, everything had been magnified ten thousand times. Jasper Lloyd had built himself an empire in his own lifetime. As we came around to the churning plant, I could see how far beyond me it was. This was the throbbing, smoking heart of it. Because of his father's fondness, because he could not possibly rise to the task of managing all of it, there was now the possibility that Whitcomb Lloyd might piss away everything his father had made.

"I know where he'll go," I said. "He'll kill the Old Man, if he hasn't already."

I pulled the Chrysler to the drive that led to the security building. Two Willys trucks were parked like a funnel at the end of the drive, and three men in dull green fidgeted nearby. They carried rifles slung over their shoulders—with some discomfort, if I could judge by the way they all messed with the straps.

"National Guard," said Federle. "Not even regular army."

One of the guards put up a hand to stop us. I put the car in first gear when I stopped and opened the window only a crack.

"What gives?" I said.

"You have some identification?"

I pressed the badge against the glass, and he peered at it intently for a moment, pursing his lips over his buckteeth.

"What's wrong with him?" he said, jerking a thumb toward Federle.

"He was up all night hugging the toilet," I said.

The guardsman looked Walker over, too, but could not in his feeble imagination rake up anything more to say. He took a step back from the car and motioned us with two fingers to pass. The other pair of sad sacks moved to the side, and I drove on along the curving drive. As the whole space was open except for a few polite trees, I could see that the other end of the drive was entirely unguarded. It was only custom that would lead anyone to choose one end of the drive over the other.

"If those ducks would let *us* through, who would they stop?" Federle said. "Himmler? I'm glad they're over here and not over there."

"We'll try to keep a lid on all the ruckus. These security guys won't be hot to give us a leg up." I was not worried about Walker, but Federle was fairly writhing in the backseat. "You put that gun up, didn't you?"

"Sure," he said.

"We'll try to keep together, Walker," I said. "If the Old Man is close by, that's where we want to be."

The old-time security man—Pickett was his name—waddled around the corner of the building and came near the car.

"Fellas, you come at a bad time," he said.

"What is it?"

"Think they'd tell me? These days I'm only parking cars."

"We need to see the Old Man, if he's holed up in there somewhere. We heard there's a place by the river."

Pickett's face went stiff, his eyes narrowed, and the corners of his mouth pressed down. He leaned on down to talk low to me. "You can't drive in there," he said.

"We can't," I said, "but I'll bet you can."

"What gives?"

"You haven't seen Whit Lloyd come through here, have you?"

"He don't ever come through here," Pickett said. "Not as I've ever seen."

"We'd like to see that he doesn't get to see the Old Man."

He stood up as straight as he could and worked his gnarled hands over his lower back. With his eyes in deep shadow under his rampant eyebrows, he scanned something far in the distance.

"All right," he said. "I'll take you."

Walker got in back with Federle, and I moved over so the security man could drive. He took us away from the big plant, and then drove north for the better part of a mile so he could come back at the river from another angle. It was a kind of service road, and though the pines and cottonwoods were close alongside, you could catch glimpses of the stacks and the broad buildings not far off. You could feel the heft of the plant.

I expected that there would be a couple of Jeeps and guards to stop us, but there was nothing. As the road curved southward toward the plant, Pickett stopped the car and unhooked a ring of keys from his belt.

"Hop out and get that chain," he told me. "And hook it back up after I pass through."

The lock was new, though the little branch road didn't look much used. All the way down to the big river, spring-grown branches clicked and brushed on the windows and panels of the Chrysler. Before too long the brush opened up, and we saw the stone castle Lloyd had put up for himself.

It wasn't a quarter the size of Whit Lloyd's place, and it was only the one structure—but still it was clear that money could cut a hole in things. The house looked like a miniature stone castle that had been plucked from the English countryside. Pickett pulled right up to the steps and killed the motor. He grunted and huffed, struggling to goad his bulk off the seat and out the door. I came out, and Walker followed.

As far as I could see from the outside, the place was cold and dead. There were no other autos, nothing stirring.

I was going to walk right in. The handle was locked though, and I had to rap with some pepper to get any sound out of the massive carved doors. I had a surge of anger, thinking that Whit Lloyd had already blown through the place.

We'll be walking into something nasty, I thought, and I turned to retrieve the pistol from the car.

The bolt clicked behind me, and the door opened inward. It was so big that I could feel the fresh air sucking past me.

I wheeled around to see an ox of a man filling the entry.

"Yah?" he said.

Walker by this time was close to me. The big man let go of the door and stood looking at me quizzically. His hands were as wide as they were long.

I was certain I had never seen the big man's face, and nothing in the way he held himself put me off. But I leapt onto him. I got my bad hand onto his neck, and I drove the heel of my other palm into his face.

We went into the house. The big man stumbled back over the edge of a rug and put out his hands as he fell. His heavy forearm brought down the antique table next to the door and the hammered copper tray that had been resting on it. I heard Walker growling or groaning behind me and Pickett cursing.

To no effect I did manage to bring down an elbow or two and a few good shots to the big man's jaw. I was on top of him, and it was easy for a time. But he had already begun to close himself off with his forearms, and he would have come up soon to tear me to pieces—if half a dozen strong hands hadn't pulled me away.

As I spun, I saw Walker with his hands raised and the old security man with his arms and legs spread like he was caught dead to rights.

I came down facing up—and before I could blink there was a gun to my temple and one to my throat. The big man scrambled like a beetle to get over, and I heard the seams of his suit rip as his tree-trunk legs flexed. A fourth man stood back with a silver pistol at his side.

"Gee-O, Caudill," he said. "You're not right in the head."

CHAPTER
27

My only worry, despite the bore of one gun at my temple and another pressed to my neck, was that Federle would burst in, shooting. He had been a raider with the marines, and it wasn't any trifle.

"Bugger me," said the big man, standing now clear of the rest, and drawing out his own weapon. "That's the last time you get to pull any of that."

The man with the gun at my temple peeled my fingers from his forearm and stood up, keeping his aim on me. He stepped over to be close to the other standing man, and I had a good picture: all four of the thugs were there, the two big men and the two smaller men—though the smaller ones were no slighter than me. Sure, it had been a dream in the first place, only a bad turn, but I was trembling. It was raw fear and panic, now turning back to rage. I'd risk a bullet—take the bullet, just so I didn't go to my end lying on my back. How quick was I? Could I take the gun at least from the fat one who now pressed his open palm on my chest?

"We're unarmed," said Walker.

"That's good for you," said the first small man.

"Not great, but good," the other said.

"It's better than being dead, anyway," said the first.

"We have another fellow out the door," Walker said. "He might be armed."

"That Federle's a raw one," the first man said.

The man I had grappled with sidled over and pushed the door closed with his foot. There was a narrow panel of stained glass to either side of the doors, too small for even slim Federle to squeeze through. The doors, I knew, were too thick and hard for the pistol to penetrate.

"Jesus Christ," said Pickett. "What's the beef? Who are you guys?"

"We're nobody," the second man said. "Strangers."

"Who did you want us to be?" asked the first.

"Well—" Pickett blinked and worked it over for himself. "What have you done with Old Man Lloyd?"

"That's a little familiar, wouldn't you say?"

"He's sleeping, as far as we know."

"Don't worry! It's not that kind of sleep. Not the bad kind."

"Not yet, anyway."

"You fuck," I said. "Get your mitt off me."

"No," said the second big man. "I like you better laying down."

"I think your friend ran off." The first big man had stooped to peer out the spy hole in the door. He pressed his fingers to his lips to assess the damage I had done, and then grabbed his nose to see if the cartilage would wiggle.

"Where would he be off to?" asked the first small man.

"Your pal Federle's been scrounging around the plant every night."

"A regular Sherlock Holmes."

"He's found something, maybe."

"What brings you here, Caudill? Why would you still keep poking into things after what you've been through?"

"Don't you think we can handle things?"

"You're in no condition."

"Why don't you sit down, Walker? You, too, old-timer." The second man waved toward the dressing bench along the wall.

"You got the drop on us," Pickett said.

"Don't be too hard on yourself."

It would make a terrific mess to kill us just then. We all had plenty of blood in us. The four of them were implacable, and seemed to act with no second thought, even without first thought. But by this time I was certain that the four of them wouldn't be likely to travel about the country chopping up women, whatever the reason.

I said, "We figure Whit Lloyd for all of this."

"That's pretty strong language, Caudill."

"But don't you work for Whit Lloyd, friend? Isn't he throwing some money your way?"

"To save your own hide, you'll turn on the hand that feeds you?"

"I don't work for him."

"Well, who do you work for?"

"They all work for me." Jasper Lloyd's warbling voice sounded from the edge of the room. "Can you men produce a court order that would excuse such a trespass in my home?"

The humor drained from the first man. "If we felt we needed a court order, we'd have one. You'd be better off to stay abed. You'll catch your death."

The weight of the big man's paw eased from my chest, and I sat upright. The ghastly figure of Lloyd stood unsteadily at the edge of a corridor that loomed like an open mouth behind him. His white fingers were like tendrils bracing him against the ornate corner post.

"Your boy's been up to no good, Mr. Lloyd," the first man said.

"I don't believe you," Lloyd said. "I don't have to believe any of it."

"You must have known all along," said the second man. "A father knows those things."

The beefy man who had been pressing me down put away his gun and lumbered over to help Lloyd. He picked up the old man gently like you'd pick up a sleeping toddler.

"I had the idea he might come over here," I said.

"Detective," said Lloyd, "I should not have lived so long."

"Take him back to his bed."

The appearance of Jasper Lloyd seemed to drop a curtain on the whole show. The two smaller men dropped their bantering act and looked around the room in exasperation.

"Jesus Christ," Pickett wheezed, "I'm too old for all of this."

"Just sit back, old-timer," the first man said. "Don't try to take over."

"We'll run the show." The second man looked down at me. "That's the way it is."

I wanted to get up from the floor but I didn't seem to have the initiative.

"We were just trying to find out something about my baby sister," Walker said gently. "We didn't mean for all of this—"

"I'm sorry about it, Walker," the first man said. "There isn't any way to bring her back."

"What do they call you, sir?" Walker asked him.

"Call me John, if it helps you."

"You can call me Mike," said the second man.

Finally I got up from the floor. I wanted to be flooded with rage toward them, but it wouldn't come. I stepped to a chair that looked like a little throne and sat down.

"Listen, Caudill," John said. "I know it can't seem right, the way we handled you."

Pickett made a move to get up and then sat back down on the bench by the door. "You guys are punks, that's all."

"Come on now," said John. "Do we really seem like punks to you?"

"You got the guns on ya," Pickett muttered crossly. "I guess you can say what you want."

"But what's it all about?" I said. "How can you do something like this?"

John put up his gun in the shoulder rig and stood in front of me. "We're all business," he said. "And that's about it."

"It's a war on, Caudill," Mike said. "You can see how some things are more important than others in a time of war."

"Punks," Pickett said. "All talk is what you are."

"Mr. Pickett," Walker said, "it's not helpful."

I said, "You should have just killed me."

"You feel that way?" John squared himself to me. "Who wants to die?"

I wanted to speak up for myself, but it wasn't any use.

John said, "You don't want to die; you want things to be better."

"Sure."

Walker said, "What will become of us?"

"Don't worry," said Mike.

"I can't help but worry."

"Look," said John, "what we're interested in is seeing to it that the plants keep working. That's what we have to do. Outside of that, we're not involved here."

"Then we're free to go?" Walker asked.

Mike and John exchanged hard looks, and the big man at the door just shrugged.

"What about your friend, Caudill?" John asked. "Do you have a line on him?"

"I don't know anymore."

"Are you all from the government?" Pickett asked. "Hoover's men?"

"Don't say Hoover," Mike said.

The big man at the door said, "That's a bad word."

CHAPTER
18

Federle had gone off in the Chrysler. When we stepped out with the two smaller men, I expected him to try a rescue, as in the movies, but he was nowhere in sight, and even a little Chrysler coupe isn't an easy thing to make disappear in an open area. There was no telling what Federle might be up to, if he was plotting an ambush, if he was taking the car to find Johnson or some other help, or if he had simply fled. The two men did not show any worry.

They weren't about to interrupt production at the plant by calling a general alert. Maybe the Lloyd plant had bunkers set up in case of an air raid. I don't think anyone in Michigan believed that the Japs or the Germans could make it so far into the heart of the country, but there were some who took it seriously. Though it was hard for me to picture the mass of men moving together in an organized way, I thought there would be enough room in all the tunnels to shelter everyone in a real emergency.

The two biggest men stayed back at the castle to sit watch over Jasper Lloyd. Walker and I and the old guard Pickett hitched a ride back to the plant, bouncing along in the hard second seat of a battered Willys that had been parked inside the garage. The car was open and noisy, and so there was no talk. John and Mike sat in the front seats without concern for us.

I was beginning to be able to discern the difference between the two of them. We drove to the corner of the complex closest to the Lloyd's hideaway castle, where food service trucks dropped their loads across four stalls, and a white company bus shuttled white-clad workers from the building to the parking lots and the rail spur, far to the other end of the plant.

John tucked the Willys alongside the building, and we all entered at the little alcove. As far as I could see, there were no guards controlling the building.

John said, "You'd better find your friend."

"Better keep him under your wing. Keep him close."

"If he's loose in here, if he's causing a ruckus—"

"He'll do more harm than good, that's what we mean."

I said, "How are we supposed to find him in all this mess?"

"Probably," said John, "you should think of what he's looking for, Detective. Where will he go?"

"Do you know much about him?" Mike said.

I said, "He lives up the stairs from me."

John said, "Do you know why he was kicked out of the service?"

"He got burned up," I said.

"He suffered some rather severe burns on his legs, it's true," said Mike.

"But that would hardly be grounds for a dishonorable discharge, would it, Mr. Caudill?"

"Wounded on the field of battle, as it were. Such a man might be made a hero."

"So what do you want to tell me about it?" I asked.

"We can't tell you anything about it. It's confidential."

"Why don't you ask him about it when you find him?"

"The hell with you guys," I said. "You remember, if I get the chance, all four of you—"

"You shouldn't talk so much," John said.

"You should try to be happy with what you have."

"You were close to being dead, but we didn't let you die."

"Now you've got the chance for a second life," Mike said. "Don't squander time looking for revenge."

The pair of them walked off and left us. The wet smell of fresh bread swallowed us. The noise in the food service building was constant but not as maddening as the din in the plant itself.

"Can you walk, old man?" I asked Pickett.

"I can do anything," he said. "It takes a little longer."

"We'll try to find Whit Lloyd. Where do you think he is, Walker?"

"I'll go along with Federle's idea. If it was me, I'd get far away. Don't they grow rubber in South America?"

The old man said, "Maybe he ain't welcome down there either. He don't keep friends for too long."

"We'll look for Lloyd at his office," I said.

"That's good for a laugh," Pickett said. "They'd grab him in a minute if he showed up there."

Walker asked, "What kind of a show would he want to put up in here? He's a desperate man, and now he's got to feel like he's backed into a corner. It might be best to back up and let him run off before he gets a mind to hurt any more people."

I said, "If he wants to go, he'll be gone already. If he's here, he'll try to make a big splash."

"You mean a blowup?" Pickett said. "We've had blowups before. Anyplace you have a furnace you could have a blowup."

I thought with dismay about the sheer size and complexity of the great plant, and about all the warrens and tunnels they had built over the years. Whit Lloyd probably knew every route, every shadowy corner, and it would be impossible to tell where he might go. Doubtless there were places in some of the buildings that hadn't been used in years, railcars parked along sidings, pump houses, shanties built and forgotten—it was like its own city, like Detroit, a sprawling blot on the landscape.

"We'll just try his office first, how's that?"

There was a moment of silence, and then the old guard turned and led us away. His spindly legs churned and churned, but the pace wasn't so fast that we ever got winded. Coming and going on the workroom floor through a number of buildings, we had only to show our badges to pass. Walker just kept between us. After a steady half hour's walk, we were inside the administration building. By this time many of the office regulars had gone out, and mop jockeys were beginning to swab things down. The smell of bleach affronted my nose.

With his ring of keys, Pickett got us up to Lloyd's floor. We stepped off the elevator, and though it seemed deserted, I could sense that it was the wrong kind of stillness. Walker sensed it, too, and we spread out on either side of the hall, leaving the old man to trudge resolutely down the middle toward the office. My hand itched for a gun.

"I'm going to need to piss before too long," Pickett said. "So you know."

One of the Lloyd security men stepped out where the hall widened in front of Whit Lloyd's office. He had drawn his gun from the shoulder rig, and now rested it casually along his backside.

"You've got no business here," he said.

"We're looking for Whit Lloyd," I said.

"You and everybody else. Seems young Whit doesn't want to talk to anybody just now."

"He'll talk to me," I said.

"Who are you?" said the security man. "I know you, you're the Old Man's monkey." To him it seemed funny.

"We'll check the office."

"You can check the door," he said. "But you won't get in. It's a regular lockbox."

I took it as an invitation to step closer. The handle was locked, and from the setup I could see how it was. I brought up a hard knuckle and rapped a few times.

"That should work," the security man laughed. "I think I would've seen if he come by me already."

Pickett stepped close and jingled his keys again. "Come on, come on. The crappers I get to work with." He worked his fingers over the keys to select the one he wanted.

"How do you come to have a key here, old man? Nobody's supposed to have any keys in this area."

"Nobody pays me any mind. I come and go where I please, and nobody pays me any mind." He added, "You motherless bastard."

He brought up the key to the polished brass plate of the door bolt. Because we were all crowding him, it seemed that his hand could not work fast enough.

"I'll go in first," the security man said. "You all hold back."

"That's all right with me," I said, thinking now that Lloyd, even if he had not managed to make it to the plant or to his office, might have left a surprise. Walker and I moved back from the door and pressed ourselves along the walls of the hall.

Pickett finally made the key work, and then turned the big handle to set the door swinging. The security man elbowed his way past Pickett's belly and peeked into Lloyd's outer office. Then he stepped in with his gun down. From where I stood, I could just see across the room, which was unlit, to the tall windows facing the jagged skyline of the plant. Clouds had moved over the sky, blocking most of the light from the low sun.

It seemed that the outer office, at least, was empty, and Pickett moved through the door too. I was about to follow after them, but I stopped to try to think. Walker stood opposite me, his mouth and lips dry, looking tired and wary.

I patted up my ribs where I would have kept a gun if I had a proper rig, and then smiled across at Walker.

"I'll go in," I said. "You find an angle out here in case he tries to come up behind us."

Walker nodded, and then he began to scan the hallway for a place to set himself. He walked toward the alcove where the security man had stood in wait. Because Lloyd's office floor was covered with an assortment of woven rugs, I could hear only the intermittent tapping of Pickett's oversized feet as he went through the outer office.

"Do you have a key to this other door?" The security man rattled the handle on the door to Lloyd's inner lair. "I don't even see a lock here."

As I came through the door, I caught from the corner of my eye a flash like lightning through the bank of windows. Where the thunder should have rumbled there was an immense shivering crack, followed closely by a blast of air that rattled the windows of the outer office. I could see, across the expanse of the plant, that there had been an explosion at the power station. The tall stacks were obscured by a swirling plume of fire and black smoke, and the nearer buildings were silhouetted and thrown in garish light.

I walked close to the windows and put my hand on the glass. The security man came quickly over.

"Good God," he said.

Pickett's foul breath wafted over my shoulder. "That's the end of us," he said.

Another blast blew out from the powerhouse, and I thought I could see two of the stacks tipping gracefully toward the river. From our position at the eastern end of the facility, we could see the power winking out from each building in the complex like a big wave had come over everything. When the loss of power hit us, the administration building seemed to shudder into darkness. For a few moments, we were lit up only by the big fire. As Walker crept in toward us at the window, an emergency generator somewhere tried to push juice through the wiring; I could feel it in the walls.

Alarm sirens began to moan across the plant. A weaker buzzer sounded in our building as a minimal flow of power helped a few emergency lamps flicker on.

Pickett said, "You really think Whit could do this?"

"It doesn't matter what I think about it now," I said. "It's done."

"You don't think it's that Federle?"

I had to give it some thought. "No," I said. "I don't know what he'd do, but I don't think he'd want anything like this."

The security man was at the window, tearing his hair and tapping his pistol to his skull. "This is a disaster," he said. "A disaster."

It grabbed him suddenly that he ought to do something.

"We'd better get over there," he said. As he jostled again past Pickett's belly, he put his gun into the holster and smoothed his hair.

Pickett stood next to me for a moment more, and then waddled off after him.

It was something to watch. The power station was caught up entirely from within by white flame.

How many men? I thought.

"Come on, Detective," Walker murmured. "We had better get out of here."

"Do you think Federle could have done this?"

"As far as we know, it could be an accident," Walker said.

"Walker, that's no accident."

As with any fire, we couldn't take our eyes off of it. Sometimes in the dead of winter the temperature is so low that the smoke belching from the stacks blows white and hangs in the air. But the smoke from the power station was black, and lit from within.

If Federle was like me, as he had always said, he would not want to pull the world down around him. If he was empty of hope, if he felt that his life had not panned out as he had dreamed it would, that he had botched up and ruined any chance for happiness, then he would want simply to be able to sleep. I thought it most likely that he had driven off in the Chrysler to some remote spot and put a bullet through his brain.

I wanted to do it, too. Not a day had gone by in the last several years without some thought of ending it all. John was right: It wasn't that I wanted so badly to die; I wanted things to be better, but I could not see how it could happen. I had been through my own fire, and it had stripped away for me the layer of illusion that makes life bearable and even happy for most men.

"We'd best be moving," Walker said, standing shoulder to shoulder with me now.

"What's the rush?"

He was looking beyond me toward the big desk that Mrs. Bates kept. He walked over, picked something up, and pulled it close to his eyes. When he brought it close to the window to catch light from the fire, I saw that it was the picture of his sister I had given to Hank Chew. His tired eyes glistened.

The moaning alarm sirens now meshed with the familiar wavering air raid sirens. I saw that they had opened up a few powerful spotlights to rake the sky. Because I had never taken the idea of an actual air raid seriously, I had never taken notice, but I thought now that there might have been some sort of antiaircraft bunker set up to protect the plant. It was not a raid, though. Enough damage had been caused to cripple the whole facility for a time, but it could not be a raid. We were in Michigan, cradled by water and by friendly relations with our northern neighbor.

The fire at the powerhouse no longer flared like an inferno, but the thick black smoke that pushed out of the place went up and spread out like a sooty layer of cloud. They would be scrambling now, telephoning the far corners of the globe in an instant to ask for help and to pass on the news of the disaster. I knew that before too long the administrative personnel would be called back to the site to start to put things right again.

"Why would he do such a thing, Detective?"

I made no answer.

"Do you think it could be the money? When I think of my own son," Walker said, "I just can't imagine it. It passes outside my understanding."

"This will be the death of the Old Man," I said. "How could he live through such a thing?"

"He's lived through the fullness of his life."

Whitcomb Lloyd darkened the frame of the door leading to the hallway. "Let me tell you something about shame, Caudill."

Walker tensed up as if he might try to make a rush at Lloyd, but he saw as I did that Lloyd held a revolver in one hand and an oddly curved blade in the other.

"You know a taste of what it means to disappoint a father so roundly. Surely you can't miss the irony? Granted, you haven't lived up your father's standard, you're a failure, but for me—well, it's a matter of magnitude. It's a matter of *degree*."

"Come on, Lloyd," I said. "What kind of man arc you?"

"A tragic man?" He smiled broadly as he said it, and raised his gun to stop Walker from creeping to the side.

"I don't feel sorry for you, however you want to think about it."

"Sorry?" He stepped into the room and with his heel closed the door behind him. Somehow he had changed into a London-cut suit and put a clean shave on his face. The hand and arm that held the knife were doused in blood, still wet. "It's a tragedy of epic proportion! The storming of heaven! Celebrate, Mr. Caudill. You'll never again see such a spectacle in your lifetime."

Walker said, "Will you kill us, Mr. Lloyd?"

"Why shouldn't I, Mr. Walker?"

"I have a wife and children who look to me to keep them from living in the street."

"I, too, am in a family way."

"You have the money to take care of them, even if you go to jail for all this."

"You should tell him not to inflame me, Mr. Caudill."

"Woman killer," I said. "And now a bomb?"

"There was no bomb," Lloyd said. "Do I look like an anarchist to you? It's a matter of throwing a few switches, opening a valve or two, and closing the vents."

"Either way, it makes you a coward."

"Coward! At least I can face up to what I am. And you? A whoremonger! A cripple—an adulterer. You've no moral standing to say a word to me, Caudill. After all this?"

He was keyed up to bursting. The light in the room was dim, but his eyes glowed with such fire that I knew he would have no trouble putting a bullet or two wherever he wanted. The gun followed every movement, every sigh Walker and I made, like it was connected by wires to us. Lloyd stepped sideways until he was away from the door.

"Pick up the statue on the desk. Yes, the woman. Pick her up and press the base of the statue over the handle of my door there."

His words were clear, and I could see what he wanted me to do, but I moved like molasses. Lloyd was not rushed, though, as he knew that he had finally come to the end of things. He meant to kill the Old Man; but he could have simply put a blade to him any time he wanted to. What Whit Lloyd wanted was to make the Old Man die of shame, of a broken heart.

"Put the base of the statue to the—it's magnetic, you see. There you have it."

The statue was around eighteen inches tall and weighed a good fifteen pounds, and when I stood it on end over the handle to the door to Lloyd's office, I could hear the lock click. I pushed the door in slowly.

Inside the outer office, the shot from Lloyd's gun blasted like a drum. The bullet passed not two inches from my ear and slapped into the door. Bits of shattered shellac and oak bit into my face. *If you care so little*, I told myself, *why don't you rush him now?*

"Don't think of attacking me with the statue," Lloyd said. "Just drop her on the floor. Or rather put her back on the desk there."

Walker and I stood before him unhappily, but there was no way to get a drop on Lloyd. I rubbed my thumb over the ample bronze breasts of the statue and put her down on the desk.

"Go on in and see how Mrs. Bates has fared."

The doorway was wide enough for Walker and me to go in together. We went slowly, in the vain hope that there might be a place to duck aside or split up so that we could scramble for something to use against Lloyd. But we were tired.

"Mrs. Bates didn't deserve to die," Lloyd said. "Certainly not Mrs. Bates. But you can see just the same she's gone."

It wasn't until I looked closely that I could see that Mrs. Bates was in pieces. Lloyd had arranged her on the floor to look like she was taking a peaceful nap, lying on her side. Her ankles were crossed, and the knees were hidden by the bottom hem of her dress, so it was not easy to see that they had been disconnected. One plump severed arm served the old woman for a pillow.

"It's no use," I said. "You can't try to pin all this on me. Nobody will believe it."

Lloyd looked at me quizzically. "I wouldn't try to pin anything on you, Mr. Caudill. I was only trying to see if you were clever enough to figure it out for yourself."

"Well, I'm sorry," I said.

"Perish the man whose mind is backward now!" Lloyd cried.

Walker took a few halting steps away from me and then crumpled down to the floor as if he had been struck low. I rolled across Lloyd's desk and down to the floor behind it, then flipped up the desk and charged it toward Lloyd. I could feel the two shots hitting the desktop but I could not see where Lloyd had gone in the dimness.

The desk came to ground on top of Mrs. Bates and continued to roll toward the door. Walker crawled rapidly to one side, and I saw a flash of Lloyd along the wall, racing toward the row of potted plants before the window. I angled myself to intercept him, intending to tackle him and smash us both through the window to the ground four floors below. But as we connected, I found that the broad window was so thick that we bounced off it.

Lloyd's gurkha knife sliced lightly through my shirt and opened a nick against my rib as we fell to the floor near the elevator, but I was worried about the gun. I got close enough in to his body to take away the angle he might use on the knife, and I smacked his head sideways as I went for the pistol. I was lying over him, trying to put my weight down, using both my arms to stretch out his gun hand so he couldn't point the weapon at me. In such a struggle it's better to have your hands free, and it was putting him at a great disadvantage to keep hold of both weapons. He wouldn't let go of the knife, which was doing some damage against my leg and back, but the gun went skittering away.

Lloyd pulled himself in and managed to slip partway out from under me. He brought the butt of the knife against the side of my head, bone against bone. I knew that Walker would get the gun if I could keep myself between it and Lloyd, so I concentrated on keeping free of the blade.

Lloyd was far more limber than I was, and faster, and he was on his feet, slashing furiously. I couldn't get up fast enough or protect myself with my hands, so I rolled backward and put my feet up to keep him back.

"Get up! Get up!" he said.

He was set to fall onto me when Walker's shot sounded close to my head. He missed with the first shot but hit Lloyd square on the kneecap with the second, knocking his leg out from under him.

Lloyd still flailed with the knife, though I could see how the gunshot had shocked him. I rolled away and came up to standing again, and Walker let loose another slug that hit Lloyd's knife arm between the wrist and elbow. I could see from the puff and spatter of blood coming out through the fine striped cloth of Lloyd's suit that the shot went through bone.

Still Lloyd would not give up his grip on the gurkha knife. If it had been a family heirloom, I could not judge. I could attest that it was sharp enough.

With my foot I forced Lloyd's broken arm to the floor and then I stepped on his writhing hand. My shoe leather was thin enough that I could feel finger bones snapping as I put my full weight on the hand. I brought down the other knee quickly to Lloyd's chest and heard the wind go out of him, and then I took hold of his throat with my bad hand and got ready to bring down a hard fist between his eyes.

"I prithee take thy fingers from my throat, for though—*ck*—*ck*—"

Whatever more he wanted to say I choked from his mind.

It was when Whitcomb Lloyd stopped wanting to talk and began to look at me with twinkling eyes that I became interested in what he had to say.

"We'll need to get this man to a hospital before he bleeds out," Walker told me.

"He won't bleed out from a shot in the knee," I said. "Let him bleed."

I eased my grip around his neck, but Lloyd held his tongue because he knew it would cost him a slap if he tried to speak. He was in great pain, I knew, because his kneecap had been clipped; and if any part had been broken off, it would likely have been pulled up the inside of his leg by the long muscles there.

"What about Mr. Federle?" Walker asked.

"Hopefully he got out."

Lloyd caught his breath at this, and I pushed his head to the floor. His wet scalp was hot against my hand.

"If he didn't get out, and he's carrying that gun, there will be trouble for him," Walker said.

"He's got a badge, hasn't he?"

"You two had better get your story straight," Lloyd hissed.

I hooked my claw hand around his windpipe and gave a squeeze.

"We should just kill him, Walker, before anyone comes up here."

"You should," Lloyd spat.

"I'm not willing," Walker said.

"He's got the dough to put off trouble."

"With the lady lying dead there, I would think that there would be cause to convict him."

"He's not stupid—are you, Lloyd?" I pressed my knee harder to the middle of his chest and turned his arm to rotate his shoulder past where it wanted to be. "He'll find a way to make it look like we did this." I was thinking of the dead whore on Lloyd's lawn, a girl I had put my pecker into not two weeks before. To my fevered mind it seemed probable that Lloyd was not merely toying with me; he might well have planted some incriminating bit of dope at my apartment or on the girl herself.

"We'll have to let him tell his tale," Walker said. "You have some faith in justice, don't you, Detective?"

"I never did."

"You should worry about your pretty Eileen—" Lloyd's choked words seemed like a whisper.

"You should worry," I said. Everything was buzzing and trembling. My lips tingled. It occurred to me that Lloyd might have had some kind of button to press or some kind of booby trap set up near his desk, and so I held the scruff of his suit and dragged him across the floor next to Mrs. Bates. I turned his head so his face could get well smeared with the old woman's blood.

"Are you certain she's safe?"

"I told you—"

"Detective, it's not right."

Walker came close enough to block the fist I was fixing to slam into the back of Lloyd's neck.

"The rest of your life in prison, Walker," said Lloyd, struggling for enough breath to speak at all.

I put my thumb hard into Lloyd's ribs below his shoulder blade until he gave a spasm of response.

"She's a plump one, Caudill."

I twisted Lloyd's arm enough to begin to separate the ball of his shoulder bone from the socket, and put enough weight onto the center of his back with my knee to prevent him from pulling in enough air to get by.

Walker stepped close and laid a firm hand on my shoulder. He was still holding Lloyd's pistol.

It felt good to be able to hurt Lloyd. His lips were pulled back, and though he was suffering to breathe, his teeth were clamped tight.

"Detective, it's over now," Walker said. "You can't just go on and kill this man."

I eased up a bit on my knee and let Lloyd's shoulder slip back into its joint.

"Can't you see the trouble he'll give us?" I said.

"We've been through trouble before," Walker said.

"You should check the furnace building," whispered Lloyd. "If you want to see something. Your friend Federle has been busy."

"He's just talking," Walker said.

I felt the space between the two bones of Lloyd's lower arm with my thumb. I found I could make the broken fingers of his right hand jump and wiggle by squeezing hard.

"Can't you stop?" Lloyd said. "I was never cruel, Mr. Caudill. Have I ever lied to you before?"

I began to settle myself. As I looked down on Whit Lloyd, I felt something for him. I could have loved him. He had suffered so much, and he had gone so far beyond any hope of redemption that he was utterly lost. He had been broken and bloodied, and he was now completely helpless except for the puffery of his words. What he had done to the women and to Chew could count against him if he went before the Lord, but there was no necessity for me to make him suffer.

"Can you keep him pinned down here until somebody comes, Walker?"

"I'm willing to have a go at it," he said.

"You'd be willing to shoot him dead if he won't go along?"

"He won't get loose from me. But if he did, I'd let him run rather than shoot him dead," Walker said carefully. "I'd be willing to shoot out his other leg."

"Put your weight down here and take the arm," I said. "Put the gun down to the small of his back and let the trigger go if he starts up."

Lloyd could not see what I was doing because his face was shoved up close to Mrs. Bates's bloody hair. I knew that he would start to talk to Walker as soon as he could hear that I'd gone out of the room, but I also knew that Walker could be as patient as any man could be.

"I'll send somebody up, Walker. I'll let them know not to plug you right off."

"I'd appreciate it sooner rather than later."

"I'd better try to find Federle before somebody else does."

"You should finish me, Caudill," Lloyd said.

"No," I told him. "I feel sick of all of it. You make me sick."

I stepped out of the office and the outer office and into the hall, holding to the weak notion that I would be able to feel it somehow if Eileen had been brought to the massive plant. Lloyd had tried to steer me toward the furnace, but as I stepped through the hallways that glowed still with dimming emergency lighting, I couldn't tell where I wanted to go. I moved my flat feet along, wishing for something more substantial than my own bloody hands and my wreck of a face to help me.

CHAPTER
29

The floor containing Lloyd's offices seemed utterly empty. I thought that Lloyd might have stopped the elevators somehow, and I was not sure that any staircase could open to the floor without a special key. I heard nothing but the wail of sirens moaning up and down the scale over and over.

I came to the elevator that had taken us up, and pressed the only button, but there was no response. There was a door close by that looked like a janitor's closet, but from its position I thought it might lead to a stairwell. I tried the handle slowly, and when it turned, I eased the door open with my foot. Though it was almost completely dark inside, I could tell by the feel of it that there were stairs. I pulled down a small painting that had been attached to the wall and used it to keep the door from closing after me.

The stairway was windowless, and the emergency lights inside were no brighter than fireflies, and so I had to feel my way downward, holding on to the rail. The staircase only went down one floor. From the inside, I was able to pull open the door with no difficulty. I peered around the corner into the hallway and found another area of gleaming floors and a maze of doorways. Again I pulled something from the wall to prop the door open, and then I stopped to listen carefully.

I don't know what it was that made me turn one way instead of another.

As my senses were reeling, I might have heard something, even the rustle of paper or a tight breath, or I might have noticed a shadow moving at the corner of my vision. I want to say that I could feel even some slight change in temperature, a waft of heated air coming from the hall to the right of me. But since I was turned around, since my sense of direction had gone the way of my common sense, I just turned right and stepped down the hall.

The whole floor seemed quiet, which was odd enough, but there was something, something that drew me on. Most of the offices had nameplates carved out of wood tacked up outside them, but I did not recognize the names until I came to the end of that hall: CHARLES HARDIMAN, ELLIOT HARDIMAN. I opened the door and stepped inside.

There was an outer office, a quarter the size of Lloyd's, that led back to a pair of offices at the window end.

"It's Caudill," I said softly. "Who is it?"

This brought some movement from inside one of the offices but no words.

"It's all right," I said.

"Don't come in, Pete."

It was Federle's voice, I thought.

"I'm coming."

"You'd better not."

"Will you shoot me?"

"Sure, I will," he said. "Ain't I crazy?"

I stepped beyond the secretary's desk and stood before the window at the back of the outer office. Federle half-sat on the long desk in Charles Hardiman's office, holding the pistol over his leg. He was facing the long bank of windows, and the light that came over him seemed to make him blue.

He didn't turn to look at me. Something thrashed and bumped on the floor before his feet, and he waved the gun softly.

"*Hnnnn!*"

"Quiet," Federle whispered.

I took just a step to get me into the frame of the door to the office. The Hardiman boys were trussed on the floor under the windows.

Federle lifted up his shaky hand and pulled a long drag from a cigarette that was almost gone. His breath was so deep that he burned the fag down to

his fingertips. He brought the butt close to his face and considered the glowing end of it. Then he pressed his fingers together and put out the fire.

"I was trying to help you, Pete. You know I was only trying to help."

"Sure. You were helping me."

"You can see about these Hardimans, right?"

"A couple of bastards, all right," I said.

Federle's face was slack, his jaw soft, and his eyes stared out at nothing.

"You should kill them, then," I said.

"I don't want to kill them! I didn't want to kill anyone!"

"They haven't done anything wrong, is that it?"

"*Hnnn!*"

"Quiet, you!" Federle turned to me and saw that I was covered with
blood. "Walker?"

"He's all right," I said.

"I shouldn't have run off on you. But I had to—"

"*Hnnn!*"

"Jesus, you stupid pansy, shut your yap!" Federle sprang up from the
desk and was across the floor and at Elliot's throat with the gun in a flash.
"You keep quiet!"

I was still at the door, but after Federle got up from the desk, I could see
a woman's hand and arm glowing white. It was too slender to be Eileen's,
wasn't it? I could see polished nails and a tiny jeweled ring on the fingers.
Her new beau's given her a ring, I thought. *Or is it Patty's hand?*

"Who's this, now, Ray? Whose arm do you have here?"

He stood up abruptly and gave Elliot a short kick to the belly. Then he
turned toward me and waved the gun stiffly. "She's— I know it was wrong,
Pete. She's nobody now." He was wound up tight. His arms came up and
then down, and the fingers of his free hand splayed out and curled up like
he couldn't control them.

"Come on, Ray, it's all over now. Walker's got Lloyd upstairs."

"All I wanted was to help you. From that first time I saw you, that's what
I had to do."

"You've been helping. You did good. But this girl ..."

"It had to be the Hardimans. *It had to be.* You said so yourself. Their father was a piece of work. Their mother—those goons—"

"It's all right, Ray."

"She was just…she was like the other girls, Pete. She was bringing shame to her family."

"I know, I know."

"I knew it was wrong."

"You put the arm here to make it easier to pin things on the brothers." Ray had been so certain that the Hardimans had killed the girls that he had killed another woman just to frame them up. "But who is it, Ray?"

His face broke into a manic smile and he began to sob.

"You got me pinned down, Pete," he said.

"Hand over that pistol," I said. "That belongs to me."

"That's just a bad idea."

I did not take a step but I shifted my weight a bit to judge how Federle would react. His gun hand went up to train the piece on me without any hesitation, and I leaned back. I could see the four glittering eyes of the Hardiman brothers. They were both working at the cords that held their hands and feet. Charles had worked off one of his burnished oxblood shoes.

Federle brought himself together a bit and leveled the gun at my belly. He picked up the arm from the desk and stood facing me.

"Get down on the floor with them, Pete."

"I won't let you tie me up like a hog."

"Just step out of my way."

Charles Hardiman worked his gag down with his jaw and said, "You're wrong about us, Mr. Federle. You're wrong about Elliot."

The sharp crack of a billy rapping on a door came from far down the hall, followed by a shout.

"Let's sit down here and talk this over," I said.

"It's no use, Pete. I'm through. You should— Can you help Patty out? Can you do anything for her?"

"She needs you, Ray. She needs a husband."

His bitter smile let me know that I had spoken poorly.

"It isn't fair, Mr. Federle. It isn't moral." Charles used his voice patiently, quietly.

"Lloyd tried to tell me that Eileen was here," I said. "He said I should look in the furnace building. We'll go together."

Federle considered it. Then he skipped toward me quickly and planted
his foot on the middle of my chest. It was enough to knock my feet from
under me, and I went backward and bounced into the doorway of Elliot's
office. Federle blew past me and was gone.

"*Hnnn! Hnnn!*"

I righted myself and tried to stand up, but the dizziness put me back to
my knees. I heaved to get some of my wind back, and then started off again
after Federle.

"*Hnnn!*"

A couple of uniformed Lloyd security men were far down the hall,
knocking on doors, yelling to find anyone who had been left in the building
when the power fell. One of them saw me as I turned down the broad open
stairway that led as far as the third floor, but he was far enough away for me
to ignore his shouting. I came down to where the staircase opened to an
impressive open area toward the rear of the administration building, and I
could see that the security men had rounded up all the stragglers in suits
and white shirts in the courtyard outside. Covered in blood as I was, I could
only hope to slip any contact with the security men or bluff my way
through. I did have my gold badge, after all, and I was in fact performing
some duty.

I knew that Lloyd had been suckering me with his talk of Eileen. It was
not possible that he could have done anything to her. If I had any confidence left in me at all, it made me sure at least of so much. I knew that my
heart would not quit seizing in my chest until I could put my hand on her
shoulder, but for now my mind was on Ray Federle.

The elder Lloyd had set up the facility so that he could see the whole
process played out before him; near the river, where freighters could slide
in and turn to dump their loads of ore and coke and scrap, they had built a
mess of rail lines and spurs to transport material inland to the furnaces and
the rolling mills. Lloyd could watch from his window as the raw earth was
dumped and hauled and charged and blasted into steel; he knew how
everything moved toward the end of the line, where in better days new automobiles rolled into great lots close to the river. These cars were loaded
onto freighters and shipped across the country, to all ports, to all cities
where the Lloyd name was known.

It was all laid out in a squared-off circle, and the administration building, where Jasper Lloyd had kept his office before turning it over to his son,
looked over it all. I knew I could get to the open hearth furnace building
through the rolling mill, which was adjacent to the building I had just left.
For Federle it would be the natural end. I huffed my way past the gaggle of
men and women who smoked and joshed each other outside the buildings,
not yet released to go home. They were lolling on the grass, and I didn't
pay any mind to what the sight of me might do to them.

The first gate I came to was manned by a couple of army men, and they
braced me as I got close. There wasn't any use in trying to blow past them.

"Watch out, now," I said. "Trouble on the other side."

"Says who?"

"Jesus, brother, look at you. There's a medic set up—"

"He's got a gold badge."

"There's a medic set up over in the glass plant. They're bringing everybody there."

"No, no—I don't have time to talk," I said. "Did you see a little fat bald
guy with a—with a sort of mustache come through here?"

"Nobody came through here except going out."

"Listen," I said, dodging my head to look at the crowd. "If you see
anybody—listen—" I got between the two of them and lowered my
voice further. "They think it might be the Germans. If you see anybody—
anybody—comes through here after me—"

"Nobody goes," said the first.

"Watch who you talk to," I said.

"Ain't you Pete Caudill?" the second soldier said.

I cocked my eye and squared him up. It was Gino Pastore, a local boy
who had joined the Detroit police force a few years after I started.

"I got drafted," he said.

"You got the easy duty, Gino."

"You look like you been put through the winger, Pete. I heard you was."

It let me catch my breath for a moment. I slapped him on the shoulder
a couple of times with my good hand. "Listen, Gino, don't let anybody
through here."

I slipped past the pair of them and cursed them for being stupid enough to let a bloody one-eyed murderer waltz through their post on a night when an explosion had taken out the power for one of the most important war production plants in the world.

Crews of mechanics swarmed all along the rolling mill, some of them wearing helmets with lamps, as if they were miners. Thousands of tiny panes of glass lined the top of the south wall, but it wasn't enough light to let me see through to the other end. I followed along the safety railing that separated the work floor from the electrified railcars that ran below, transporting ingots and bars of hot steel away from the river. As I made it to the end of the building close to the furnaces, the fresher ingots still glowed from within, dull orange.

There was an unguarded gangway between the rolling mill and the furnaces, and I walked across it without looking up toward the splash of timid stars. I could hear voices down by the cool river, hearth men enjoying a rare night of ease and fresh air. Inside the furnace, it was quiet except for a deep hum, almost a vibration. It made me tremble and want to piss. Since there was still no power, I thought that the hum might have been caused by the slowly cooling ladles of steel that hung from the giant craneway. The biggest of the ladles held seventy-five tons of metal, and without electricity there was no way to pour out the ready steel into ingot molds.

I had never been in the furnaces, and I had to stop to orient myself. Panels of windows in the roof were made to rise up and down to vent the superheated air from the place as needed, and this allowed some light to pour down. Some of the ladles cast up a glow, too, and I could see outlines and shadows well enough to get a picture of the place.

There was a metallic clanking that came irregularly from down below, but I could not say if it was a workman or if it came from ingots shrinking as they cooled. To my eye there was not another man in the building, and I wondered idly if it was because of the danger of an explosion.

There atop the catwalk across the very center of the building I could see a white figure pacing. For many years my eye had not been sharp enough to see at any distance, but I knew it had to be Federle.

The staircase leading up to the catwalk turned and turned like a fire escape, four sets of stairs that led to a walkway all down the length of the building and across the open space at intervals. Federle had placed himself as far from the walls as he could, and he continued to pace as I crept toward him. The heated steel made a wind that went straight up to the roof, and the draft fluttered up the tattered legs of my trousers.

Federle had pulled off his clothes and shoes, and now prowled in bare feet over the waffled steel of the catwalk. As I drew near, I could see that he still carried the pistol.

"Ray."

He seemed impossibly tall and slender, and the orange glow from the ladle below could not warm the unbearable whiteness of his skin. I saw what the fire had done to the lower part of his body.

"Come on, Ray."

He turned toward me and made a couple of halting steps my way.

"Stop, now."

From his ankles to his waist the scars swirled like the flames that had made them. In the dim light, I could see how black his eyes had become. At his crotch, though, I could see that the flames had not touched him; his balls hung low but they had not been burned. His prick was gone. Just a nub remained, but I could see that it had not been burned away.

"Why would you, Pete?"

"What?"

"Why would you go on living if you were in my kind of shape?"

I didn't move any closer to him. I would have backed up if he had come any closer to me.

"You can see, can't you?" he said.

"I see, Ray."

"There's your buddies." He gestured to the floor below with the pistol.

I saw something, maybe a pair of figures, maybe John and Mike, the two smaller thugs.

"I was sorry to have to lie to you, Pete," said Federle. "Sometimes you have to lie. You know it as well as anyone."

"It's all right."

"They cut my pecker off."

"Don't worry about it now."

"Come on, Pete! Can't I tell you?"

I could make out the woman's arm Federle had carried with him from

Charles Hardiman's office. It lay over the pile he had made of his clothes on the floor of the catwalk.

"I strangled a whore in Hawaii—after I got burned—that's the kind of man I am. I strangled her. She wouldn't look at me. She laughed! It was a lie I told you about the fire burning my pecker off. Her men came in and found her, and they cut me short. If it wasn't for the MPs—they got me out of the mess but it wasn't something that could be—"

He stopped abruptly and went back to pick up the arm. He pushed it up over the side fence of the catwalk and it fell to the center of the open ladle below us. For a moment it lay on the thin crust over the molten steel, and then a whitish flame came up and seemed to pull the arm down.

"I wanted to help you, Pete. That's all there was."

He scooped up his clothes without taking his awful eyes off me, and hoisted them up and over, too. After a few seconds they burst into flame and made a puff of smoke that rose and blew away through the roof.

"I hope it isn't too late for Eileen," he said, leaning against the woven metal fence. "I couldn't find her."

"She's all right, Ray."

John and Mike had come up on either side of us and now stood some distance off. I could see John's head bobbing at the far end of the gently bowed catwalk.

"What a thing to do, Ray. What a thing to do."

"It's not the same for you," he said. "You're not the same as me."

He flipped the pistol over the fence, and I heard the crack it made as it hit the crust of hardening steel in the ladle. Then he put his hands to the top of the fence and pulled himself over in one smooth motion. I was fast enough to get a grip on his ankle, and I held fast as his weight pulled him down with enough force to snap the joint of his knee at the top of the fence.

He gritted his white teeth and looked at me fiercely through the fence. His hands braced off the fence and he arched himself away. The scarred flesh of his ankle was smooth and slippery, but I thought I could get the other hand on him and maybe come up on the fence to get him back over.

"No, Pete," he said. "I had to find you. I had to see if I could help you."

"Ray."

His face went softer. "Now we're square."

I stared hard into his eyes and let him go.

The surface of the hot steel was maybe twenty feet below, and Federle landed flat on his back. It didn't seem to hurt him.

"Find your family, Pete," he said.

The metal cracked slowly from his weight, and flakes of the surface tipped to let him slide down a bit as he melted away. The steel was too heavy to allow him to sink into it, but it was still hot enough to pop and spit as the watery parts of Ray Federle came out from his scarred skin. I watched him as long as I could and wondered if my own end would be so unbearable.

"Your woman is all right," John said at my elbow.

"The coppers have her."

"It's too bad about your friend, Caudill."

Mike said, "You can't have enough friends in this world, Caudill."

I was too empty. I could not tell how to answer them. Even if it had been possible, I don't think I wanted to throw them over the fence. I didn't want to go over myself anymore.

"Caudill, I'll tell you just the one thing," said John. "From what I knew about your brother Tommy, I could see he was a good Joe."

I looked at him closely and thought I could see something human in him, despite what he had done to me. It was clear to me that the pair of them would fall back into the vaudeville routine if I tried to get anything more out of them, so I just turned away.

They let me go, thumping and dragging my numb feet across the catwalk and down the winding staircase to the regular world.

CHAPTER
30

I held on to the badge that gave me access to any Lloyd plant, though I could not be sure it would continue to hold the same sway for long. They let Walker and me through to Lloyd's castle a couple of weeks after the explosion, just as the last of the operations went back up. General Motors and Chrysler had sent over men and a number of smaller generators to cobble a working system into place until the main power plant could be repaired or replaced. The transformers that had blown out in almost every facility had been in need of replacement all along, and the Lloyd Motor Company made use of generous government money to do so. I could not hope to understand what deals had been made to secure the money, what control would be given up, or what new monster had been created.

Walker had dressed up in his Sunday best for the visit, and he sat next to me in the Chrysler without much comment. He had purchased a new hat, I saw, to match his older jacket and trousers, and had put a smooth shine on his shoes. Everything I wore reeked as new, even the patch over my eye. I had wanted to make a fresh start, and the poor condition of everything that had touched my grimy flesh made me want to burn it. Walker retained his thrift, though, and his steady nature. He had not thought of changing himself, only of continuing the most sober course he could see ahead.

Though old Lloyd was not yet dead, the air in the house and the attitude of the servants told me that soon enough there would be a funeral. Of course there was no trace of the tussle we had with the goons inside the doorway, and the goons themselves had slipped away just as mysteriously as they had come. Pickett, the old parking guard, had worn himself down with worry, and kept vigil over his beloved boss in an armless leather chair at the end of the hall that led to Lloyd's chamber.

"Okay, fellas," Pickett said. "You came through it all right, then."

"We're just fine, Mr. Pickett," Walker said. "We trust that things will work out for the best. It's the only way."

"My old wife passed," he said. "That same night."

"My condolences," Walker said.

"That's too bad, Pickett."

"It was her time, anyway."

"How's the Old Man?"

Pickett looked up at me pathetically. "They've got him fixed up pretty good. He's—" Pickett's gnarled hands had worn through the racing form he held with his fingertips. "He's lived through his years, hasn't he?"

"He's earned his rest," Walker said.

I knew I couldn't say anything hopeful, and so I just nodded to Pickett.

"You fellas can go on through. James is up there by the door."

"Take care of yourself, Mr. Pickett."

The hall was wide and lined with stone. The vaulted ceiling was marked along its length with fancy plaster carvings, the sort of thing that you wouldn't care about after you'd lived with it for a while. There were paintings, too, and photographs along the walls, each with a little lamp that drooped light down onto its face. I might have stopped to look over the pieces because I knew that I would likely not have cause to walk the hall again. But I kept shoulder to shoulder with Walker until the secretary moved from his office outside Lloyd's suite.

"Gentlemen," he said. "It's good of you to come."

"It's an honor to come," Walker said. "A pleasure."

"He called us over, and we came," I said.

"You can go in," said James. "Mr. Caudill, if you'll stop by to see me after you're finished."

"Sure."

He pushed the tall door open for us, and we went in. It was a regular church inside, with flowers making a powerful stink and ceilings I judged to reach fourteen feet. Tall, narrow windows covered with gauzy drapes let gray light filter in from the cloudy sky. Lloyd's bed was not tucked away in a private corner or behind a screen, but had been placed to one side of the great room with space left at the head for an assortment of medical machines. Walker and I stepped over the antique rug toward the bed.

Estelle Hardiman sat primly beside the bed in a chair that looked French to me. Her posture was impeccable and—from some distance—she seemed radiantly beautiful. It was a trick of the light and of her own art as a woman. As I came close, I saw what a wreck she had become.

"Mr. Caudill," she said, "you're doing well."

"Better."

"Jasper has been asking for you. He's been restless all along."

"I'm Jonah Walker, ma'am."

"Pleased." She held the Old Man's hand carefully in her own, stroked the ragged veins and bulbous knuckles as if she really loved him.

Lloyd's eyes were closed. His skin was ghostly white and draped close to the bones and cartilage of his skull. Most of his meat had gone away, and not much more than gristle and bone was left. His nostrils and his lips were pink and moist, and tears clung to the white lashes of his eyes.

"I know you think I brought those men to harm you, Mr. Caudill. But I didn't—I wouldn't—they just arrived of their own accord. I know you hate my sons."

"That's not worth going over," I said.

"Can't we be civilized?"

"You can have a go at it," I said, "but it's too much to remember for me. I'll just be regular."

She had tried with lipstick and makeup to approximate what she had looked like thirty years earlier. She knew enough to wear modern clothes to cover what time had done to her body, but she could not well hide her face.

"I'd like to hear you say you don't mean to harm my boys."

Lloyd's eyes were open, but there was nothing to show that he could understand what was happening.

"I don't have any business going after them," I told her. "But I don't lay off the possibility that I'll need to mop the floor with either one."

"You're a tenderhearted man, Mr. Caudill, masquerading as a brute."

"No."

"Your father was a dear as well," she said. "But he didn't feel the need to be cruel."

I moved within an arm's reach of her.

"He was as handsome as you are, I'd say, though obviously not so damaged by wear."

"Estelle," croaked Lloyd.

"She's had it," I said. "Now she's too old to have it anymore."

"Please, Caudill. Please." It was a chore for Lloyd to pull enough air into his flaccid to make the words.

Estelle Hardiman rose up from her chair. "I'll go, Jasper. It isn't good for you to be upset."

"Don't, Estelle. Don't."

"I'll come back tomorrow." She leaned delicately over to place a kiss on Lloyd's bony forehead.

He closed his eyes and smiled as she did it, and the breath in his lungs rattled like a cat's purring.

"Can't we start anew, Mr. Caudill? Can't we make a fresh start from here?"

"I'm not willing," I said.

She seemed genuinely hurt. "Someday, Mr. Caudill, you'll understand. I'm sure you will. Good-bye for now, Jasper."

She walked out of the room with some dignity. I watched her as she went, as her crisp dress and her hair and her figure grew hazier and softer to my eye. Walker's reserved gaze seemed to accuse me; I had no real cause to be so harsh with the woman. I could see that the murder of her daughter Jane still cut her deeply, and I could believe that she might once have loved her husband Roger. A kind word from me might have helped her. But as with my mother, I always held back from that kind of gesture. It made me a coward, a moral coward.

Old Man Lloyd fluttered his fingers to draw Walker and me closer to him. Estelle Hardiman's perfumed odor still whispered at the bedside, not yet wiped over by the sickly stench of the cut flowers.

"Mr. Walker ... we haven't properly met, have we?"

"No, sir. I'm Jonah Walker." He bowed his head for the old man.

"Caudill—this Federle? Can you tell me—"

"I can't say I understand it," I said.

"It's the war," said Lloyd. "That's what it does."

"Roger Hardiman was never in any war," I said. "And look at the kind of man he was."

"That's hurtful, Mr. Caudill. You speak ill of the dead."

I don't think Lloyd was crying, really, but liquid brimmed over his pink eyelids and he worked his thin lips back over his teeth. Someone had done a poor job of shaving his slight whiskers.

"I've done bad things," I said. "I don't excuse myself from it all."

"Do you believe that the Lord is just, Mr. Caudill?"

Walker made a motion to say something, but thought better.

"I have to believe it, don't I?"

Lloyd managed a smile. "That's the boy," he said.

"What will happen to the company now, Mr. Lloyd?" Walker asked.

"Oh, I shouldn't worry over it. Perhaps my daughter and my daughter-in-law ..."

The Old Man's eyes had never lost their peculiar yellow color. He trained them on me and lifted a finger to call me closer still.

"Estelle did know your father. It's true."

"It seems like everyone knew my father," I said.

"It's a pity, a pity." He drew up his strength and seemed almost to glare at me. "You never really knew Jane, did you, Mr. Caudill? How could you have known her? That's the pity. She was a wonderful girl. I knew her when she was a baby."

I pictured her again in my mind: the one time I had seen her in life, bright, open, and sure of herself. Then I saw her as Bobby and I had found her, spattered with her own blood.

"I had thought— In his younger days I thought my Whit was a shining star, such a perfectly charming boy. I wouldn't want to hurt you, Caudill. I'm nearing the end of my days."

"I wish I could have been more use to you," I said.

"It's all right, Mr. Caudill," Lloyd said. "You don't need to worry any-more. Your work here is finished."

I felt like I should thank him or curse him, or at least tender my best wishes, but it was as if I was speaking to a man who had already fallen from a great height. What could I tell him? He had only to make the best of every moment in his life, and he had tried to do so. Now that it was over, there was only the formality of waiting for his breath and his heart to cease.

"If you'll see James as you go," Lloyd said.

"I will." I turned away from them and stood for a moment to allow Walker to make his courtesy.

"I will pray for you, Mr. Lloyd," he said. "My wife and I will pray for you."

"Yes," said Lloyd.

Walker and I stepped away from him. It was enough to think about, enough to occupy my mind for another year if I let it. We went out the door and closed it after us, and then I turned to enter the cubbyhole that James used for his papers and his desk during the Old Man's dying.

"Mr. Caudill, I have some papers for you. Mr. Lloyd has dictated some information about your father and his involvement with Frank Carter. He wanted you to have it. Some of this is possibly incriminating, and so—"

James was offering me a packet of papers about as thick as his polished thumbnail was wide. It had been sealed with a button of pressed wax and a gold-threaded ribbon.

"Mr. Lloyd thought you might want to know the truth."

"The truth," I said. "You've read this?"

"I took the dictation myself. There is no other copy, and no one else has ever been privileged to—"

"I'll take it," I said. "When I'm old I'll read it."

"As you wish, sir."

"What will you do now?"

James looked surprised at the question. "There will be a great deal to attend to," he said. "I'll continue in my capacity until my services here are no longer useful."

"It's all right for me to keep the Chrysler?"

He thought for a moment. "I can't see any reason why you shouldn't."

"Thank you."

"Thank Mr. Lloyd."

"No, I mean to thank you, James," I said. "Thank you. Thanks for everything."

"I haven't done anything more—"

"You've done a good job here for the Old Man," I said.

"You should stop interrupting, Mr. Caudill," said James. "Polite conversation is a skill like any other."

"It's too late for me."

"No," he said. "You're a gentleman at heart."

I took the packet of papers from him and tucked it under my arm. Then I walked out and picked up Walker as he was admiring a photograph of Jasper Lloyd and Mae West against a backdrop of some desert scene, with foothills in the distance.

"Are we finished?"

"I guess so, Walker."

"It's a shame, isn't it?"

We said our good-byes to Pickett and got ourselves clear of the cold stone mansion. Walker and I did not need to speak during the long trip back to his apartment. The Chrysler puttered quietly along and I was left to pass the time lost in thought.

CHAPTER
31

Some parts of the city and the area girdling the city are foul with smoke and runoff from the plants. In some places downriver, where the houses are thick together like a checkerboard, the air is so thick with soot and grit that it crunches on your teeth; it gathers on the sheets of your bed as you sleep. You can think of the way water drains all of it soon or late, how even farmers have manure that runs off in a big wash of a storm sometimes. Blood spilled on bare ground soaks in and gets to be something else. It grows up into the sap of trees. They've got a system in the cities to funnel all that washes away down through pipes and tunnels underneath it all. They try to control it. But nothing ever just disappears. Traces of it gather below the ground or at the bottom of a lake, and sometimes it comes back to the surface to affect things or to blow things apart.

Where I grew up on the east side, we always called it Belle Island. When we had the fare, we rode on streetcars right to the foot of the bridge and walked over to spend the whole day exploring the place. If you knew how to do it, you could hop on without paying the fare. Belle Isle is stuck right there close to the Detroit side of the big river, and the water on either side is deep enough to make you think of it like a moat—like a place protected from the ugly life of the city that could be seen from almost any point on the island. We felt like kings, Tommy and I and our cohort, and we wished for a castle on the island. We thought that somehow we might own the place someday, when we'd conquered the city, when we could claim our spoils.

It never happened. Tommy was gone. Our father was gone. Our mother...

Eileen had invited me for a picnic to meet her beau—Eugene was his name. He was decent enough. Though his mustache put me off, and though his eyes seemed to bulge too much, he seemed sensible. His own wife had died during a bank robbery in Oklahoma ten years earlier—right before his eyes, he said, not two months after they had been married. He had taken out a mortgage on a nice home in Highland Park, he kept a pair of German short-haired retrievers in a kennel in the back.

"That breeze doesn't quit, does it?" Eileen said. "It's making a mess of me."

"It keeps the bugs away," Eugene said. "If you go up into the trees, you'll get eaten alive."

"Sure," I said. "It's fresh air."

"Mother seems to be enjoying herself."

My mother and her friend Paulette sat on a bench looking over the water. They wore scarves and sweaters and housedresses, and seemed happy just to sit.

There were dozens of small boats and canoes tacking back and forth across the water on the Detroit side, and larger sailboats and freighters moved up and down the river in the deeper channel on the other side of the island.

"We should try to make it a regular thing," said Eileen. "We should have a picnic every Sunday. Look at mother kicking her legs like a school girl."

"Sure. It seems like a good idea. But you can never tell what will come up."

"You could get a regular job any day of the week, Pete," Eugene said, his little mouth pulling into a natural smile. "We've got men pulling eighty hours every week. If you start in, you'll make a decent salary right away, and you can arrange to take Sundays off."

"All right, Gene, I'll think it over."

"You could get a job anyplace. It doesn't have to be over here." He waved to the stacks of the Jefferson plant, not far up the river. "It's a good time to get in somewhere."

"It's so far away, isn't it? We can sit out here without being afraid." Eileen looked over the spread she had made for the picnic: roasted chicken, greens, potato salad. "It's almost hard to imagine how the fighting could be." She glanced over at me and smiled. "Pete knows about fighting."

"It's a nice little island here," I said. I was thinking about Whitcomb Lloyd and Ray Federle. "We should enjoy our peace while we have it."

"You're right, Pete. You're sure right about that." Eugene picked up a greasy leg and pulled it apart politely with his little teeth, wiping his mustache clean after every bite.

"It will be summer soon," Eileen said. "They say the Japanese are on the run."

"They ought to be," Eugene said. "With what we're sending after them."

"The Germans, too."

I lifted my iced tea as a toast. "Here's to the end of it all," I said, "whenever it may come."

They lifted their cups and drank and seemed happy enough.

Eventually, before any lull or silence in the conversation could let lurking darkness break into our day, I wandered off toward the water and sat on a hard bench watching the gulls cry and fight over bits of food. I felt the damage that had been done to my ears; the wetness in the air seemed to swell the inside of my head, and I heard all the sounds of the water lapping and children playing like it came through a cardboard tube. But it didn't bother me overly.

Since Lloyd's secretary James had given it to me, I had kept the packet of papers inside one of the cubbyholes of the Chrysler—unopened. My father had been a good man. He had been bad at times, but from what I knew about the way he had lived his life, he had on the whole tended toward the good.

For some years after it had happened, I had believed that he had killed himself out on Fighting Island. I wondered now, why had I ever been willing to believe such a thing? This was the sharpest kind of betrayal, really, to show your back to your own family, and there wasn't anything I could do to take back or change the wrongness of what I had done to his memory. Worse, now, I could feel from my own bad urges that maybe my father had really thought of ending his own life. He had chosen to go on living, and I knew now that he must have fought hard against those men who roped him up on that tree.

Maybe all of it would be laid out in words in the papers Lloyd had given me. It might explain or excuse what Lloyd had tried to do, what my father had been thinking. Maybe the papers would show me something of my father that I had been too stupid or too proud ever to see for myself. Lloyd was a great man in a time of change for the city. When I thought of how much he had done compared to the great mass of workaday laborers here and across the country, how he had been able to amass and arrange so much—no one could say that he had been born with the silver spoon. So far as I knew, he still held on to his life at the castle at the edge of the plant. Maybe he could look out at it through a little window.

Lloyd had been a great man, a truly great man.

But my father had been a good man.

I knew what I had to do to be a good man. Though I had failed to stave off the riot the previous year, and I had failed Ray Federle, and I had failed to help Jasper Lloyd in any way, I had at least one task left.

Alex's mother was laughing across the grass with her new beau. She could laugh even though such a part of her was missing, had been torn away too soon and with too much wrongness. Alex was thinking of her, he had to be, even if his life with her seemed far away to him now, wherever he roamed. I knew that it would be easier and easier for him to stuff the feeling away deep inside himself over time, and so I felt the urgency.

Such a perfect day—a day to eat and rest and to patch up the social bonds I always left untended. The breeze seemed to clear away everything else.

There would be time to read Lloyd's papers. If I had to spend the rest of my days scouring the earth for my nephew, there would be time. For now, I rested on my bench. I felt the weak April sun soaking into my back, and I tried hard to remember.